CRIME SCENE

A BUCK TAYLOR NOVEL

BOOK 11

BY

CHUCK MORGAN

COPYRIGHT © 2023 BY CHUCK MORGAN

Printed in the United States of America

First printing 2023

ISBN 979-8-9862066-9-1 (eBook)

ISBN 979-8-9881613-4-9 (Paperback)

ISBN 979-8-9881613-5-6 (Large Print)

ISBN 979-8-9881613-6-3 (Hardcover)

LIBRARY OF CONGRESS CONTROL NUMBER

2023913258

DEDICATION

Dedicated to the men and women who scour crime scenes to find the smallest pieces of evidence.

Chapter One

The noise is almost too much to bear. It's the same thing day and night, day after day, and it makes you want to do crazy things. The noise is worse today than it ever has been, and there's only one thing that will make it better. But I hesitate. The memories that accompany the noise are too painful.

I remember when the noise started. It was the laughter that made it worse. My parents owned a bar downtown. I was alone most nights while they worked, but Saturday nights were the worst. On Saturday night, they hosted vaudeville night. It was very popular, and even people in the audience would sometimes dress up. There were clowns and comics and singers and dancers. There were men who dressed up as women and women who dressed as men.

The worst part came after the show was over. My parents would bring home several of the male entertainers, and they would drink, and then they would have sex with my mother. Two, sometimes three men at a time, and all the while, my father would be sitting in his chair drinking and cheering them on. I would be in my room and would wake up to the moans of the men and my mother, men in dresses, or garter belts, all with painted faces. They would never even close my door, so I would sit next to the door and watch the vulgar acts, and sometimes my mother would look over at the door, see me there, and smile.

That was the first time I heard the noise in my head, but I was too young to understand it. It was something that made my head hurt, and I would have to close my eyes and hide my head under the pillow to make the noise go away, but it never completely went away. It was always in the background. As I grew older, it would take an act of savagery to calm the noise.

On Sundays, following the night of debauchery, my mother would drag me to church. My father was always too drunk to go. She would scream at me the entire time to hurry, or we would be late. Unlike the night before, in the morning, she would have on her high heels, her hose, a pretty skirt or dress, and her white pearl necklace. All the way to church, she would tell me I was bad, or I was evil and that God would punish me for the things I did. The things that quieted the noise.

We were members of the Evangelical Church of the Risen something or other. All I can remember about that time was sitting there in a jacket and tie and listening to the Reverend Max Turner telling us for two hours or longer that we were all going to hell if we didn't put more money in the collection plate. It was terrible and made me feel like a worthless piece of humanity, but the noise grew louder each Sunday.

I don't remember when I realized that the Reverend Max Turner was one of the regulars who would show up at my house on Saturday night and take part in banging my mother. It just sort of happened one day as my brain started to go to sleep during the service. I was looking at the reverend with his arms raised towards the almighty, and I suddenly pictured him with a clown face and a big . . . red nose.

After that, it made going to church easier because I

would picture him and the other men. I would sit and look around the congregation and wonder how many of the other men in the audience had been with my mother. It helped me to pass the time. After the service, my mother would take me to meet the reverend behind the church, and she would tell him about all the bad things I had done during the week. He would yell at me and tell me that I was so bad that even the devil had no place for me in hell, then he would pull off his belt or pick up a thin stick and beat me. He said it was to drive out the evil spirit. Sometimes I wondered if he just liked to see my bare behind all red and bleeding. Then he would drop his pants and rub himself against my bare ass. What a sick fuck. My mother always stood in front of me and cried, like she was sad that it was happening. I think she enjoyed it.

It wasn't until that one summer day that I was able to rid myself of some of the noise. I was riding my bike and spotted the reverend down by the river fishing. He was so focused on what he was doing that he never saw me come up behind him. He sure knew I was there when I hit him in the back of the head with that rock. He dropped his pole in the water, fell to his knees, and grabbed his bloody head. He looked up at me, and I hit him again and again. It was incredible. The noise had disappeared, and for a few minutes, I was free.

Because of my age, the judge sentenced me to a juvenile detention home, where I would remain until I was eighteen. Dr. Oliver Martin thought he could cure me of the noise in my head, but he made things worse. He believed in the power of corporal punishment, and he made sure to use me as an example for the other boys at the facility.

The pills he forced me to take didn't help. It didn't make the noise disappear, but it made me groggy and dopey. I realized that Dr. Oliver Martin wasn't making me any better, so I stopped taking the pills and planned my escape. The night came when I found out that the youngest kid in our room was being abused by staff members. We found him sitting in a corner in our room, crying, and I decided that now was the time.

After lights out, I got dressed and put everything I needed in a plastic bag I found in the trash. I snuck out of my room and entered Dr. Oliver Martin's room. He was sleeping soundly, but the noise in my head prevented me from hearing his snoring. I had stolen the hammer from the big toolbox the maintenance man kept in the basement. I stepped up to his bed and slammed the hammer into his head. I never heard him scream. When I was finished, I left the hammer next to his pulverized head, and, using his ring of keys, I unlocked the outer door, ran across the yard to the woods, and disappeared for good. I changed my name and never looked back.

I didn't think I could live with the noise, and then one day, while clicking through the internet, I discovered my salvation. It came in the persona of Donny Truex and his This Is What's Wrong with America *podcast. I listened for hours that first night, soaking up all his messages about the evil trying to ruin our country. I felt like he spoke directly to me.*

He had spent hours talking about the evils of drag queens and how they were all pedophiles and they were trying to seduce our children and sell them to rich Asians and Europeans who would turn them into sex slaves. They were vile and disgusting people and needed to be dealt with. Then he mentioned that a new drag club was opening just outside town and that the grand opening was at the end of the week. He said someone should stop them, and then the noise in my head got louder and louder. I could hear my mother moaning along with the men dressed in women's clothes, and I knew what needed to be done.

And here I sit in my car outside this fancy new club as I watch hundreds of people—perverts and pedophiles—congregate to celebrate their vile actions. I can't believe how many cars are in the parking lot. The phone on the seat next to me rings again. I look at the number. This is the eighth time the nursing home has tried to reach me. I know what they are calling about. They want to tell me that my mother has been murdered. Funny. I already knew that.

Now the noise is getting worse, and I hear my mother yelling and the Reverend Max Turner and Dr. Oliver Martin yelling at me and hitting me, and I can't make the noise stop. I put on my headphones and open the latest podcast from Donny Truex, and he's telling me what I need to do. I want to scream, but Donny needs me. The world needs me. I have to save all those kids from becoming sex slaves. And the noise gets worse through the headphones.

I exit the car and open the trunk. Everything I need to accomplish my mission for Donny Truex and the children is in the black duffel bag. I pull out the pistols and screw on the suppressors, and I load up my ballistic vest with magazine after magazine. I do a quick count in my head, and I figure I have enough ammo for everyone in the place. I run through my mental checklist. I have barricaded the door behind the club so no one can leave that way. I have loaded both pistols with extended magazines and have many more to replace those.

The noise has gotten intense, and I turn up the volume on my phone, but it does little good. The noise has taken over, and it is time to do what I came to do. I close the trunk and head for the door. I have a pistol in each hand as I approach the large man with the beard who is guarding the door. From twenty feet away, I fire three shots into his body, and blood sprays all over the wall. The big man falls to the floor. I push his legs out of the way and open the door.

The laughing and the bright lights confuse me. It sounds like people are having fun, but how can that be? These are perverts and pedophiles, and the laughter reminds me of the men having sex with my mother. The noise is made more intense by the flashing lights, and the laughter makes my head hurt, and I rub my temples. I can't lose focus now. The children need me.

I step up to the double doors and stop to catch my breath. I pull open the doors and step into the room. I walk past the bartender and down the hall to the dressing room. I push open the door, step inside, and the first three people die. I know where to go because I helped build the building. The fancy lighting and sound system are all mine, and I will use them to my advantage. I walk back to the bar and shoot the bartender. He's a nice young man, but he works for the perverts. It's a shame he had to die. I step to the front *of the bar and fire into the crowd enjoying all the debauchery.*

The screaming begins.

Chapter Two

Buck Taylor sat in his lounge chair reading the latest national crime report from the FBI. He had the TV tuned to 9NEWS out of Denver and had the volume turned low so it was acting as background noise.

He had reached for the last of the Coke in the bottle sitting on the table next to him when something flashed in the corner of his eye. He grabbed the remote instead, pointed it towards the TV and turned up the volume.

Across the bottom of the screen was a crawler that said BREAKING NEWS. He put down the report and listened to the news anchor.

"We are just getting word of breaking news out of Mesa County. We are hearing reports of an active shooter situation at a brand-new drag club located outside of Grand Junction. Early reports are multiple dead and several hundred injured. We have teams en route and will update you as soon as we get more information. Please stay tuned to Nine News for additional information."

Buck's phone, sitting on the table next to his Coke, chimed. He picked it up, looked at the number and answered.

"Yes, sir," said Buck.

"Hope I didn't wake you," said Director Kevin Jackson. "Turn on the news."

Kevin Jackson, the director of the Colorado Bureau of Investigation, had been the youngest person to run the bureau when he was appointed by Governor Richard J. Kennedy. He'd had a stellar career with the Colorado Springs Police Department before being tapped for the top post at CBI. He was more bureaucrat than cop, having spent most of his career on the administrative side at CSPD, but he was well respected in the law enforcement community, and Buck was impressed with him.

"Already on, sir. A mass shooting in Mesa County," said Buck.

"Yeah. The governor wants us all over it. This one's bad, Buck, not that any of them are good. I just spoke with the sheriff. He's calling for ambulances and doctors from all over the state. I need you out there right away."

"No problem, sir. I'll leave now. Can you text me the address? Will you call Bax and Paul and get them rolling and also call Franklin and have him call out the forensic team?"

"Anything else?" asked Director Jackson.

"Yes, sir. You may want to put out a call for additional forensic pathologists. Sounds like Sima is going to be up to her elbows in dead bodies. She could use the help."

"Good idea, Buck. Once you get there, let me know what else you'll need."

Buck disconnected the call and dialed his son David. He knew David was working, and he didn't want to call and wake up his daughter-in-law Judy since she was probably already in bed. David was the oldest of Buck's three children and the only one to follow in his footsteps and enter the law enforcement field. He was a patrol sergeant with the Gunnison Police Department and worked as the night shift supervisor.

Cassandra was Buck's middle child, and she was every bit a middle child. In high school, she'd played soccer, ran track and played volleyball. She lettered in all three sports. She was also the one who got in trouble for violating curfew, drinking and whatever other mischief she could find to get into. Buck was surprised when she was accepted to the University of Arizona with a full scholarship for volleyball. He was even more surprised when she was accepted into law school. Cassie was never much for regimented education.

Two years ago, she'd dropped out of law school and her career path took a different track. She joined the Forest Service and was now working as a wildland firefighter with the Helena Hotshots. The Helena Hotshots were one of the elite firefighting teams based out of Helena, Montana. Buck was not surprised. He never saw her sitting behind a desk as a lawyer. She loved the outdoors, and she was as tough as they came. Lucy wasn't pleased that she'd quit school without any discussion, and she worried whenever Cassie was called out on a fire, but she also knew her daughter, and if this was where she was happy, then so was her mom.

Jason, his youngest son, was an architect, and he lived in Boulder with his wife, Kate, and their three children. Of all of Buck's kids, Jason was the most sensitive, always worried about Buck's job. He was also the one who had continued to follow Catholicism, just like his mom, and seemed to get more involved in his church after Lucy died.

David answered on the first ring. "Hey, Dad. You heading to Grand Junction?"

"Yeah, I didn't want to wake Judy. There're some steaks in the fridge that need to get eaten. Since I'm not sure when I'll be back home, have her pick them up and you guys eat them. I'll call and let you know what's happening."

"Be careful, Dad. The latest report is that the shooter hasn't been found yet."

"Thanks, David. Stay safe, and I'll call when I can," said Buck.

He hung up, grabbed his pistol and badge and clipped them to his belt. He walked into the bedroom and stuffed some additional clothes into his go bag. He went out the back door, locked it, climbed into his state-issued Jeep Grand Cherokee and pulled out of the driveway.

Grand Junction, Colorado, was about two hours from Buck's home in Gunnison. Highway 50 was a two-lane road for the entire distance and was not built for speed, but Buck was familiar with every section of it. He turned west onto the highway, and once clear of the town limits, he flipped on his flashers and hit the gas.

Buck's phone chimed, and he looked at the message. The director had sent him the address of the club, which was south of Grand Junction at the intersection of Highway 50 and County Road 141. Buck made the drive in a shade over an hour.

Highway 50 was closed a mile south and north of the club. Buck pulled up to the roadblock and held up his badge and CBI ID, and the deputy logged him in on his laptop. He told Buck to park wherever he could find a space. Flashing red, white, and blue lights lit up the night sky, and he found a spot and pulled in behind a couple of ambulances. He grabbed his backpack and slid out of the Jeep.

The western slope of Colorado had been having some of the hottest weather on record, and even this late at night, the air was uncomfortably warm. Buck noticed that the firefighters and paramedics weren't wearing their turnout gear but were wearing uniform pants and T-shirts with the Grand Junction Fire Department logo emblazoned on the shirt. They looked uncomfortable, even dressed like they were, and Buck felt bad for them.

Buck made his way to the Mesa County mobile command center parked down the street from the club. He climbed up the steps and pulled open the door. The cold air hit him like he was walking into a refrigerator. It was almost too cold. He stepped inside and closed the door.

Sheriff Jackson Foley looked up from the plan table, stepped around the table and reached out his hand.

"Buck, good to see ya. Director Jackson said you were on the way. You made good time."

"Jack," said Buck. "Good to see you."

He put his backpack on the floor next to the plan table and shook hands with the people gathered around the table. Jackson Foley was in his second term as sheriff. He was six feet tall and had a slim build. His hair was still brown with little gray, and he had a brown mustache. Tonight, he wore jeans and a sheriff's department polo shirt. Standing next to the sheriff was Ellen Thompkins, one of the three county commissioners. She was a thin woman with angular features and wore jeans and a Mesa County Emergency Services polo shirt. The third person in the room was Commander Raul Martinez. The SWAT commander was five foot nine and had a muscular build. He had jet-black hair cut short, and he was dressed in his call-out gear.

"Sorry I'm late to the party, but do you want to give me a rundown of where we are?" asked Buck.

"Yeah," said Sheriff Foley. "We are deep in the shit. We have a mess of dead and wounded, and we can't find the shooter."

Chapter Three

This was fun. It was wild and insane and exhilarating and dangerous as hell, and I loved every minute of it. The voice is almost silent. I guess enough blood, death and destruction can satisfy anything.

As soon as I started shooting, their world turned upside down. I learned from reading about other mass shooters that the secret is to not let anyone get too close. And believe it or not, it worked. The screaming started after the first shots rang out. Most people headed for the back exit, but they couldn't open the door since the old pickup truck was parked against it.

They started running for the front doors, and I mowed them down. One of the first people I killed was the bartender, and then some people in the dressing room. The bartender was a sweet young man named Jeremy, and I hated to do it, but the voice was relentless. Once he went down, I stood near the bar and shot people as they ran past. Because of the suppressors and the noise in the club, it took some time before people realized what was happening. A lot of people died in those first few minutes.

Anyone who tried to get to me was shot immediately because they were all in front of me. That one asshole in the three-piece suit tried. He had a gun, and I guess he figured he was the good guy with the gun and was going to save the crowd. Boy, was he mistaken. The first shot destroyed his right kneecap, and the second shot destroyed that stupid mustache he wore. What the hell was he even doing here in his three-piece suit? He looked so out of place. Maybe he was looking for a date.

It was hard to kill the entertainers. They were just doing what they loved. Funny how, in the end, they tried to be real men. Someone threw a chair at me, and I emptied what was left of both magazines into him. I dumped both magazines and reloaded. Having thirty rounds in each magazine sure helped. I could kill a lot of people without reloading.

I was on my fourth and fifth magazines when the light stopped flashing. Someone tried to run behind the bar and hit the wall switches to turn on the house lights. I blew him away before he had a chance. I liked the effect and the atmosphere. Flashing lights, loud music, people screaming. It was calming in a weird way. My therapist would have had a field day with that image.

Three young men with muscles and spandex tried to rush me. They went down in a pile. I stepped from in front of the bar and shot each one in the head. What a rush. I ejected the eleventh and twelfth magazines, reloaded and moved towards the crowds trying to get out the front door.

By now, people had managed to get out the front doors, and I could hear the sirens in the distance, although the music kind of drowned them out. I looked at my watch and counted down three, two, one. Bingo. There was a loud pop from behind the stage, and the lights and the music died together. It was suddenly eerie, with all the people moaning and screaming in the pitch blackness.

Someday someone will ask me why I did it. Did I feel any remorse for causing so much death and destruction? I'll have to think about that, but right now, I am enjoying myself too much to stop.

I made my way past the bar and towards the area behind the stage. I found a couple more entertainers hiding in the dark, lit them up with a flashlight and shot them dead. The busboy, Ramone, tried to throw a bus tub full of glasses at me. He died for his efforts. He was kind of cute. I might have saved him, but he got stupid.

I worked my way towards the dressing room, shooting anyone I encountered. The floor was slick with what was probably blood, but it was hard to tell in the dark. Good thing I knew where I was going.

I stepped into the dressing room, where I had killed the two entertainers and the guy wearing workout clothes who was hiding behind the clothing rack. I remember him begging for mercy, so I gave it to him. In this one place, at this one time, mercy was mine to give or not to give, and it came out of the end of my gun.

The screaming had subsided in the main show area, but I heard some people in the hall. I opened the door a crack and spotted three Hispanic women trying to make their way in the dark behind the dim light of a cell phone. I slid the pistol through the crack in the door and fired three times. The women dropped like they had been hit with a hammer. One of them started to crawl away, leaving a trail of blood. That's why it took four bullets to kill the three. She died without ever looking up at me.

The voice in my head was calm, and with the music off, I could hear sirens coming from all directions. I took one of the pistols and threw it into the kitchen. I heard it hit metal objects and then some plates or cups breaking. The second pistol I threw down the hall towards the bar area.

I stepped back into the dressing room and stripped out of my clothes, hanging each piece amongst the entertainers' clothes on the racks. Under my clothes, I had worn a women's bra, panties and hose. Using the flashlight app on my phone, I checked the clothes rack and found a dress in my size. It was a pretty floral number that stopped just above my knees. I pulled a pair of shoes off one of the dead entertainers and slid them on. They weren't a perfect fit, but they would do.

I used my flashlight to put on some lipstick and foundation and then pulled a big red-haired wig off a wig stand and put it on. I put some mascara around my eyes, then took some water from a bottle on the counter and dripped it onto my face, making everything run.

I moved to my hiding space, a janitor's closet behind the dressing area, and settled in, waiting to be rescued. It took the cops longer than I expected, and I sat there for almost two hours before someone yanked open the door and shined a flashlight in my eyes, blinding me. When I could see again, two cops were standing there with guns pointed at me. I acted like I was never so glad to see anyone in my life after the ordeal that I had been through.

They helped me up, asked if anyone else was hiding in the closet and then led me through the dressing room. Someone had thrown a couple of old blankets over Chastain (Billy) and Rosebud (Tommy). The guy behind the rack was just lying there. They checked me for weapons, then led me past the rest of the bodies and the injured and turned me over to a detective. They were amazed I had survived. They didn't know the half of it.

Chapter Four

Buck Taylor was six feet tall and weighed in at 185 pounds—very little of it flab for a sixty-two-year-old man. Buck's hair was salt-and-pepper, with what seemed like a lot more salt than pepper, and he wore it longer than was typically the fashion of the day. Buck was always pleased when he looked in the mirror since, other than getting older, he was in as good a shape as he had been when he played defensive linebacker for the Gunnison High School Cowboys, what seemed like a long time ago. He still tried to jog five miles every day when he could, and he tried to ride his mountain bike every weekend, weather permitting. Except for a couple of sore knees coming from age, Buck was in good shape, which was important in his line of work.

Buck Taylor was an investigative agent for the Colorado Bureau of Investigation. He was assigned to the CBI field office in Grand Junction, Colorado, but he hadn't been in the office much during the past year. Somehow, he had become the favorite "go-to" guy for the governor of Colorado, Richard J. Kennedy, who was one of "those" Kennedys. The governor was in his second term in office, and Buck had been instrumental in closing several high-profile investigations during that period, which made the governor look good. As a result, when a situation came up that might get a little hairy, the governor always asked to have Buck assigned.

Buck had been married for thirty-four years before breast cancer stole the one person he cared about most in the world. He missed Lucy every day, even after all this time.

If you asked Buck, he would tell you that he fell in love with Lucinda Torres on the first day of their senior year in high school. On the other hand, Lucy always told people that Buck stalked her the entire senior year before she gave in to shut her friends up and agreed to go to the movies with him. She had always considered him just another jock, another football player who was too full of himself.

What she found on that first date was a shy, unassuming gentleman, for lack of a better word, who, it seemed, cared more about pleasing her than bragging about his prowess on the football field. She would tell people it was love at first sight that had taken a year to accomplish. From that day forward, they were inseparable.

During senior year, Buck had been approached by several college football scouts who wanted to sign him to play for their schools. Gunnison High School was a small school back in 1978, and Buck and his family were amazed at how many schools had recruited him, but for Buck, college wasn't in the cards.

Buck and Hardy Braxton had been on-again, off-again friends since kindergarten. They'd played football together for the Gunnison High School Cowboys. They were the team's defensive backfield and were called the "Wrecking Crew" during senior year. Between them, they broke every defensive high school football record in the state, many of which stood to this day.

Buck hated school and spent a lot of time getting himself out of trouble instead of getting an education. When he found something that interested him, he had no problem learning all he could about the subject, but regular schoolwork just bored him. After several long heartfelt discussions, first with Lucy and then with his parents, he decided to join the army after graduation. Surprisingly, no one was surprised.

Buck spent four years after high school in the army, and by the time his enlistment was up, he had been promoted to first sergeant. He spent three years of his enlistment in the military police and took to police work. That was when he decided to apply for a position with the Gunnison County Sheriff's Office.

Since he was already well known in the county, he had no trouble getting a job as a deputy. He proposed to Lucy the night he received the call that he had gotten the position. His life and career were set. He made the most of his time with the Gunnison County Sheriff's Office, becoming the undersheriff in charge of the Investigation Division and coming to the attention of the Colorado Bureau of Investigation.

Buck had worked with the Colorado Bureau of Investigation on several cases inside the county and had earned the respect of the investigators he had worked with.

As twilight started to fall on Buck's career, he knew that unless he wanted to go into politics and run for sheriff, he had reached the highest position in the sheriff's office that he could obtain. He loved his job, but when the first offer came in from CBI, he sat down with Lucy and had a long heart-to-heart talk.

He'd spent seventeen years in the sheriff's office and had always figured he would retire from that job. They had three children, two in high school and one not far behind, and he was a well-respected member of the community. Did he have the right to disrupt their lives, pick up, move someplace else and start all over? The kids had friends. Lucy owned a small deli/ice cream parlor, and they had a nice life.

He could stick it out for another ten years and retire, and they could travel and see the world as they had always planned. Twice he turned down the offer from CBI, although more and more, he felt like he was trapped behind a desk instead of doing what he loved, which was investigating crime.

The final offer came from Tom Cole, then-director of the Colorado Bureau of Investigation. Buck always remembered that day. The Denver Broncos had just lost another game, the third one in a row, and his friends had all packed up and headed home when there was a knock at the front door.

Now, anyone who lives in a small community knows that no one ever uses the front door, and no one ever knocks. So, who could this be this late on a Sunday evening?

Buck answered the door and was surprised to see the director of the Colorado Bureau of Investigation standing on his front porch. The director smiled and said, "Before you close the door in my face, please listen to my offer."

Buck invited him in, and he and Lucy sat on the couch and listened as the director laid out his plan. He was opening a new branch office in Grand Junction, Colorado, that would house five agents and a small forensic unit. Buck could continue to live in Gunnison but would have to report to the office in Grand Junction twice a month. Otherwise, he would be free to work from his house. There would be no disruption in his life other than spending time on the road as his investigations warranted. He would work alone, but he would have all the branch office's resources at his disposal.

Before Buck could say a word, Lucy said, "Buck, this is what you have been waiting for, a chance to be a real investigator again. You have to take this." That was one of the things that made him love Lucy every day. She always knew what he was thinking and understood what drove him. She had nailed it this time. Buck looked at the director and replied, "Well, I guess it's settled; looks like you have a new investigator on your team."

That was twenty-three years ago, and Buck had never looked back. He had made the most of those years and was one of the most respected and feared investigators in the state, but all that work couldn't make up for the loss he suffered.

Lucy was diagnosed with metastatic breast cancer following a routine mammogram, and they set off together on their next adventure: the quest to beat the dreaded disease. After a double mastectomy and five years of chemo, they knew their time was drawing to a close when the cancer returned several times to her brain and was no longer controlled by the radiation.

Together, they decided to stop all treatment, even though they had always told the family that the decision was Lucy's alone to make. Lucy spent the last couple of months of her life taking care of her small business and spending as much time as she could with her children and grandchildren.

The end came quietly one spring night. Lucy had been sleeping on and off for twenty or so hours a day in the end. The night she died, Buck had been lying in bed next to her, reading a report, when she snuggled into his arms and rested her head on his shoulder. Sometime during the night, Buck had fallen asleep. When he woke up, Lucy was gone, and his world was shattered.

They say that time heals all wounds, but Buck wasn't sure that was the case when you lost your closest friend. And even now, all these years later, he missed her more and more each day.

Buck always thought back to that Sunday morning when the family had gathered for a private ceremony at the little dock along the Gunnison River to scatter Lucy's ashes. Each family member got to say a few words about Lucy, and when they finished and turned to go, they were stunned to see several hundred of their neighbors and friends standing silently behind them in the park. Word had gotten out about their private service, and everyone turned out to pay tribute to Lucy. The affair turned into a huge party, with plenty of food and drinks. Lucy never wanted any kind of service, but Buck figured she would have loved this spontaneous outpouring of love.

Chapter Five

Buck looked at the floor plan of the building, which the sheriff had spread out on the table. Since it was a new building and had completed its final inspections the week before, the building department had the plans readily available.

"Can we get in the building yet?" asked Buck.

"We've cleared the building," said Commander Martinez. "The forensic pathologists are inside trying to sort things out. We are still finding injured amongst the dead."

"Do you have a count?" asked Ellen Thompkins.

"Not final," said Sheriff Foley. "So far, we have seventy-five dead and two hundred and forty injured, some serious. It's hard to believe one person could cause this much damage."

"Are you certain there was one shooter?" asked Buck.

"That's what the witnesses are telling us. One shooter with multiple handguns and extended magazines," said the sheriff.

"Have my people arrived yet?" asked Buck.

"Yeah," said Sheriff Foley. "Your forensic team is standing by until we can get into the building. I have Bax and Paul covering a section of the search area."

The door to the trailer opened, and a deputy stepped in. "Sir," said the deputy. "Dr. Kalishe asked me to let you know you can enter the building now. She has a ton of work to do, but she doesn't want to hold us up."

"Thanks, Deputy," said the sheriff.

The sheriff opened a drawer behind him and pulled out two Tyvek suits, booties and face masks. He handed a set to Buck and looked at Ellen Thompkins.

"Sorry, Ellen. You'll have to stay here if you want to hang out."

Ellen Thompkins nodded and pulled out her phone. She sat in one of the chairs and opened her news app. Buck and Sheriff Foley pulled on the Tyvek suits, slipped on the booties and pulled up the hoods. Commander Martinez opened the door and led the way to the building. He wasn't dressed in Tyvek since he was coordinating the search for the killer.

They approached a big man dressed in Tyvek, who was speaking with the forensic teams from the county, the city of Grand Junction and the Colorado Bureau of Investigation. They waited until he was finished.

"Okay, folks. You have your sections; let's see what you can find, and remember, all eyes are on this, so we need everything by the book."

The teams finished suiting up, grabbed their gear and headed into the building. The big man walked over to where Buck and the sheriff were standing. He stepped up to Buck and reached out his hand.

"Buck, good to see you. Wish it was under better circumstances," he said.

Buck shook his hand. "Duke. You the lead on this?"

Detective Sergeant Duke Morgan stood six foot four and had a football player's physique. He had blue eyes, dirty blond hair, and a warm and comforting smile. He had been with the Mesa County Sheriff's Office for fifteen years and had an excellent closure rate. Buck was glad to see he was going to be the lead detective. From the sound of things, this investigation would need the best the department had to offer.

Buck excused himself and walked up to Franklin Williams. Franklin was the lead forensic tech based out of the CBI office in Grand Junction. He was a distinguished-looking black man who stood about four inches taller than Buck but weighed about the same. He had short gray hair and a gray goatee. He had been with CBI for more than thirty years.

"You got everything you need?" asked Buck.

Franklin smiled. "We shall see. This one is going to be tough."

"Okay," said Buck. "You let me know if you need anything."

Franklin nodded, shook Buck's hand and headed into a horror show, the reality being far worse than anyone could imagine. There were bodies everywhere, and the smell of gunpowder, combined with the coppery smell of blood, made the scene grisly.

The county public works team was working to get power and lights into the building, but for the time being, everyone was using flashlights, which made the scene even worse, as it highlighted specific views.

Buck, Duke Morgan and Sheriff Foley put on their

masks and followed the forensic teams into the dark space. Buck had been at some terrible crime scenes in his long career, but he had to stop at the door and take it all in. He panned his flashlight around the space and was stunned by what he saw in the small circle of light. He could imagine the nightmare the guests had experienced as they fought to get clear of the building.

The forensic teams were bagging evidence and recording the locations of individual bodies as Buck and the others slowly walked through the space. Buck spotted a short woman in a white Tyvek suit. He stepped away from the others and approached the woman, crouched over one of the bodies.

"Sima," he said. "How are you doing?"

Dr. Sima Kalishe pulled a red Sharpie from her pocket, placed a small red x and a number on the victim's neck and stood up. The technician standing next to her made a note on the form with the corresponding number on his digital tablet and saved the form. Dr. Kalishe stood about five foot two. She had medium-dark skin and jet-black hair tied up in a bun, but her most striking feature was her blue eyes.

Dr. Sima Kalishe was a forensic pathologist. She worked under contract with the Mesa County coroner, based in Grand Junction, Colorado, and several other counties in the area, including Montrose County.

Colorado was one of about a dozen states that still used the coroner system instead of the medical examiner system. The coroner for each jurisdiction was an elected official, and that person did not have to have any experience or even be a medical professional.

Anyone could run for coroner.

The system was evolving so that the coroner was required to complete a formal training program in death investigations, but it was a slow legislative process. Unlike in the medical examiner system, and since the coroner did not have to be a doctor, coroners would contract with a licensed forensic pathologist to handle any investigations that required an autopsy.

These forensic pathologists were highly trained doctors who split their time among several jurisdictions to keep costs down. Many forensic pathologists were current or former medical examiners, and several were retired, working part time to keep their hands in the game. Sima Kalishe, in Buck's opinion, was one of the best.

Dr. Sima Kalishe pulled down her mask and smiled. "We'll be all right, Buck. I've got a lot of help coming, and we have a plan to handle the workload. That being said, I don't expect to sleep much over the next few weeks."

"Was the director able to get you some more pathologists?"

"Yeah. I've got four additional pathologists from the surrounding counties. The director is sending four more from the front range, and the governor has authorized four additional National Guard pathologists. The National Guard is providing a mobile surgical facility that can handle three autopsies at a time and a refrigerated morgue trailer that can hold up to one hundred bodies."

"I'm glad to hear you're getting what you need. Let

me know if you need anything else, and I'll take care of it."

She thanked Buck, pulled up her mask and moved on to the next closest body. Buck turned and headed towards the stage area. He was almost there when the overhead lights came on. He stopped and looked around. With the bright lights opening up the space, the gravity of what they were all facing became evident. He noticed that most of the forensic techs had also stopped what they were doing and looked around. They were in for a long couple of days.

Chapter Six

Buck pulled out his phone, opened his camera and took pictures as he moved around the bodies. As he walked, he tried to get a feel for where the shooter had been by how the bodies fell. After looking at the wounds on several bodies, he stood up and looked towards the bar.

He was developing a picture of those first few moments. Either the shooter had a detailed plan about what he intended to do, or he got lucky. With the number of people in the building, he could have been overwhelmed at any point. He walked towards the bar and stopped at one male body. He took a picture of the man in the three-piece suit and the object lying partially under the body. He waved and caught Dr. Kalishe's attention, who held up two fingers and marked the neck of the body she was kneeling next to.

Dr. Kalishe stood and walked over to Buck. She looked at the body and then at Buck.

"Sorry, Doc," said Buck. "This body looks out of place. Most of the other folks here are in costume or casual clothes. This guy is in a three-piece suit, and there is the grip of a gun visible under his hand. I need to move the body and check for ID, but I don't want to disturb the scene."

"No worries, Buck." She asked her technician to open a new file, and she kneeled next to the body. The technician used the camera function on the tablet to document the man's face, the bullet hole in his knee and the one under his nose.

Dr. Kalishe felt the pockets of the victim's jacket and found a wallet. She lifted the right side of the jacket and reached into the inside pocket. As soon as she pulled out the bifold wallet, she knew this was going to be trouble. She looked up at Buck and held up the wallet.

Buck took the wallet in his gloved hand and opened it. "Oh, shit."

He showed the badge and ID inside the wallet to the tech, who used the camera on the tablet to photograph them and log them in the file.

Buck put the wallet in an evidence bag he got from the tech and noted the number on the bag, which matched the number Dr. Kalishe had written on the victim's neck. He stepped over to the bar, laid the wallet on the bar top so the badge and ID were visible, pulled out his phone and took a picture. He then dialed a number and waited.

"Hey, Buck," said Director Jackson. "How's it going?"

"Slow, sir," said Buck. "We are in the building, and it is worse than I could have imagined. The shooter was incredibly efficient, but that's not why I'm calling. We may have a problem. I just sent you a picture of a badge and ID. I was hoping you could make a call and find out what his assignment was and why he was here."

There was silence on the phone while the director looked at the picture Buck sent him.

"Fuck, Buck. This is going to be bad," said the director. "I'll make a call and get back to you."

Buck thanked him, picked up the ID and returned to the body. He spotted Sheriff Foley and Duke Morgan and waved them over. They stepped up next to him and looked at the body and pistol the tech was placing in an evidence bag.

"He doesn't look like he belongs here," said Sheriff Foley. "Good guy with a gun?" he asked.

Buck handed him the evidence bag, and he stared at it for a moment, then he handed it to Duke Morgan.

"Fuck, Buck," said Duke Morgan. "Do we know who his protectee is?"

Buck explained that he had asked Director Jackson to make the call and see what information he could get. The expectation was that somewhere amongst all the bodies was someone under the protection of the Colorado State Patrol executive protection division. Only the governor could assign protection for someone in Colorado, and there had to be a damn good reason for the request.

Buck's phone rang, and he looked at the number. He stepped away from the group and answered the call.

"Governor," said Buck. The governor seldom called Buck, but when he did, it usually meant that whatever investigation he was on was about to take a turn, not usually for the best.

"Buck," said the governor. "I'm afraid I am going to throw a wrench into your investigation. Corporal James Cordova was assigned to Congressman Royal Sanders. The congressman's office contacted me two days ago and requested protection because the congressman had been receiving death threats. Corporal Cordova started his protection detail yesterday morning when the congressman arrived in the state. Buck, what the hell was he doing in that club?"

"That's a good question, Governor. The first thing we need to do is find out if the congressman is outside with the survivors, is being treated with the wounded or if he is dead inside. Once we know that, then we can start to figure out why he was here."

"Okay, Buck. Let me know as soon as you can make that determination, and Buck. Let's keep this under the radar until we can find out the circumstances."

The governor disconnected the call, and Buck walked back to the group. They all looked at Buck.

"What I am about to tell you stays within this group for now. That was the governor on the phone. The protectee was Congressman Royal Sanders, and we need to figure out if he is alive or dead."

Duke was the first one to break the silence. "The same Royal Sanders who is trying to pass national legislation outlawing drag shows?"

Buck nodded. "Yep. That Royal Sanders. And now you understand why we need to keep this low-key."

Congressman Royal Sanders was an ultraconservative Republican congressman representing Colorado's third congressional district and, of late, an outspoken critic of anything related to drag. He had already proposed legislation banning drag queens from reading to kids in libraries or schools, and he was preparing legislation to propose to Congress to ban drag shows with harsh penalties for any violation. The likelihood that either piece of legislation would pass was slim to none since Democrats held a slight advantage in each house, but it was legislation guaranteed to fire up his base. The question now was, why was he there? Who was he with? And how was his office going to spin it?

Buck was never interested in politics, and since he didn't have a dog in this fight, he would follow the evidence wherever it led. If the congressman and his staff were worried about his reputation, then he should have thought twice about where to spend his evening.

Buck called over Franklin and had him bag and tag the gun. Franklin sealed the bag and signed across the top. He marked the bag with Dr. Kalishe's victim number and handed it to her technician.

Buck stepped away with Detective Morgan and Sheriff Foley. "Looks like we need to find the congressman. Duke, can you check outside with the medical personnel and see if he is either being treated or has been transported to a hospital? Jack, let's you and I continue looking in here."

Duke nodded and headed for the door. Buck and the sheriff split up; Buck headed for the stage area while Sheriff Foley headed towards the kitchen and dressing areas. A large pile of bodies was lying in front of the rear emergency exit. Buck stepped around them and pushed the panic hardware mounted to the door. He heard the lock click, but the door wouldn't budge.

Sheriff Foley stepped up behind him. "Bastard

parked an old truck against the emergency door. Everyone had to pass by the shooter to get out of the building. You need to follow me."

They walked away from the door and headed towards a back corner. They found Dr. Kalishe working on an older dark-haired man. He had the rugged good looks of a man who had spent a lot of time working outside. Dr. Kalishe handed Buck the man's wallet.

"Shit," said Buck, looking at the ID in the plastic window. "Looks like we found our congressman."

"One bullet hole in the chest. Probably nicked the heart," said Dr. Kalishe. "I'll mark him to get on the table first."

Buck thanked her and looked at the two other men who had been sitting at the table with him. The older, gray-haired man who had been wearing a cowboy hat was slumped in the seat with a hole in his chest. The second man, about the same age as the congressman, had fallen across the bench seat and had a bullet hole just over his left eye. There was no obvious exit wound.

Sima Kalishe removed the older man's wallet from his pants pocket and handed it to Buck. Buck pulled out his phone and took a picture of the ID. He handed the wallet to the tech.

Dr. Kalishe leaned over the second man, slid his leather vest out of the way and stopped. "Buck," she said.

Buck walked to the opposite side of the bench seat

and looked where she was pointing. The black pistol clipped to his belt was undisturbed, so Buck pulled it from the holster, dropped the magazine and ejected the round from the chamber. He handed both to the technician.

Dr. Kalishe looked at him. "No wallet or ID."

Buck raised his phone and took a picture of the man. Luckily the damage to his head didn't make getting a good picture of his face too difficult. He stood, stepped away from the table and placed a call. Melanie Hart answered on the second ring.

"Hey, Buck. How bad is it?"

"Bad, Mel. I need you and George to run an ID and a picture for me." Buck clicked a few buttons on his phone and hit send.

George Peterman and Melanie Hart were the CBI cybersecurity team based out of Grand Junction, Colorado, and they couldn't be more different.

George Peterman had joined CBI after retiring from the navy, where he'd spent his entire career working in cybersecurity. As far as Buck was concerned, George and his partner, Melanie Hart, were two of the best computer people he knew. Paul Webber was good. Ashley Baxter was better, but these two were world-class.

Melanie Hart was about five foot two, with shoulder-length black hair; she wore black jeans and dark gray hoodies and had several piercings. Anyone meeting her for the first time would think she was a high school kid, but she had received her doctorate in computer science from MIT about a dozen years ago. She'd joined CBI right out of college.

George Peterman could have passed for her father. George was about the same height as Buck, a shade under six foot, but where Buck still weighed what he'd weighed when he played football in high school, George had added a few pounds over the years.

"Got them. We'll run background on the ID and run the other through facial rec. We'll call when we have something."

Buck thanked her and disconnected the call. He wondered if the guy with the gun and no ID was with the congressman or the older man—one more mystery to add to the growing list of mysteries.

Chapter Seven

One of the Mesa County forensic technicians approached the group and tapped Detective Morgan on the arm. Duke turned to face him.

"We found two pistols, one at the bar and one in the kitchen. Thought you'd want to see them before we process the scene."

The tech headed off, followed by Duke Morgan, Buck and Sheriff Foley. He stopped at the end of a long hall near the bar and pointed to the black pistol under the footrest. Buck pulled out his phone and took pictures of the pistol. The tech reached down and picked up the pistol.

"Nine millimeter US Arms model 17." He hit the magazine release, dropped the extended magazine and showed it to the group. "Empty," he said. "This makes magazine eleven we've found so far."

Buck looked down the hall. "Where is the second pistol?" he asked.

The tech sealed the evidence bag and headed down the hall. They passed the dressing room and the restrooms and entered the kitchen. They could see some damaged plates and cups lying on the floor, along with a couple of small pans. The pistol was under one of the stainless steel prep tables.

Buck took some more pictures, and the tech followed the same routine as he had with the other pistol.

"Twelve extended magazines," said Sheriff Foley. "This guy came ready for war. Do you think he ran out of ammo, and that's why he stopped shooting?"

Buck looked back down the hall towards the bar. "Could be, but I'm wondering why he threw the pistols in opposite directions and why he left them at all?"

He looked at the two bodies lying on top of each other in the hall and then at the third woman, who had tried to crawl down the hall after being shot, based on the blood trail. He looked around and pushed open the restroom doors. The angle was wrong based on the blood splatter on the wall. He walked to the dressing room door, pushed it open, turned and looked down the hall.

"This was the last place he shot from," said Buck. Everyone turned to look at him. "It's the only angle that works. Let's do a gunshot residue check on the door and the frame."

He looked behind him and spotted the three bodies lying on the floor. "What do we know about these three bodies? Are they entertainers, audience or something else?"

"No idea yet," said Duke Morgan.

"No worries," said Buck.

Buck stepped into the hall. "Why throw the guns in opposite directions? The shooter knew we would find them, eventually. What was he hoping to accomplish, and where did he go after he got rid of the guns?"

"With the lights out," said Sheriff Foley, "he could have gotten out with the crowd that made it to the front doors. No one would know since no one saw him to begin with. Our descriptions of the shooter are all over the board. The only thing anyone agrees with is that he had two pistols with extended magazines, and we feel that is true based on finding two pistols with thirty-round magazines."

"What if he didn't leave," said a voice behind them.

Ashley Baxter and Paul Webber, dressed in Tyvek from head to toe, walked up to the group and looked at the bodies in the hall.

CBI Agent Ashley Baxter had worked with Buck on many interesting cases over the years besides working on her own cases. At thirty-four years old, she was the youngest agent in the Grand Junction Field Office. She'd joined CBI straight out of college, and, having had no experience in the field, she valued the time she got to spend with Buck because she learned so much about running an investigation.

Bax stood about five foot six with blue eyes and blond hair that she often kept tied in a ponytail that hung through the hole in the back of her CBI cap. Some people would describe her as husky, or what used to be called having a "mountain girl" figure. She wasn't gorgeous, but she was pretty enough to turn men's heads when she entered a room until they spotted the badge and gun clipped to her belt. She had been with the Colorado Bureau of Investigation for eleven years and had earned Buck's respect.

She was also a whiz at doing deep background searches—a talent Buck did not share, so he relied on Bax to help him. They worked well as a team and collaborated more and more as the years rolled by.

Paul Webber was over six foot four with a muscular physique. He had joined CBI seven years earlier after spending ten years with the Dallas, Texas, police department. His last post had been as a homicide detective. Paul may have seemed like a giant, but those who knew him knew he was a pussycat. He was one of the most soft-spoken men Buck had ever met.

"We checked every video camera we could find in the area," said Bax. "No sign of anyone leaving the club either on foot or in a vehicle."

"If he parked a truck against the back door," said Paul, "how did he leave?"

Duke Morgan pulled down his mask. "Our first deputy arrived about five minutes after the shooting started. We received the first nine-one-one call at eleven thirteen P.M., and the caller said the shooting had just begun. The first deputy was here at eleven eighteen P.M. The following deputies blocked off all the exits so no cars could leave. Grand Junction police officers arrived two minutes later and corralled everyone running out of the building, and the first deputies entered the building minutes later, so about eleven twenty-five P.M. As far as we know, no one left the property. Now, it was pretty crazy, so anything is possible."

"So, we have three options," said Buck. "Either the shooter is inside dead, he was transported to the hospital with the other wounded, or he was still in the building when your deputies entered. Duke, can you have the first deputy to enter the building meet us outside?"

Duke pulled his radio from his pocket and stepped away from the group. Buck and the rest of the group headed for the front doors so the forensic team could process the hall and the bodies.

They stepped outside into the heat and were approached by a young deputy. "Sheriff, Detective Morgan called me to meet him here."

Sheriff Foley introduced them to Deputy Steven Tolliver. Buck pulled off his mask and pulled the Tyvek hood back. It was still warm for this early in the morning, and he was sweating under the jumpsuit, which he unzipped.

"Deputy," said Buck. "You were the first deputy to enter the building?"

"Yes, sir. Deputy Steely and I entered the building as soon as the Grand Junction cops arrived."

"You didn't wait for SWAT?" asked Bax.

"No, ma'am. People had just started running out of the building, and it sounded like someone was using a machine gun. We didn't want to wait."

Buck smiled. "You did the right thing, Deputy. You should be proud of yourself."

Deputy Tolliver lowered his eyes and scuffed the ground. "Wish we could have gotten here sooner. A lot of people died," he said.

The sheriff patted him on the shoulder, and Tolliver wiped the tears from his eyes.

"Deputy," said Buck. "How long after you entered

the building did the gunfire stop?"

Tolliver thought for a minute. "Not more than a minute. It was dark, and people were still running for the doors, so we got held up in the lobby. We thought the shooting was finished, and then we heard four shots, three close together and a couple of seconds later one more. That was it."

Buck looked at the group. "That was the last four shots in the back hall. We know the shooter threw the pistols away right after that. So where did he go?"

"He had to still be in the building when SWAT arrived," said Duke Morgan. "We need to get a list of all the survivors we interviewed and are interviewing. The shooter might still be here or at the sheriff's office."

"We also need the registration for the truck," said Buck. "Bax, can you and Deputy Tolliver check the truck parked at the back door and see if the registration is in it?"

Bax and Tolliver headed around the building, and Duke Morgan called the office and told one of the other detectives not to let anyone leave after being interviewed. He disconnected the call.

"Shit," he said. "They've already released several of the people who were interviewed. No reason to keep them."

"Duke," said Buck. "Check with SWAT and see if any survivors were found inside after they started to clear the building."

Bax and Tolliver came around the building. "We

found the registration in the glove box," said Bax. "I called the office to get a copy of the owner's driver's license."

She looked at the picture on her phone. "Norman Wingate," she said. "Lives in Fruita. We're gonna need a warrant."

Duke Morgan looked up. "I'll call my mom and get one."

Duke Morgan's mom was District Court Judge Jane Morgan. Jane and Buck had been friends for years, and she had helped him out on several cases, both in her capacity as a judge and as an advocate. She and her husband ran a shelter for abused women and children, and even though she wasn't a trained psychologist, she had a way with people that made her good at both jobs.

"Bax, you and Paul take Deputy Tolliver and a couple of SWAT officers and head for the address on the registration," said Buck. "We'll call you when we have the warrant. Let's see what Mr. Norman Wingate has to say about his truck being here."

Things were starting to move, but the little bug in Buck's brain that let him know when things were going to break was quiet.

Chapter Eight

The two SWAT cops who found me cowering in the janitor's closet were so nice and compassionate once they figured out I wasn't a threat. Scared the shit out of me when they opened the door and shined their lights into the darkened space. I think they were as surprised to see me as I was to see them.

The tears and the running mascara made the fear so real. They were quick to assess the situation and then helped me to my feet, frisked me, and led me through the darkened building to the light at the end of the tunnel; well, actually, it was the light from the front entry doors.

I was barefoot when I walked out into the parking lot. The shoes I had taken off of the dead entertainer hurt my feet, so I dumped them in the closet. Made it seem much more real. An EMT put a blanket around me and led me to a large white tent that had been set up in the parking lot. The SWAT guys kept reinforcing that I was safe now and no one would hurt me. I felt like telling them I was well aware I was safe now, but I figured I'd save that for another day. They asked me my stage name, and I told them it was Boobies Galore, and I showed them how the inflatable bra worked. It was good for a laugh and released a little of the tension in the room.

Two of the girls who I knew were entertainers sat in the chairs opposite me and then kept glancing over at me like they knew something wasn't right. I wish I had kept one of the guns. I would have killed them right there, right then, but that would ruin my escape.

Psychiatrists would be reviewing this event for years to come and would have a hard time figuring out my motivation. They would find it hard to believe I wasn't suicidal and that I wasn't looking for attention or to get caught. I guess most of the mass murderers had some kind of death wish. I didn't. I just wanted to kill as many people as possible to quiet the noise in my head. With the political climate and the violence that had joined the political discourse over the last few years, what better place to make a statement than at a drag club?

Proponents of the drag movement would decry the violence perpetrated against them, and opponents would offer up hopes and prayers while secretly applauding the action of one deranged gunman. What a fucking joke.

One of the detectives called one of the entertainers to a small cubicle, and she let go of her friend's hand and followed the detective. The entire time she talked to the detective, she kept glancing over her shoulder and looking at me.

A female detective came out of the other cubicle and asked me to follow her. She was a pretty brunette with shoulder-length hair. She wore jeans and a T-shirt with the Grand Junction Police Department logo emblazoned over her petite left breast. I kept staring at the logo.

She asked me to take a seat in front of a makeshift desk and asked if she could get me anything. I almost told her what she could get me, but then that would have ruined the moment.

She asked me to tell her how I came to be found in the janitor's closet, and I explained that I had gone into the dressing room to get changed and was standing behind the clothes rack when all the lights went out. The two other entertainers were sitting at the desk putting on makeup, and they both looked around, not knowing what to do.

I told the detective, Jenny was her name, that we heard shooting and screaming coming from the other side of the door and that we thought we would be safe in the dressing room. At some point, I heard someone coming down the hall and decided to hide. I wasn't sure how I found it in the dark, but I felt the doorknob to the closet, and I stepped inside. Within a minute, I heard the dressing room door open, and then two shots rang out. I heard the two entertainers hit the floor, and I huddled under the big sink, trying to hide.

I told her I heard more shots and was so scared that I started to shake. I let the tears flow, and she handed me a tissue from the box on the corner of the desk. I asked her what kind of person could do such a thing, and she told me the person must have been crazy. I almost laughed.

I gave her my name and address, and she asked about my stage name. I showed her how the small pump that was hidden under the dress inflated the fake boobs, and she laughed. She entered my name into her computer and, a few seconds later, showed me a picture of my driver's license. I acknowledged that the picture was me under the makeup.

When we were finished and I signed the statement, she called over a young Hispanic officer and asked him to give me a ride home. He was a nice young man, and he let me keep the blanket. He dropped me in front of the house and asked if he should wait until I got inside, but I thanked him and told him that wasn't necessary.

Thank god it was still dark when I slid out of his patrol car so no one could see me disappear around the corner and head towards my actual address. I crossed the street and went through the side gate. I'd left the back door unlocked and entered the house. I left all the lights off and headed upstairs to shower. I knew the nitrile gloves and the old coat would catch most of the gunshot residue, but a quick shower would make short work of anything that might have gotten on my face or arms.

I stepped out of the shower, toweled off and slipped on a pair of sweats. I headed for the kitchen. I could not believe how hungry I was. Killing people must be good for the appetite. I devoured the scrambled eggs and bacon and then turned on the news to see if the story had gained traction. I opened my laptop, and the story was everywhere.

I knew I should sleep, but I was too amped up. My adrenaline was pumping, my heart was pounding, and for the first time in a long time, the voices in my head were quiet. I hoped that would last, because I wasn't sure what I was going to do as an encore if they came back.

Chapter Nine

Bax turned off Highway 50 at Pine Street in Fruita and followed it north until she got to the left turn for East Grand Avenue. She parked behind the Fruita Police SUV and slid out of her seat. Paul exited the Jeep right behind her. Deputy Tolliver, in his MCSO SUV, and the two MCSO SWAT officers in their black SUV pulled in behind them. They all exited the vehicles and shook hands with Fruita Sergeant Gabe Espinoza.

Espinoza pointed to a gray house, the fourth one from the corner. "That's the address Dispatch gave me. I drove by and there were no lights on. Do you have the warrant?"

Bax nodded. "We just got the call. I have the warrant on my phone." She handed her phone to Espinoza, who read the warrant and handed her back her phone.

"Since it's pretty early, I'd like to keep this low-key if possible. Let's try not to wake up the neighbors."

Paul looked at all the other members of the group. "No problem, Sergeant. Your town, your rules."

Espinoza smiled and looked at Deputy Tolliver. "Steve, you and the SWAT team take the back of the house. We'll approach the front, knock and see what happens. Be ready for anything since we have no idea what, if any, involvement Mr. Wingate had in the events last night."

Everyone nodded and returned to the vehicles. They

pulled up the street and parked in front of the Wingate house. Deputy Tolliver and the SWAT officers moved silently up the driveway and disappeared behind the house. Sergeant Espinoza, Bax and Paul walked up the front walk and stepped onto the small front porch. Bax stepped to one side of the door, and Paul stayed at the bottom of the stairs with his hand on his pistol.

Espinoza looked at them and knocked on the door. He waited a few seconds, heard nothing from inside the house and knocked harder. The third time he made a fist and used the side of his fist in a typical cop knock. That got the owners' attention, and the front porch light came on and a sleepy voice behind the door asked what they wanted.

"Police, Mr. Wingate. We want to ask you some questions. Please open the door." Espinoza held his ID up to the peephole in the door.

They could hear a second voice inside, a woman's voice, asking what was going on.

"I don't know," replied Wingate. "They said they're the cops, and they need to ask me some questions."

"Well, open the door and see what they want, you old fool," said the female voice.

They heard the door unlatch, and it opened partially, held in place by a silver chain. A grizzled face looked out. "What d'ya want at this ungodly hour?"

Espinoza, in uniform, stepped closer to the door. "Mr. Wingate, we need a word. Please open the door."

The door closed, and they heard the chain slide off and the door opened. Wingate, who stood about five foot ten, stood there in a plaid robe and black socks. The woman standing behind him was five foot five and heavyset, with short gray hair. They both looked like they had just woken up, which they had.

Espinoza introduced Bax and Paul and asked the Wingates if they could come in. Mr. Wingate stepped aside, and they entered a small but well-kept living room.

"What's this about?" asked Mrs. Wingate.

Bax looked at Mr. Wingate as Tolliver and the two SWAT officers entered the house. The Wingates looked at the new arrivals and their eyes got wide.

"Folks, we have a warrant to search your house," said Bax.

Mr. Wingate shook his head as if he hadn't heard correctly. "A warrant to search for what?"

Bax asked the Wingates to sit on the couch, and she sat opposite them in an old, well-worn armchair.

"Mr. Wingate, your truck was discovered at a crime scene this morning, and we need to know how it got there," said Bax.

Mr. Wingate looked at her like he wasn't comprehending. "My truck at a crime scene? That's not possible. It's in the garage out back. Must be some mistake."

Bax nodded to Tolliver, and he walked out of the room, followed by one of the SWAT officers. Paul and the other SWAT officer searched the rest of the house. Bax pulled out her phone, opened the gallery and showed Mr. Wingate the picture of the truck blocking the back door of the club. Wingate picked up a pair of glasses off the table next to the couch, put them on and looked at the truck.

He shook his head. "Sure looks like my truck, but there's no way. It's in the garage."

Bax put her phone away. "Mr. Wingate, where were you between ten and midnight last night?"

He looked at his wife. "We were right here. We watched the news at ten o'clock and then went to bed."

Mrs. Wingate nodded in agreement.

Bax continued, "And you never left the house after the news?"

"No, never," said Mrs. Wingate. "Sure, we get up during the night. At our age, it's a fact of life, but we never leave the house. What's this about?"

Tolliver stepped back into the living room. "There's no truck in the garage, just a Subaru Outback."

The Wingates looked at each other. "That can't be," said Mr. Wingate. "I put it in the garage last night after work. That can't be."

Paul looked at Bax and then back at Mr. Wingate. "Sir, where do you keep the keys for the truck?"

"I leave them in the ignition. The garage is locked, and I don't have to remember where I put them. You can check the Subaru. Those keys are in the ignition too."

"Who else has access to the garage?" asked Paul.

Mr. Wingate thought for a few seconds. "Just the

wife and I. Oh, and one of my former employees. But Bryce would have no reason to take my truck. He grabs some tools occasionally, but that's it."

"What do you do for a living, Mr. Wingate?" asked Bax.

"I'm an electrical contractor. Well, used to be. Now I do small electrical projects, kind of semiretired."

"And this Bryce, he's an electrician also?" asked Paul.

"Yeah," said Mr. Wingate. "He works for Tyson Electrical Contractors. They specialize in fancy lighting and sound systems. Very technical work. Not something I would do, myself."

"Do you know if he worked on the new drag club?" asked Tolliver.

"Yeah, they did. Bryce was very proud of that project. Put a lot of time into it."

"Mr. Wingate," said Bax. "Do you have Bryce's last name and current address?"

"Yeah. His last name is Tanner. He lives near Lincoln Park. Not sure of the address. What do you think he did?"

"Sir," said Paul. "Last night, there was a mass shooting at the new drag club. There are lots of people dead and injured. We're trying to figure out who was responsible."

Mrs. Wingate raised her hand and covered her mouth. Mr. Wingate looked bewildered. "You can't believe that Bryce could have had anything to do with that. He's a good kid. Worked for me for years. He never caused a bit of trouble. No. It's not possible."

Bax looked at Paul, and he nodded, pulled out his phone and stepped out of the living room onto the front porch.

Bax looked at Mr. Wingate. "Sir, do you own any guns?"

He looked up at Bax with suspicion in his eyes. "You think I had something to do with this?"

"No, sir," said Bax. "We just need to cover all our bases. So, do you?"

"Yeah, I have a rifle I use for elk hunting. That's it. Do you want to see it?"

Deputy Tolliver nodded, and Mr. Wingate stood up, and they headed towards the back of the house. They returned a few minutes later.

"Rifle's locked in a small gun safe. It's clean," said Tolliver.

"Mr. Wingate, what kind of person is Bryce?" asked Bax.

"You know," said Mr. Wingate. "He's a normal kid. He was never any trouble when he worked for me. He was easygoing, seemed to make friends with the other guys on the crew. Never got into any fights. Nothing like that."

Mrs. Wingate looked uneasy sitting on the couch. Bax leaned closer. "Mrs. Wingate. Do you have something you'd like to add?"

Mrs. Wingate hesitated. She wrung her hands

together and looked at them as she was doing it. "I heard he might have been in reform school when he was younger. I don't know the circumstances, but he might have been abused as a child."

Mr. Wingate stared at her, and she looked up. "Just something he mentioned at one of the weekend barbecues we used to have for the employees," she said. "I don't know anything more than that."

"Is he a local boy?" asked Tolliver. "Does he have family here?"

She thought for a few seconds. "He mentioned that his parents were both dead. I don't know if he was local or not."

Paul stepped into the living room and stood next to Bax. He leaned towards her and whispered, "We have an address. We need to go."

Bax thanked the Wingates, apologized for the intrusion and said they would be in touch. They headed for the vehicles, and Bax thanked Sergeant Espinoza for his assistance. Bax slid into her Jeep, and Paul held up his phone with the address and directions. She put the Jeep in gear and headed for the highway. It was time to find Bryce Tanner.

Chapter Ten

Buck stood next to the black Suburban and looked at the neighborhood map Grand Junction SWAT commander Phil Black had pulled up on his phone.

"Several ways out of here, and we're spread pretty thin to cover them all."

"What do you suggest?" asked Buck.

They were parked along the curb on Chipeta Avenue between North 15th Street and North 16th Street. The house they were looking at was one block south of Chipeta Avenue on North 17th Street. It was a quiet residential neighborhood that was just waking up. The sun had crept over the mountains to the east, and the streetlights had all turned off.

Phil Black, a tall thin black man with a bald head and trim goatee, enlarged the map of the house. "Nothing easy about this, so I think we send four of my guys into the backyard from the neighboring house, and we take the direct approach and walk up to the door. If he doesn't answer, we have the ram with us. We'll hit the door and enter the house. Do we have the warrant?"

Buck checked his phone and nodded. He hated going into an unknown situation, but they still might have the element of surprise on their side. Commander Black keyed his mic and gave out the assignments. When he felt his backyard team had had enough time to get into position, they slid into their vehicles, drove one block over, turned right onto North 17th Street and pulled in front of the third house on the right.

The SWAT officers bailed out of their Suburban, pulled the forty-pound ram from the back of the vehicle and headed for the door. Buck, wearing his ballistic vest and CBI windbreaker, followed Commander Black as they approached the door. Using the side of his fist, Buck knocked hard on the door and stepped to the side.

"Bryce Tanner, police. We have a warrant," said Buck.

Receiving no response from inside the residence, Buck nodded to the SWAT officer carrying the ram, who stepped up to the door and smashed the ram against the door. The door exploded inwards and slammed against the wall. Commander Black and three SWAT officers raced into the house.

"POLICE. WE HAVE A WARRANT" was heard throughout the house as the officers entered and cleared the rooms.

"CLEAR. CLEAR. CLEAR" came from several directions.

The officers reconvened in the tiny living room and stepped outside, where they had room to move.

"Looks like no one is home," said Commander Black. "What do you want to do?"

Buck stepped to the front door and looked at the neighbors who had come out and were standing on the sidewalk.

"Have your guys talk to the neighbors. See what they can tell us about Bryce Tanner."

Buck looked around the living room. "Doesn't look like anyone lives here. I'm going to look around. Also, have your backyard guys check the rest of the property and make sure we didn't miss a hidey-hole."

Commander Black keyed his mic as he stepped out the front door onto the sidewalk. He huddled with his officers and relayed directions to the backyard team. Buck put on black nitrile gloves and stepped into the kitchen. He opened the refrigerator door, which was as empty as the freezer. He looked inside the oven, which looked like it hadn't been used in years. He opened all the cabinets and found nothing. If anyone was living here, they didn't cook or eat here.

Bax, Paul and Deputy Tolliver walked into the kitchen and looked around.

"This is cleaner than my house," said Paul. "Nobody home?"

Buck nodded. "Check the rest of the house and let's see what we can find."

He stepped into the living room as Bax headed one way and Paul another. Tolliver was looking at some pictures that hung on the wall.

"These are old pictures. Look at the clothes. I wonder if they are Tanner's family."

Buck pulled out his phone and took pictures of the pictures. He dialed a number and waited as it rang.

"Hey, Buck," said George. "What's up?"

"Hi, George. Can you run background on Bryce Tanner? We're at the address you sent Paul, and it doesn't look like anyone lives here. Also, see if anyone by that name owns other property in the area."

"Will do," said George. "By the way. We're still running facial rec on the guy at the club. Nothing yet. I'm going to expand the search to the military database. Mel just sent you the link to the investigation file. She uploaded the background package on George Billings. Take a look and let us know if you need more."

Buck thanked George for the information and told him to thank Mel for opening the investigation file. Around the CBI office, Buck was known as a technological dinosaur. He was happiest when he had paper files and his little notebook, but the times were changing, and Buck tried to change with them.

CBI had gone digital a couple of years back, so instead of having a blue binder for each case, Buck just had to open a program on his laptop. The new case was automatically assigned a case number, and Buck would list everyone who needed access to the file and send them email invites. All evidence, lab reports, photos, etc., that were part of the case would be uploaded into the file, and anyone who needed access just had to open the file. That was much better than the old system, where everything had been placed in the binder by hand, and Buck would spend half his time tracking down who had the binder.

For a tech dinosaur like Buck, this made his life so much easier, and he had ready access to anything he needed. Buck just had to click on a file and open the chronology page, which was the first page in the file. Nothing was ever entered into the file without a note entered in the chronology first. The chronology kept track of everything that happened in the investigation.

Buck was meticulous about his case files and had never lost a case in court in all his years in law enforcement because something was missing from his files.

Buck clipped his phone to his belt and pulled off the nitrile gloves. He looked at the neighbors across the street as they spoke with the SWAT officers. The SWAT officer spotted Buck and waved him over. Commander Black was talking with two older women who were wearing floral bathrobes. Buck was surprised until he realized most of these folks had just woken up.

Commander Black introduced Buck to Marla Scott and Helen Chancellor. "Ma'am," said Commander Black. "Can you repeat what you just told me for Agent Taylor?"

Marla Scott looked at Buck. She had a warm smile and short silver hair. "Roger hasn't lived here for a long time. He didn't get along with his folks after what happened."

"Roger who, ma'am?" asked Buck. "We're looking for Bryce Tanner. This is the address we were given."

Marla Scott looked confused. "That's Olivia Shipman's house. I don't know any Bryce Tanner. Olivia has a son named Roger, who hasn't been around in years. Some kind of falling-out."

"What happened, ma'am?" asked Buck.

"Olivia, that's Mrs. Shipman, told us that Roger was in reform school in Ohio until he was eighteen, which was about twelve years ago. I don't know all the details, but . . ."

"We heard he murdered someone when he was young," said Helen Chancellor. She could have been Marla's sister, except for the Southern accent she had that Marla didn't.

"Now, Helen. We don't know if that's true or not. Olivia never wanted to talk about it," said Marla.

Helen looked at Marla. "She told me one night when we were drinking in the backyard. She said he killed a preacher. And it wasn't Ohio; it was Michigan or Kentucky."

Helen was obviously the neighborhood gossip, and Buck smiled. "They moved here while Roger was still in reform school. I heard he was wanted for killing another man, some doctor." She leaned closer to Buck. "I don't think their last name was Shipman. Might have been in witness protection or something like that."

Marla looked shocked. "Where do you get this stuff from?"

Helen just shrugged her shoulders.

"Anyway," said Marla. "Roger never lived in this house. Olivia told me he was supposed to take care of it if anything ever happened to her, but then she got transferred to the nursing home, and the place went to hell. My husband keeps the lawn mowed and makes sure no one goes near the place. Haven't seen Roger in years."

"Do you know what nursing home Mrs. Shipman is in?" asked Buck.

Helen answered first. "St. Theresa's on North

Avenue. She's been there a couple of years. She had a stroke and never really recovered. She was a wonderful person before the stroke."

"What about Mr. Shipman?" asked Buck. "Is he around?"

"We haven't seen him around for years," said Marla. "One day he was here, and the next, he was gone. I guess he left about the time Roger got out of the reform school. Olivia couldn't understand why he just up and left one day without a word to anyone. Strange if you ask me."

Buck thanked the women and walked back across the street to the Shipman house. Paul and Bax walked through the door and pulled off their gloves.

"Place is clean," said Paul. "Maybe the forensic team can get something, but the place is spotless. I doubt even Franklin can find anything."

Bax nodded in agreement. "What's next?"

Buck explained what the neighbors had told him and that he was confused. He hoped that maybe Mrs. Shipman could shed some light on the problem.

"I'm gonna go back to the club. According to the ladies across the street, Mrs. Shipman is in St. Theresa's nursing home on North Avenue. See if you can track it down and pay her a visit. She had a stroke, so you may not get much, but let's see if she has anything to say."

They both nodded and headed for Bax's Jeep. Buck waved over Commander Black. "Phil, unless you see a reason to stay, release your team, and thanks for the assist."

"No worries, Buck. You let me know if you need us again."

He keyed his mic, rounded up his team and they headed for their vehicles. The police handyman was fixing the broken lock on the front door, and Buck made one more circuit through the house. He walked out, thanked the handyman and headed for his Jeep.

He wondered where this investigation was headed.

Chapter Eleven

Harlan Groves rose early like he did every morning. He liked the peace and quiet of the compound before the others woke up and started their day with meditation, yoga, and all that other spiritual stuff. The barn was his sanctuary, and he got all the meditation he needed taking care of the livestock.

He never thought of himself as a farmer, having spent thirty years working as an aeronautical engineer for Martin Marietta in Denver. When it came time to retire, his wife decided they needed to move someplace with less snow, so they packed up and headed for Arizona. His wife, Fran, connected with a group of what Harlan used to call hippies, and when she suggested they join their commune, Harlan was amazed that he agreed to do it. That was almost twenty years ago.

Except for the five years he spent fighting in Vietnam with the Marines, he was a peace and love kind of guy, and this was important to his wife, so he went along, unwillingly at first, but over the years, the place had grown on him. He let his hair, which was still mostly brown, grow long, wore it in a ponytail and grew a beard. Now he spent his days in quiet reflection while caring for the livestock.

He was feeding the horses when he heard the phone in his house ringing. He checked his watch. The sun was barely over the horizon, so he wondered who would call his wife this early. He'd just put the hay in the trough when he heard his wife yell his name. He put down the water bucket he had picked up and walked towards the house. At his age, he didn't go anywhere quickly.

He walked through the kitchen door, and the smell of fresh bacon cooking on the stove filled his nose. Fran was leaning against the counter by the sink talking on her phone, and she pointed to his chair. He sat. Fran reached across the counter and turned on the small television hanging on the wall above the countertop. She flipped to the local channel and caught a breaking news story out of Colorado. Harlan looked at the TV.

The story was about a mass shooting at a drag club in Grand Junction, Colorado, and he heard the news anchor mention that there were almost a hundred dead and several hundred wounded. He wondered why this story had caught his wife's attention.

Fran disconnected the call and stood silently watching the news report. The fried eggs in the pan on the stove sizzled, and she reached over and turned off the flame.

"Fran, what's going on?" he asked.

She seemed distracted as she watched the news, like she was looking for some piece of information that hadn't revealed itself yet. The station went to a commercial, and she turned the TV off. She scooped his eggs out of the pan, set them on a plate with the bacon and placed them in front of him.

"That was Molly," she said. She wiped a tear from her eye with her apron and sat down opposite him. "That club they were just talking about. That's the new club that Jeremy was working at. Molly can't reach him, and she's worried sick."

Molly was Fran and Harlan's oldest daughter. She lived with her family in Colorado Springs, Colorado. Jeremy was her oldest son, and Fran could remember a few weeks back when he called to tell her that he had gotten a bartending job at a new drag club in Grand Junction, Colorado, and was excited to be moving to a place of his own.

He would be sharing an apartment with several of the performers from the club. Fran wasn't sure if Jeremy was into drag or if this was just a good job, and she never felt comfortable asking. Jeremy was always, what her father would say, a little girly, but she never took him for being anything other than her grandson. Now she might never know.

Harlan sipped his coffee. "What do the cops say?"

"Molly hasn't been able to get through to either Jeremy or the sheriff's office. Frank was loading up the car and was going to head over that way. She said it's a couple of hours' drive. He wants to see firsthand what's going on."

Fran's hand shook as she picked up her coffee cup and took a sip. Harlan looked at her while he bit into a piece of bacon. "Let's not panic until we have some more information. Molly will keep us in the loop, and then we can decide what, if anything, we need to do."

Tears filled Fran's eyes. "He was always such a fragile boy." She stood up and went into the living room. Harlan stood, walked into the living room and hugged her. "Why don't you pack some things for a couple of days? That way, we are ready to travel if the worst has happened."

Fran nodded, wiped her eyes and headed for the bedroom. He would need to gas up the old van and check the oil and the tires to make sure it could make the trip. He walked back into the kitchen, finished his breakfast, cleaned his plate and mug and headed back to the barn. Harlan was a practical man who would wait until they received word, but he needed to be ready for his wife's sake.

Chapter Twelve

Bax turned off North Avenue and pulled into the driveway for St. Theresa's Convalescent Home, a modern two-story stucco-and-wood building that would be more at home at a ski resort than in Grand Junction. She stopped short of the porte cochere because the drive was blocked by several Grand Junction police cars, unmarked SUVs and the coroner's van.

Bax and Paul slid out of the Jeep, grabbed their backpacks and headed for the front door. Their way was blocked by a young police officer with a clipboard, who told them the building was closed.

They flashed their badges and asked the young man what had happened.

"I heard one of the residents was beaten to death last night. You'll need to talk to the detectives if you want more information."

Bax spotted one of the detectives she knew and called him over.

"Hey, guys. What brings you here?" asked Detective Mark Ridgeway. Ridgeway was average height and wore a wrinkled suit. He didn't look like he had slept much in the last couple of days.

"We came to see a resident," said Bax. "What's going on?"

"Sometime during the night, one of the residents, Mrs. Olivia Shipman, was beaten to death with a hammer. She wasn't found until this morning."

Paul looked at Bax and then at Detective Ridgeway. "You did say Olivia Shipman was the victim?"

"Yeah, why?" asked Ridgeway. He stopped for a few seconds. "Is that who you were coming to see?"

Bax nodded. "Want to tell us what happened? Last we saw you, you were taking statements at the drag club."

Detective Ridgeway smiled. "As you can imagine, we're a little shorthanded right now. I got the call just after five this morning, and I was pulled off the drag club and sent here."

He called over one of the forensic techs and asked him for some Tyvek booties and gloves, which he handed to Bax and Paul and told them to follow him. He filled them in as they walked.

"Mrs. Shipman, according to the doctor on duty, suffered a stroke several months back and was pretty much a vegetable. This was her second stroke. The first happened a couple of years ago. Her daughter refused to pull the plug on her. Guess she was waiting for a miracle or something. Late last night, someone slipped into the building without setting off any alarms, put Mrs. Shipman in a wheelchair and took her to the basement to a mechanical room. Once there, that person proceeded to beat her with a hammer. She wasn't found until the custodian arrived for his shift."

They stopped at the door marked MRS. SHIPMAN and stepped inside. Two forensic techs were pulling fingerprints off several surfaces while a third was bagging up all the clothes and linens in the room.

"Like looking for a needle in a haystack," said Ridgeway. "We probably have fifty sets of prints in here."

Bax stepped around Paul and walked over to one side of the bed. She looked in the drawers on the nightstand and looked at the pictures sitting on the windowsill. She picked up one of the pictures and motioned for Paul, handing him the picture.

"Think that's her son, Roger." She looked at Detective Ridgeway. "Do you have the sister's name?"

"Yeah. Marybeth Johnson. We spoke with her this morning. She lives someplace in Michigan. She's gonna fly in as soon as she can get a flight. She said we should call her brother, Roger Shipman, but we haven't been able to reach him. She said they haven't spoken in years."

Bax made some notes on her phone, and they followed Detective Ridgeway into the hall. He stopped at an elevator, pushed the down button, entered and pushed the button for the basement. They exited the elevator into a beehive of activity. Police officers and forensic techs were looking in every nook and cranny.

From down the hall, they could hear the deep voice of Detective First Class Jessie Maldonado, and they followed Ridgeway until they came to the open mechanical room door. They stepped inside.

Jessie turned and looked to see who was intruding into her space. She smiled when she saw Bax and Paul. Jessie was a large woman with a booming voice. She could have played on the offensive line for the Denver Broncos. What most people couldn't see under her saggy suit was a hard body. Jessie was not fat. She was a weight lifter and had won numerous regional competitions. Her long black hair hung past her shoulders, and she wore tortoiseshell glasses. Jessie was a first-rate detective, and both Bax and Paul had worked with her on several cases.

She walked over and shook Bax's and Paul's hands.

"What brings you guys here?" she asked. "Thought you were working the drag club; man, what a mess."

"We were," said Bax. "We came to talk with your victim, Mrs. Shipman. We are trying to locate her son, Roger. Why are you here? Thought you were on vacation."

"Was on vacation," said Jessie. "That damn drag club pulled in everyone we had. Got the call at five A.M. from the chief that my vacation was canceled, and here I am. What's your interest in her son?"

"His name came up as part of the investigation," said Bax. "We spoke with the owner of the truck that blocked the rear exit of the club. The truck's owner had no idea it was gone until we showed up with the SWAT team and told him. He put us on to a guy named Bryce Tanner, who was an electrician working on the construction of the club."

"I got Roger's phone number from his sister," said Jessie, and she rolled her eyes. "But the number is out of service. What a real charmer she is. She was more pissed off this morning that her brother wasn't here than she was that her mother was dead. I don't think there's any love losts amongst all of them. What's this Bryce Tanner got to do with Roger Shipman?"

"We went looking for Bryce Tanner this morning, but the address we had for Tanner, according to the neighbors, is for Roger Shipman's family," said Paul. "Place was spotless. Doesn't look like anyone has lived there for a while. Neighbors said they hadn't seen Roger Shipman in years. We have no idea what Bryce Tanner has to do with Roger Shipman. Do you think Roger Shipman did this?"

"Good a guess as any at this point. Don't know why anyone else would go through the trouble," said Jessie.

She stepped out of the way so Bax and Paul could get a better look. The body was lying on the concrete floor with her legs twisted to each side. There was blood splattered all over the walls, the pipes, and even some on the ceiling, and there wasn't much left of Mrs. Shipman's head. The bloody hammer lying on the floor next to the body was covered with blood and brain matter. The assault had been vicious.

"Looks like rage," said Bax.

"Yeah, our thoughts as well," said Jessie. "Someone hated this woman."

They all stepped into the hallway so the pathologist and her assistant could get the body into the body bag and onto the gurney.

"You let me know if you find the brother," said Jessie. "Got a couple of questions I'd like to ask him."

Bax nodded. "You do the same."

Bax and Paul left Ridgeway and Jessie in the hall

and headed for the elevator. They waited until they were back on the main floor before they removed the gloves and booties. They walked down the hall and past a door that said ADMINISTRATION. Bax turned the knob, and they stepped into the office.

"May I help you?" asked a young woman sitting behind the desk.

Bax and Paul flashed their badges. "We'd like to talk to whoever is in charge."

The young woman lifted the phone on her desk, said something and hung up. Before she could say anything to Bax and Paul, the door behind her desk opened, and a tall thin woman with strawberry blond hair wearing too much makeup stepped out of the back office and introduced herself.

Elaine Crenshaw was intense, and she was not happy about what had happened at her facility.

"Are you people going to be here long?" she asked. "This is very disruptive for our residents."

Bax stared at her. "Mrs. Crenshaw, a woman was beaten to death in your basement. The police will be here as long as it takes to figure out who did this. I am sorry if that is disruptive to your patients."

Elaine Crenshaw looked taken aback. "I am sorry. What can I do for you?"

"How long has Mrs. Shipman been a patient here?" asked Bax.

"Like I told the other detective, this time, she has been here about eight months."

"This time," said Paul.

"Yes. This was her second stroke. The first was two years ago. She was a patient here for about a month before her son took her home. Her daughter was not happy about that move and threatened to sue us. The son told us he had arranged for round-the-clock care at her home. Who was I to argue?"

"Why was she brought back here the second time?" asked Bax.

"Her second stroke was far worse than the first one. I guess her son felt she would get better care here than at home. Her doctor referred her back to us, and luckily, we had a room for her."

"Mrs. Crenshaw, who pays her bills each month?" asked Bax.

"Her son sends us a check every month. We have never had an issue. He even helped us out when our security system needed to be upgraded. He sent around an electrician to help us out. He was always so nice. Who could have done such a terrible thing?"

"Have you ever met Roger Shipman?" asked Bax.

"As a matter of fact, no. Each admission was handled over the phone or online. I don't think he ever came to visit his mother either time."

"You don't happen to remember the name of the electrician he sent to help you?" asked Bax.

She thought for a minute, then held up her finger and opened the center desk drawer. She pulled out a large checkbook ledger and flipped through a few pages.

"Here it is," she said. She turned the ledger so Bax could see it and pointed to an entry.

Bax looked at the name. "Bryce Tanner," she said and looked at Paul.

"Did you contact her son when the body was discovered?" asked Paul.

"We tried several times, but we never reached him. The detectives contacted her daughter, who is a most unpleasant person."

"Why do you say that?" asked Bax.

"All she was concerned with was why her brother wasn't here and how inconvenient it was at this time for her to travel out here. This was her mother, and all she cared about was the name of our attorney."

Bax and Paul stood, took Roger Shipman's contact information, thanked her and left the office. They thanked the receptionist, who was wiping tears from her eyes, and they walked out of the building into the sunshine. Bax pulled out her phone and dialed Buck. This case had just taken an interesting turn.

Chapter Thirteen

Buck was talking with Sheriff Foley and Duke Morgan about the address confusion and the situation with Bryce Tanner and Roger Shipman when his phone chimed. He answered the call, spoke for a few minutes then disconnected the call and clipped his phone to his belt. He walked to the table in the center of the mobile command center and spoke to Sheriff Foley and Detective Duke Morgan.

"Bax and Paul swung by St. Theresa's nursing home and walked into a crime scene. Olivia Shipman was beaten to death last night."

Sheriff Foley's face showed his surprise. "Fuck, Buck. Who killed her, Roger Shipman or Bryce Tanner? And are they working together, or is this something else entirely?"

"Not sure," said Buck. "We need to figure out the connection between these two guys."

"We need to determine if either of them was here," said Duke Morgan.

"Let's get all the interviews that have been completed so far and review them," said Buck. "We need to focus on what the survivors saw."

Duke Morgan clicked some keys on his laptop and brought up the interviews that his detectives and the detectives from Grand Junction had completed. Since interviews were still ongoing, they would not, as yet, have a complete picture, but it would give them some place to start.

The door to the trailer opened and Bax and Paul walked into the command center. Buck filled them in on the plan, and they pulled out their laptops and coordinated with Duke Morgan to split up the reports. They pulled up stools around the table and went to work. There were a lot of reports to get through.

Buck looked at his watch and realized that none of them had eaten anything. He pulled out his phone, opened a delivery app, ordered several sandwiches and drinks and went back to reading reports on his laptop.

When the sandwiches arrived, they all took a much-needed break and used the time to clear their heads. They had been going at it for hours and were no closer to finding anything that indicated that anyone had seen Bryce Tanner in the building during the shooting.

They were at a serious disadvantage. All the reports they read indicated the shooter was of average height and probably white, although many survivors were unsure. Most of the survivors assumed it was a man; he wore clothes that covered all of his body parts and he wore a ski mask. The lights flashing, followed by darkness, and the sound system screaming in their ears didn't help with perception, and many of the reports conflicted with others.

While they ate, they discussed what they had read thus far, and the results were much the same. People were scared, hiding, and the last thing they were focused on was what the shooter looked like. Most of those interviewed wanted to get home to their loved ones, and the detectives helped to make that a reality.

Paul had been unusually quiet while he ate. He

looked deep in thought. Buck took a sip from his sixth bottle of Coke. "Paul, what's on your mind?"

Paul leaned back from the table. "Two things. All the interviews we've read so far talk about only one gunman. Now, it was late, the flashing lights and the loud music could have made it seem like there was one shooter, but we did find two guns, which leads to my second thought. I'm stuck on why the pistols were found in different locations in that back area. Why do that? Throw them away?"

"Good questions," said Duke Morgan. "Two shooters and they each toss a gun to confuse us, or one shooter who tossed both guns, also to confuse us. If it was a lone shooter, he was finished with a specific plan, and he wasn't going to risk getting killed or captured."

"But why throw them at all?" asked Bax. "The smart decision would have been to hide the guns and then run out with the last survivors. The shooter could have gotten boxed into the back hall and been unable to escape the building."

The little bug in Buck's head jumped up and kicked him. "Maybe the plan wasn't to escape." They all looked at him. "Think about it. We had cops all over the outside of the building and were in the process of moving inside when the shooting stopped. What if the shooter was concerned that we might check everyone coming out for gunshot residue? Easy to get off hands, but not so easy to get off clothes."

"You think he or she dropped the clothes," said Bax.

"More than that," said Buck. "What if the shooter

got rid of the guns and the clothes and hid somewhere waiting to get rescued?"

"Son of a bitch," said Sheriff Foley. "Our guys might have rescued the shooter and led him or her to safety. That's ballsy; pardon my French."

"Most people fled the building under their own power," said Duke Morgan. "There can't be that many reports from people our teams rescued. I'm going to run out to the interview tent and see if anyone took a report from someone that was rescued from the building."

Buck stood up, dropped his sandwich wrapper in the trash and faced the group.

"Keep looking for any reports that meet our discussion. I'm going to head back into the building."

Buck walked out the door while everyone else got back to their laptops. He had a hunch that he wanted to check out. The temperature outside the command center was brutal, and Buck hoped the public works guys had been able to get the building systems working. He knew they had lights on, but air-conditioning would be nice. This late in the afternoon would mean another hot night in Grand Junction. He wiped the sweat from his brow and entered the building.

He spotted Dr. Kalishe and stopped for a minute to talk with her. She told him they were just finishing up with the last victim and she would gather up her team and they would get some sleep. She had another team of pathologists from the Colorado National Guard performing autopsies at the coroner's office. So far, there were no surprises.

Buck thanked her for all her efforts and told her to have a good night. He had the same kind of conversation with Franklin and his team. They had done all they could do at this point and were going to get some rack time. They would be back in the morning and make sure they hadn't missed anything.

Buck continued walking through the building. He was grateful that the air-conditioning was working; otherwise, the heat of the day would have made working in the building unbearable. As it was, the smell of death was strong throughout the space.

Buck put on a pair of black nitrile gloves, walked around the bar and headed for the back hall. He stopped at the dressing room door and looked at the cards taped to the wall, identifying the three Hispanic women who had been killed in the hall. The one blood trail on the floor led towards the kitchen, away from the dressing room. He looked back towards the bar. The more he looked at the scene, he felt certain that the last women killed were shot from the dressing room. It was the only thing that made sense.

Buck turned the knob and pushed open the dressing room door. He looked at the edge of the door and noticed slight scarring on the wood. He unclipped his phone from his belt and called Franklin.

"Hey, you still in the building?" asked Buck.

"Just walked out the door. What do you need?"

"Did you guys get to the dressing room yet?" asked Buck.

"Not yet. That's on our agenda for tomorrow morning. You find something?" asked Franklin.

"Yeah. I think I have gunshot residue on the door."

"We'll be right there," said Franklin.

Buck disconnected the call and clipped his phone to his belt. He didn't want to enter the dressing room without the forensic team there, so he stood outside the door and waited. He didn't have to wait long.

He looked at the tired faces of Franklin and two of his technicians and apologized for dragging them back. He pointed to the small dark mark on the edge of the door.

Franklin pulled a swab from his kit, placed a drop of liquid on the tip and touched it to the small smudge. He pulled it back and put a drop of liquid from another bottle on the tip. The tip of the swab turned purple.

"Gunshot residue," he said to Buck.

Franklin and his team pulled up their hoods, put their masks back on and pushed open the dressing room door. Buck stood in the doorway and watched as they methodically went through the room, placing various items in evidence bags. After two hours, Franklin pulled down his mask and told Buck it was okay to enter the space. Buck stepped into the room and circled the space with his eyes.

He walked around the space and then stopped in front of a rack of dresses. One of the victims had been found behind the clothes rack. Something seemed odd, and he slid each dress aside. He wasn't sure what he was looking for, then it hit him.

Almost all the dresses were bright and colorful, with big flowers, butterflies and even dinosaurs printed on them. He slid one pink dress aside, and there on the rack was a black jacket with a hood and a pair of black pants.

"Franklin," he said.

Franklin walked over to the rack and looked where Buck was pointing. He looked at the rest of the clothes on the rack and smiled. "Which of these things is not like the others," he said.

Buck smiled. His five-year-old granddaughter Rosie always used that line, and it always made him smile.

Franklin put his mask on, removed the hanger with the coat and carried it over to the dressing counter. He laid it flat and set one of the sleeves on the front of the coat. One of his technicians handed him a sterile pad and placed a couple of drops of liquid on the pad. Franklin wiped the sleeve, focusing on the area around the cuff. The technician handed him a second wet pad, and he did the same with the other sleeve.

He placed the pads on the counter next to the coat and placed a couple of drops of the second liquid on each pad. The pads turned purple. He looked up at Buck, who nodded.

"Let's bag these up, and I'll have Bax call for a secure courier. I want these at the State Crime Lab tonight. He stepped away as Franklin and the tech placed both garments in large bags, sealed them and signed the chain of evidence flap. Buck walked around the room and noticed the small janitor's closet a little farther back in the room. He called Franklin and asked him to process that space as well. He accepted the two evidence bags from Franklin and headed for the door. He felt that his time in the dressing room was well spent.

Chapter Fourteen

Buck entered the command center and placed the two evidence bags on the desk. Everyone stopped what they were doing and looked at the two bags. Sheriff Foley picked up the first bag and turned it over in his hands. He looked at Buck for an explanation.

"Bax, can you call for a secure courier? We need to get these to the State Crime Lab ASAP," said Buck. Bax picked up her phone and dialed a number. She stood and walked to the other end of the trailer, spoke with someone, returned to the table and nodded to Buck. He picked up the second bag. "Our shooter was clever. He hung these on a clothes rack in the dressing room amongst a bunch of other clothes. Franklin did a rapid test, and there is gunshot residue on both sleeves." He looked at Duke Morgan. "Did you get any more reports from the interview tent?"

"Yes. We just finished logging them into your investigation file."

"Great, let's focus on anything that has to do with the dressing room."

They spent the next half hour reading report after report until Paul said, "I think I have something."

Paul finished reading the interview. He plugged a cable into his laptop and put the report up on the big-screen TV.

"One of the entertainers was found hiding in a janitor's closet in the dressing room. SWAT found him in tears, sitting on the floor," said Paul.

They all read the interview notes. "Fuck," said Buck. "Like we discussed, our SWAT guys escorted the shooter to safety."

"Shit," said Duke Morgan. "They would have had no way to know."

"That was what the shooter wanted," said Buck. "No one is at fault; we just underestimated the shooter. Can you get the detective who did the interview in here? And see if the SWAT guys who found him are still around?"

Duke looked at the signature at the bottom of the interview form, pulled out his phone and made a call. Sheriff Foley called Commander Martinez and asked him to find the two SWAT officers mentioned in the report. They all took a breath and waited.

Detective Jenny Porter walked into the command center and looked like she had been called to the principal's office. She took a seat at the end of the table and looked at his report on the big screen. Detective Porter was in her mid-twenties, short and thin, with medium-length brown hair. She had been a detective for three years. She looked around the table.

"Detective," said Buck. "First, loosen up. You're not in any trouble." Detective Porter's shoulders dropped, and her face lost all the tightness it had when she walked into the trailer. Buck smiled at her.

"Detective, do you remember the person you interviewed in this report?"

Detective Porter looked closer at the screen. "Yes, sir. SWAT found her—sorry, him—in a closet in the dressing room area. He said he had been hiding in the closet for a long time and was near hysterics when they found her—sorry, him. He told me his name was Roger Shipman, and he lived in Grand Junction."

"Did you confirm his identity?" asked Duke Morgan.

"Yes, sir. I followed the procedure we were given last night. Everything checked out."

"Was there anything unusual about the interview?"

Detective Porter looked confused. "No, sir. Not that I recall. It was just like the other interviews I did. What am I missing, sir?"

"This person might have been the shooter, so I want you to think back on the interview and see if anything stood out that you didn't think was important at the time," said Sheriff Foley.

Detective Porter looked at the sheriff. "He might have been the shooter, sir? Fuck. How did I miss that?"

"Don't beat yourself up, Jenny. We just discovered this ourselves. No one is looking to blame you, but now that you know, is there anything that stood out about the person or the interview?" asked the sheriff.

Detective Porter looked deep in thought. They could see she was running the interview back in her head. She looked up at those gathered around the table and opened her mouth but stopped before she said anything and thought again.

"There was one thing, sir. Now that I have time to think about it. His hands were rough. He had a callus on his right pointer finger."

She looked at her hand and rubbed the callus on her trigger finger between the first and second knuckle. "My callus comes from a lot of time on the range. He had a callus on the same finger, but his hands were also rougher."

"Why did that stand out?" asked Buck.

"Most of the other entertainers I interviewed had soft hands, more in keeping with the characters. When I first shook his hand, I thought that this guy must have some kind of labor job where he works with his hands. That's when I noticed the callus on his finger."

They discussed the interview for a few more minutes, but nothing else came to light.

"Detective, what did you do with him when you were finished?"

"I had one of the Grand Junction cops take him home since he didn't have a car." She pulled out a small notebook from her back pocket and flipped a couple of pages. "Here it is. I turned him over to Officer Trujillo, badge number ten forty-seven."

Sheriff Foley picked up his phone, stepped away from the table and placed a call. Buck thanked the detective, who stood and headed for the door, which opened as she reached for it. Commander Martinez and two SWAT officers stood back to let Porter leave, and they entered the command center.

"Deputies Malone and Folsom," said Commander Martinez.

Malone, a medium-height blond woman, and Folsom, a short, stocky black man, took seats at the end of the table.

"Guys, we appreciate you taking the time to chat with us," said Buck. They both nodded.

"You guys found a survivor hidden in a closet in the dressing room, correct?"

They both nodded.

"Can you walk us through it?"

Malone started. "Yes, sir. Folsom and I were assigned to clear the back hall leading to the kitchen. It was pretty dark back there until the lights came on. We found three women, all deceased, in the hall by the dressing room door. One looked like she had tried to crawl away after being shot and was shot a second time. Per procedure, we cleared the dressing room before we cleared the rest of the hallway."

Folsom took over. "Inside the dressing room, we found two entertainers dead on the floor, right by the counter. We confirmed they were deceased and then moved farther into the room, where we found another man behind a clothes rack. He had been shot once and was also deceased. We checked the rest of the room and noticed a door farther back. We opened the door, shined our lights into the space and spotted a guy in drag sitting on the floor, cowering under a sink. The poor guy looked scared to death."

Malone continued. "He looked like he had been crying; there were mascara streaks down his face. We asked him who he was and to step out of the closet. I frisked him, and we led him out of the dressing room. He told us he had been getting dressed when someone came into the room, shot the two entertainers at the counter and shot the man behind the clothes rack, who we guessed was looking for a place to hide. He said he remembered the janitor's closet and ran in before being spotted. He said he'd been in there for hours. We led him to the interview tent and turned him over to Jenny Porter."

"Anything out of the ordinary that you noticed or sensed when you found the guy?" asked Buck.

Malone and Folsom looked at each other, and then Folsom spoke. "No. He said his stage name was Boobies Galore." Folsom laughed. "He even showed us this pump under the dress he used to pump up the fake breast. He said he did a bit where each time he came onstage, his boobs would be bigger until they were huge. It was kind of funny. Anyway, we thought the sequence of events seemed odd. We wrote it off as fear or stress and didn't think much about it after that. We were kind of busy clearing the rest of the building."

"What seemed off?" asked Bax.

"Just the timing," said Malone. "All three victims were cool when we found them. Now, we're no experts, but it seemed to us that they had been dead for a while. The other odd thing was that if he were in the back getting changed, which seemed odd to us anyway, he would have been spotted when the third victim was shot. It's about fifteen feet from the clothes rack to the door, and even with the lights out, he would have been visible."

"You know what else was a little strange," said Folsom. "The two entertainers who were shot at the counter had duffel bags next to their seats that had their normal clothes in them. We checked the bags for weapons. There were no other duffel bags in the space. Where were the survivor's civilian clothes?"

"Good points, Deputies. Thanks for taking the time to talk with us," said Sheriff Foley.

Malone and Folsom stood, nodded at the group and left the trailer.

"Interesting conversations," said Paul. "Now, what do we do about it? Was the survivor Bryce Tanner or Roger Shipman?"

Sheriff Foley's phone rang. He picked it up, spoke and wrote something down on his notepad. He thanked the person on the other end and disconnected the call.

"That was Officer Trujillo. He dropped the survivor off at the address on North Seventeenth Street that you guys hit this morning. He said he had another call and didn't stick around to see if the guy entered the house. The procedure this morning was to do a DMV check and confirm addresses and faces. A lot of people did not have IDs on them, so it was the only way to be sure. The name and address that Detective Porter took down matched the DMV record, yet the address is the same one we have for Bryce Tanner. So, is Shipman Tanner, or are we completely off base?"

Paul sat back and stretched. "We know he didn't have a car since the officer had to take him home. If he didn't go into the house, which we know didn't happen, then where did the guy go? It was still dark outside, but someone could have seen him walking around the neighborhood. Did he have a car nearby, or does he live on a different street?"

Buck compared the DMV picture of Bryce Tanner to the picture Detective Porter had taken at the interview. Then he compared both of those to the picture of Shipman they had gotten from the DMV during the interview. He hooked his laptop up to the cable and put the three pictures on the big screen.

Sheriff Foley was the first to respond. "Could be the same person, but could they be twins? I think the makeup is throwing me off."

Bax had the same comment, and so did Paul. Buck picked up his phone and dialed the office.

"Hey, Buck," said Mel. "What's up?"

"Hey, Mel. If we send you a couple of pictures, can you and George do some computer magic and see if the pictures are of the same person?"

"No problem, Buck. Send them over. By the way. We've finished the deep dive on Bryce Tanner. We were able to go back twelve years. Before that, there is nothing. We're gonna try some other sources, but for the most part, he's a ghost. No priors that we can find."

Buck clicked on the driver's license image for Roger Shipman and posted it to the investigation file.

"I just sent you an image, one of the three we just discussed. This Roger Shipman could be Bryce Tanner, or they could be twins; either way, run a background check on him, and let's see what you get."

"Will do, Buck." Mel disconnected the call, and Buck looked at the group. He looked at his watch.

"We have no indications that there are twins involved," said Bax. "The neighbors never mentioned the Shipmans having twins, and the nursing home only had contact with Roger, although that doesn't mean much since everything was done online or on the phone."

"Right," said Buck. "But we need to confirm that. Let's get some sleep and pick this up in the morning. By then, we might have some forensic results that could send us in the right direction."

Chapter Fifteen

Buck stepped out of the trailer and took a deep breath. This case was getting strange, and he needed to take a minute and put it in perspective. He looked across the parking lot and saw Bax handing off the two evidence bags to the secure courier. She signed the chain of custody receipt and walked to Buck.

"Courier should have the packages at the lab by eleven P.M. Do you want to call Max and fill her in?"

Buck pulled out his phone, hit the number two on speed dial and waited. Max answered the way she always did.

"Buck Taylor. How's my favorite cop?" asked Max Clinton. "What the hell have you gotten yourself involved with this time?"

Dr. Maxine Clinton was the director of the State Crime Lab and one of Buck's oldest and dearest friends. She was a matronly woman in her late sixties, about five foot five, with short gray hair. She thought she carried around an extra fifteen pounds she didn't need, but she was still a handsome woman. Married for forty years, Max had four children, eleven grandchildren and six great-grandchildren. She lived in a one-hundred-fifty-year-old farmhouse in Pueblo, where she liked to tend her garden and sit on her porch and drink iced tea. She was also a bourbon girl and could drink most people under the table. She was loud and outspoken, but she knew her job.

Max had received her PhD in biology from the

University of Colorado and worked as a biology professor for twenty years before joining CBI. She was the head of the State Crime Lab, which she thoroughly enjoyed. She was a tough taskmaster, but she had a belief system that didn't allow for defeat. Her goal was to give the crime investigator, no matter which department or municipality they worked for, all the information they would need to solve any crime. She held that as a sacred obligation to the victims. She was dedicated to her job and her staff, and the team at the lab practically worshipped her.

Buck would have been included in that group. Many times, during a challenging investigation, it was Max and her team that lit the spark that led to a breakthrough. Max was one of Buck's favorite people, and she felt the same way about him.

"Hey, Max. I've got some samples headed your way," he said.

Buck gave Max a debrief about the case and the possibility that the clothes might have been worn by the killer. He explained he was looking for any DNA information her lab might be able to find. Buck was confident that if Max couldn't get the answer from someone on her staff, she would have an outside source that would know.

The people Buck worked with always joked that there wasn't anyone in Colorado that Buck didn't know. But the truth was, Max was way ahead of him in that department. She had contacts all around the world, and she never failed to get him the answers he needed.

During one recent case, Buck was looking for information on infrasound weapons and what effect they would have on the body. Within a couple of hours, Buck was on the phone with a colleague of Max's who was an expert in those types of weapons.

Max told him she would get her team on it as soon as the samples arrived at the lab, and Buck thanked her. She ended the call the way she always did. "You're a good man, Buck Taylor; God will watch over you."

Buck wasn't much of a religious man. He hadn't been to church in forty years. He had been raised Catholic but left the church right after confirmation. He always had too many questions about the teachings and too many people telling him that he had to have faith. That wasn't the answer he was looking for. He had a lot of friends, Max among them, who had always offered up a prayer when Lucy was dying. He never once rejected any of those offers, often smiling and thanking them for their kind thoughts.

Buck had realized long ago that it wasn't God and faith he had a problem with; it was organized religion. In his many years in law enforcement, he had seen too many times the aftereffects of someone's religious beliefs. It amazed him that so many people of faith could cause so much hatred and crime. But then, nonbelievers created just as much havoc.

Buck always believed there was a higher power, but he didn't believe that whatever that power was, it cared about one individual over another. His football coach always offered up a prayer before each game, asking for help in defeating the other team. He always suspected the other team's coach was doing the same thing. So how did God decide which team should win?

He knew a lot of people who said a lot of prayers for Lucy over the five years she was sick, but in the end, she still died. And she was the last person who should have gotten cancer. But Buck didn't carry any hatred. Whom could he get mad at? Whom could he blame?

Buck believed that there were spirits or a force all around us, and he always thanked them for allowing him to enjoy the hike or for allowing him to catch fish or see the sunrise and the sunset. It wasn't religion. It was something deeper. Something Buck didn't understand. He just accepted it. But no matter what, he always appreciated it when Max told him that God was watching over him. After all, what could it hurt?

Buck disconnected the call and was about to put his phone away when it chimed with an incoming call. Buck looked at the number and answered.

"Yes, sir," said Buck.

"Hey, Buck," said Director Jackson. "Hope it's not too late, but I wanted to let you know that the internet is blowing up with rumors and innuendos about the shooting."

Buck looked at Bax and shook his head. She smiled.

"Good or bad, sir?" asked Buck.

"Mostly good, but the radical right is screaming that it's a false flag operation to mislead the public so the president can take their guns. They're saying that it didn't happen, that no one was killed. You know—the usual crap. The coroner has started calling relatives of those killed, and the families are talking about holding a memorial on the site. The other side is calling for people to show up to protest the fake news and offer proof that nothing happened. Wanted you to be aware there could be a conflict."

"Thanks, sir. We'll keep an eye on things."

Buck gave the director a quick debrief of where things stood with the investigation, and they spoke for a few minutes about the suspect or suspects they were working on.

"Twins is an interesting angle," said Director Jackson. "Let's see what George and Mel can come up with on the faces. If they can't do it, no one can. Then we can figure out the next steps. Get some rest and call if you need anything."

The director disconnected the call, and Buck clipped his phone to his belt. He looked at Bax.

"I'm starved. You want to grab some dinner before you head home?"

"Yeah," said Bax. "Paul headed home to see the kids before their bedtime. You up for a steak? I know just the spot."

She texted him the address of the restaurant, and they headed for their Jeeps. Tomorrow was going to be another long day.

Chapter Sixteen

Harlan Groves had turned off the evening news and was locking the doors to get ready for bed when his cell phone rang. He looked at it for a minute, almost afraid to answer it. This late at night, he knew it wasn't good news. Fran came out of the bedroom, pulled on her robe and looked at the phone and him.

Harlan answered the phone. "Hi, Molly."

He listened while Fran stood next to him, trying to hear what their daughter was saying. Harlan told Molly he would let her know and disconnected the call. Tears flowed down Fran's face.

"Well?" she asked.

Harlan choked back his tears. "Jeremy is dead. The coroner's office confirmed it to Frank, and then they called Molly."

Tears flowed like water. "Do you think he suffered?" asked Fran.

Harlan looked cross-eyed at her. "Fran, he was shot. What do you think?"

Harlan realized how bad that sounded and walked over and wrapped his arms around Fran. They held each other for several minutes, and then Harlan let go.

"Some of the families are planning a vigil at the site tomorrow afternoon. If we want to participate, we must get on the road."

Fran nodded and headed for the bedroom. She had

packed several suitcases, which were sitting by the bedroom door. She put their cosmetics, shampoo and medications in another bag and told Harlan she was ready. She found her phone and sent a text to her friend and neighbor, letting her know they had to make an emergency trip to Colorado and would call when they were settled.

Harlan rolled the bags out and put them in the old van. He pulled the van out of the garage and parked in the driveway. Fran exited the house, locked the door and climbed into the van. They backed out of the driveway and headed for Grand Junction.

They drove for a couple of hours, and then Harlan pulled into a rest area, so they could grab a couple of hours of sleep. He figured they would arrive in Grand Junction in time for the vigil, and at their age, he didn't want to push too hard.

Across Colorado, families were waking up to find that one of their members was deceased. The coroner's office had people working the phones all night, making notifications to the families as soon as they were able to identify and autopsy the victims.

A web page had already been established on social media to memorialize the victims and comfort the families. Many families had planned to attend the vigil later in the day, and it was expected that as many as several hundred people could show up.

Sheriff Foley had assigned one of his tech people to monitor the internet and social media and keep track of what the families were discussing and planning. He also had the tech monitor the social media pages of numerous right-wing hate groups. He hoped to avoid any confrontations at the vigil, but after arriving back in the office, he was stunned by how rapidly the opposition had mobilized the hate speech. He had serious concerns that the vigil could become a powder keg.

He walked to the dispatch office and asked the two dispatchers to contact all his deputies and let them know that everyone needed to be in the office before the vigil started. All time off was canceled. He would meet with all his senior officers in the morning to review contingency measures.

He returned to his office, turned off his lights and headed home. Today had been one of his worst nightmares. He'd always feared that he would be involved in a school shooting. He never expected that a shooting at a drag club would be the worst incident to occur in his long career in law enforcement. He knew the first thing he was going to do when he got home was hug his wife.

Chapter Seventeen

I fell asleep on the couch while watching the late-night news. It was the same story on every channel. All they could talk about was the number of dead and injured. It was almost like it was a competition. They kept comparing the numbers to other mass shootings. So far, I was winning. Too bad they had no idea what this was all about.

The local news ran a story about some old lady who had been beaten in a nursing home. The footage from the home showed two of the detectives who were at the club walking through the parking lot. I wonder if they are starting to put it together. Well, if they were hoping Olivia would be able to give them some answers, they were sadly mistaken. I didn't realize when I started hitting her how deep the rage ran. I thought I had contained all that years ago. It was just like hitting the director of the youth home. I wonder what she felt in the end. I wonder if she had any remorse for the shit she put me through.

I cooked up a big plate of scrambled eggs and bacon, sat at the table and watched the news on my phone while I ate. The story had made the national news. Depending on which feed you watched, I was either a hero or a monster. I thought about it for a minute and didn't feel like either. I just did what I had to do to quiet the voices.

I replayed the whole event in my head while I cleaned up the dishes. I still can't believe how easy it was to get away. Everyone I met just wanted to help and make me feel safe. What a load of crap. What they needed to understand was that no one is safe, ever. It was fun watching the cops raid the house on Seventeenth Street. I bet they were surprised when they realized no one had lived there since we moved Olivia to the home. I'll bet they were even more confused when they got the second name and address from the lady detective and saw it was the same address. What must be going through their heads right now?

I sure hope Mr. Wingate gets his truck back. He loved that truck.

I stood for a minute and debated whether I should go to work. Wouldn't the cops be shocked if they showed up at Tyson and I was there just working like normal? I wonder if they would arrest me on the spot. Maybe I'll call in sick this morning.

I sat at the desk, opened my laptop and clicked the favorites link for the This Is What's Wrong with America *podcast. I wondered if Donny Truex had heard about the drag club shooting. I hoped he liked what he heard. This should be right up his alley.*

I clicked on the podcast and sat back, but what I heard shocked me. I leaned forward and turned up the volume.

". . . and so, my friends. Don't believe the crap the lamestream media is telling you. This attack never happened. This was all a radical left Hollywood conspiracy to promote gun safety and make it easier for the radical liberals to come and take your guns. It's incredible the expense the lefties must have spent to create such a production. It will probably show up in

a movie in a year or two. We've heard that they have a suspect. Some radical liberal loser named Bryce Tanner. Well, our team of intrepid investigators did their research, and no one named Bryce Tanner lives in Grand Junction or anywhere else in Colorado. This loser has no social media presence or background our team could find. He is a fabrication of the liberal fanatics. If you want to end this left-wing garbage and help take back America from the lefty fanatics, join us at the so-called family vigil this afternoon and help us show America that there are still people who believe in this country. Let's show the families of these people who supposedly died at this drag club that we are prepared to expose their lies to the world."

I could not believe what I was hearing. Donny Truex was my hero. He was the one who led me down this path, and now he was saying this was a fraud, and he was calling me a loser and said I didn't even exist.

I lost my temper; I pushed the laptop off my desk and stared at the mess on the floor. I stood and swept everything else off my desk onto the floor. How dare he say such things. I did this for him and his followers. I should be praised for what I did, and all he did was call it a Hollywood production and a hoax. How could he be so wrong?

The voices in my head came raging back, and I fell to the ground and screamed. Once the pain subsided a little and I was able to think, I realized I needed to do something to show Donny Truex and his followers that I was serious, and when I finished, the whole world would know I existed.

Fuck work. I needed to develop a new plan, which

had to be bigger than the last one. No one gets away with saying I don't exist. I'll show him. I needed to lie down until my head cleared, and then I would start working on my next big event. Watch out, world, because no one is safe.

Chapter Eighteen

Buck and Bax finished their meal at Darcy's Steakhouse, and Bax told Buck she would meet him at the command center at six. Buck settled the bill, left a nice tip for the waiter and headed for the parking lot. The temperature hadn't changed much from the afternoon, but the night was almost bearable since the sun wasn't beating down.

He leaned against his Jeep and stood for a moment. This investigation was complex, and he felt like the worst was yet to come, which was scary since what had happened the night before was far worse than anything he had seen in his career.

He slid into the Jeep and took a long drink from the warm bottle of Coke that sat in the cupholder. He put the Jeep in gear and headed towards the command center.

He pulled into the parking lot, grabbed his backpack and slid out into the night. He walked to the club door and signed in with the deputy on duty.

"Anything I can help you with, Agent Taylor?" asked the deputy.

"Thanks, Deputy. Just want to have another look around."

Buck pulled open the door and stepped into the lobby. He left the lights off and let his vision acclimate. He walked through what they knew so far. The first person to die was the bouncer at the door. Fast and efficient. Did the shooter wear a mask, or did the bouncer recognize him? The shooter entered the lobby, masked up and opened the double doors.

Buck pulled open the double doors and stepped into the club. According to witnesses, the shooter walked to the bar and shot the bartender. He positioned himself with his back to the bar and had a view of the entire club. He started shooting two pistols with extended magazines. People ran away from the shooter and jammed up at the back door. The shooter picked them off one by one.

At some point, Corporal Cordova approached the bar and was killed. Why did he leave his protectee and approach the shooter? His job was to protect the congressman. Why did he leave him unprotected?

Buck pulled out his flashlight and shined it towards the other side of the huge space. The beam landed on the congressman's table. Witnesses said that the shooter stood in front of the bar and shot into the crowd until they realized they couldn't get out the rear door, and the mob moved towards the front doors. He looked from the back door to the congressman's table, and then he looked back at the bar. With the flashing lights and loud music, that would have been a hell of a shot. So how did the congressman die? The unidentified male with the pistol hadn't pulled his gun. Which would mean that they were killed shortly after the shooting started. Why didn't he pull his gun?

Another thought hit Buck. If they died right after the shooting started, why wasn't Corporal Cordova also killed? Why was he able to pull his gun and approach the shooter, and why not shoot at the shooter from across the room instead of approaching him? Buck didn't like where these thoughts were taking him.

Buck turned his attention to the back hall. He stopped where they'd found the first pistol. It had landed in front of the bar and was lying under the footrest. He shined his flashlight down the hall towards the dressing room door. It was an easy throw from there to the bar. He moved down the hall and looked at the blood splatter on the wall and the bloody path on the floor.

He decided that their conjecture about this incident was correct. The shooter opened the door to the dressing room, shot three times and then stepped into the hall to shoot the woman who tried to crawl away.

He pushed open the dressing room door. His flashlight beam landed on the counter where the two entertainers were killed. They had to die before the three women in the hall, or they would have tried to hide. They were shot where they sat. Why didn't they try to hide when they heard the first shots?

He looked behind the clothes rack. Why was the third man in the dressing room? Where did he come from? He wasn't an entertainer or a cook, which meant he would have had to walk right past the shooter to get down the hall. That didn't make any sense.

Buck shined his light on the janitor's closet door. The SWAT officers were correct. The door was less than fifteen feet from the dead man at the clothes rack. They'd confirmed that Roger Shipman was involved. He had shooter's hands, but was he the only shooter? One more question that Buck needed to figure out.

They knew Bryce Tanner had wired the sound and

lighting for the building and that whoever set the charge that took those circuits out knew what they were doing. But was it Bryce Tanner?

Buck walked back to the front doors. He had more questions than when he'd first walked into the building, and he needed more information to answer some of those questions. What he needed was some sleep, but his brain was working overtime, and he knew sleep would not come.

He said good night to the deputy on duty and walked back to his Jeep. He sat for a minute, pulled out his laptop and opened the investigation file. He looked through the crime scene photos that had been posted so far. He wasn't sure what he was looking for, but he looked anyway. Next, he pulled up the list of evidence that had been tagged. He had a crazy hunch and waded through the evidence until he found what he was looking for.

Corporal Cordova's pistol had been logged into evidence, but according to the note in the file, it hadn't been processed yet. He looked at his watch. It was too early to call Max Clinton, so he sent her a text. Now he had to wait.

He looked at the communications folder and opened the deep dive report Mel had sent for Bryce Tanner. It was exactly what she had said. The report went back twelve years and then nothing. Bryce Tanner didn't exist. Buck unclipped his phone and dialed a number.

He had no idea how she did it, but the few times he had contacted Harriet, he always got what he needed. Harriet was a voice with a touch of a Southern accent, who was at the other end of a number he had been given by the U.S. Marshals Service.

A year or so back, Buck had been testifying in federal court in Denver during the murder trial of a survivalist drug dealer who had killed a DEA agent. One day, after court was dismissed, Buck and Jess Gonzales, the special agent in charge of the DEA's Grand Junction Field Office and one of Buck's closest friends, were talking outside the courthouse. Suddenly all hell broke loose, and people ran for cover. The marshals who were escorting the prisoner were ambushed in the parking garage, and Buck and Jess raced to their rescue.

Once the dust settled, the prisoner, one of the marshals and the ambushers were dead, but a lot of people in the garage that afternoon survived, thanks to Buck and Jess. To honor Buck, the U.S. Marshals Service made him a full-fledged deputy marshal, and as part of that award, he was given a special number that he could call anytime, day or night, and Harriet would get him whatever he needed. He had used the number several times and often wondered if Harriet was one woman or an entire team of women, but whatever she was, he appreciated the help.

"Good morning, Deputy Taylor. How can I help you?" said Harriet.

Buck explained what he was looking for, and Harriet told him she would see what she could find out. She told him she would get back to him as soon as she had something to report.

Buck disconnected the call and sat back. For some

reason, he always felt like he was making progress when he spoke with Harriet. He hoped it would be the same this time. He closed his eyes and drifted off to sleep.

Chapter Nineteen

The sun was shining through the Jeep's window, and it woke Buck up. He slid out of the seat and stretched the kinks out of his back and arms. He was getting too old to sleep in cars. He looked around the parking lot and waved to the night deputy. His stomach growled, so he looked across the street to the fast-food restaurant on the opposite corner. He walked over to the night deputy and asked if he wanted something to eat. The deputy said he would, so Buck took his order and walked across the highway. He brought back the breakfast sandwiches, a coffee for the deputy and a large Coke for himself.

Finished with breakfast, Buck saw Bax pull into the parking lot, and he walked towards the command center. They met at the door.

"You look like you slept in your clothes," said Bax.

Buck laughed. "I had some things I needed to check out and came away with more questions than answers. Let's wait for the others to arrive, and then we can get into it."

They entered the command center and waited for Duke Morgan, Paul, and Sheriff Foley to arrive. Once they were all there, Buck ran through his observations.

Duke Morgan spoke up as Buck finished. "You know, I wondered the same thing after reading through the witness statements. There is no way the shooter hit the congressman and his guests from across the room. Do we have any information on the two guys who were killed with the congressman?"

Bax opened her laptop and clicked on the investigation file. She clicked on a tab for background checks and opened the file Mel had uploaded for George Billings.

"According to Mel, George Billings is a multibillionaire out of California. He made his money in aviation technology. He owns Globestar Industries. Mel checked with Globestar and he is supposed to be on a fishing trip in Colorado. They also mentioned he was semiretired as of several years ago."

Paul looked up from his laptop. "You think he was supposed to be on the same trip as the congressman?"

"Why would a staunch ultraright conservative be meeting with a liberal billionaire from California?" asked Duke Morgan.

Before anyone could answer, the door to the command center burst open, and a short bald guy wearing glasses and a white shirt with a red, white and blue bow tie stormed into the space.

"Is it true?" he asked no one in particular. "Is Congressman Sanders dead?"

"Sir," said Sheriff Foley. "You can't be in here. You'll need to step outside."

"Governor Kennedy called me and told me to get here ASAP. He told me the congressman is dead."

"Who are you?" asked Buck.

"Sorry, this is just so horrible. This is going to be a public relations nightmare. I'm Darin Phelps. I'm

Congressman Sanders's chief of staff; now, can someone please tell me what's going on?"

The man looked like he was going to pass out, and Duke pulled over a stool and told him to sit down before he fell down. Bax handed him a bottle of water from the refrigerator, and he drank half of it down in one gulp.

Buck waited until he set the bottle on the table. "Congressman Sanders was killed last night during the club shooting."

Darin Phelps stared at Buck. "That can't be. He is supposed to be at a private fishing lodge up north of Steamboat Springs."

"Did you check with the lodge to see if he was there?" asked Bax.

Darin Phelps wiped the tears from his eyes. "I got a text from them when I got off the plane that the congressman had never arrived. What's going on?"

"We're hoping you can tell us," said Buck. "The congressman's body was discovered late yesterday amongst the victims of the shooting. He was identified by his Colorado driver's license, and his body was autopsied late last night. The preliminary cause of death was a gunshot wound to the chest."

Darin Phelps shook his head. "That can't be. Why would he be in a drag club? That goes against everything he believes in."

"We need some answers that maybe you can provide," said Buck. "What can you tell us about the congressman's trip?"

"The congressman needed a break. His schedule with the drag legislation and committee hearings has been hectic, and he needed some downtime. He arranged the fishing trip himself and announced two days ago that he would be out of touch for a few days. He typically didn't carry his phone when he was at the lodge fishing. He told me he was picking up his truck at home and not to try to reach him."

"Was it unusual for him to arrange a trip like this on his own?" asked Buck.

Darin Phelps was having difficulty focusing and shook his head and looked at Buck. "I'm sorry. As a matter of fact, it was unusual. Usually, he has one of the aides make the arrangements. None of this makes sense." He looked bewildered.

"So, you would have no idea why he requested a security detail from the governor?"

Darin Phelps looked at Buck like he had two heads. "A security detail. No. Why would he request a security detail?"

"Your boss requested one from the governor because of death threats he had been receiving," said Duke Morgan. "You didn't know?"

Darin Phelps shook his head. "He gets threats all the time, but he never mentioned needing security. Can we talk to the security guard and see what he says?"

"Unfortunately, the security guard was also killed, as was the person he was meeting with."

Darin Phelps looked like he wanted to faint. "Meeting with. Who was he meeting with?"

"Does the name George Billings mean anything to you?" asked Buck.

Darin Phelps had buried his face in his hands. He looked up at Buck. "George Billings, the billionaire. There's no way he would meet with George Billings. They hate each other. This makes no sense."

"Mr. Phelps. You don't seem to be very well informed about your boss's activities. Why is that?" asked Buck.

Phelps sat for several minutes, deep in thought. "The congressman has seemed a little off lately. He is the chairman of two significant committees and has been working on numerous pieces of legislation, including the bill to ban drag shows and clubs. I thought he was just tired. Now I wonder if it was something more."

"Any idea what that something more might be?" asked Buck.

Buck watched Darin Phelps, and when Darin responded that he had no idea what was going on, Buck knew he was lying. He decided not to push it.

"Has his family been notified?" asked Darin Phelps.

Bax looked at her laptop and clicked some keys. "Yes. The coroner spoke with his wife a few hours ago. She is making arrangements to have the body picked up. For right now, he is in a cooler at the coroner's office, and his name has not been released to the news media."

"Mr. Phelps," said Buck. "Where can we reach you if we have more questions?"

Darin Phelps pulled a business card out of his pocket and handed it to Buck. "I will head over to the congressman's house. I need to work on a statement for the press. What a nightmare."

He stood up and walked to the door. He looked back at the table, shook his head and pushed open the door. He stepped out into the morning sun and closed the door. Buck looked around the table.

"Thoughts," he said.

"I think the congressman left his chief of staff in the dark about whatever was going on," said Bax.

They all agreed.

"I think he was not being honest with us when he said he had no idea what was bothering the congressman," said Buck.

"You think he realized he no longer had a job?" asked Duke Morgan.

Buck laughed. "No. I think it was more than that. Bax, go visit the congressman's wife. See if she can shed some light on why he was here." Bax nodded.

"Paul, head over to Tyson Electrical Contractors and see what you can find out about Bryce Tanner. Duke, can you see if the coroner has an ID for our mystery man and the guy in the dressing room?"

Buck stood up to stretch and his phone chimed. He looked at the number and answered the call. Everyone stopped moving.

"Hey, Max."

"Buck Taylor, how's my favorite cop, and why

were you sending out texts at three A.M.?"

"Couldn't sleep. Were you able to answer my questions?" asked Buck.

"Yes. I had the team process the gun right after I got your text. The corporal's gun was fired. He fired three rounds. We compared them to the rounds taken from the three victims you asked about, and the answer is yes. The bullets were a match. You want to tell me who those victims are?"

"I wish I could, Max, but right now, I'm not sure what's going on, and until I am, I need to keep this one close."

"A bit of intrigue. Now you'll have me thinking about it all day. Also, we got back the DNA from the coat and pants you sent over. The DNA belongs to one Roger Shipman. He has a juvy record in Michigan. We are working to get it unsealed, but that could take a while."

"Max, you're awesome as usual," said Buck.

"You're a good man, Buck Taylor. God will watch over you." Max hung up, and Buck looked at the people at the table.

Buck was about to dial a number when his phone chimed. He checked the number and answered.

"Good morning, Harriet," said Buck.

"Good morning, Deputy Taylor. I have the information you requested. The Shipmans were not one of ours. We have no record of them ever being in or requesting witness protection. I took the liberty of checking news articles from the time. There is an article from a local Michigan newspaper that reported the murder of a prominent preacher. The article does not mention the offender's name because of his age. There was a second article a few years later regarding the murder of the director of a juvenile offender facility in the same area. I could not determine if the two were related."

"Thanks, Harriet. That helps."

Buck disconnected the call and dialed a number. George answered.

"Hey, Buck."

"Hi, George. Any luck with the background on Roger Shipman?" asked Buck.

"We ran into a sealed juvenile record. Mel is on the phone as we speak with a judge in Marquette, Michigan, to try to get it unsealed. We can't find any record of Roger Shipman after we hit the juvy record, but the timeline works with when we first pick up Bryce Tanner. Looks like Roger Shipman changed his name and disappeared, only to show up in Colorado a year or so later. We ran background on the Shipman family." Buck put his phone on speaker and set it on the table.

"James and Olivia Shipman ran a series of nightclubs in Marquette, Michigan. They had two children, Roger and Missy. Missy is six years younger than Roger. From what we found, the clubs were notorious for illicit activities, and this might be interesting. One of the clubs was a burlesque club. Mel found an old newspaper ad for the club promoting cross-dressing and strippers. They left Michigan about fourteen years ago."

Buck told George about the articles Harriet had found, and George said he would look into them a little deeper. He said he would call as soon as Mel had more on the juvy record. "By the way. We looked into other property in the names of Roger Shipman and Bryce Tanner and found no record of either of them owning any property in Colorado."

Buck disconnected the call and looked around the table. Duke Morgan was the first one to talk.

"So, it looks like the idea of Tanner and Shipman being twins is off the table. We pretty much confirmed that Bryce Tanner is Roger Shipman. Would be nice to see that juvy record."

"I think it's interesting," said Bax, "that his family ran a burlesque club. From what I remember about old movies, a lot of the entertainers in those clubs were cross-dressers. That could explain a lot."

"Right," said Buck. "But why now? He's been bouncing around for more than ten years. What set him off?"

"That's a good question," said Sheriff Foley. "But we're not going to find the answer sitting here."

They all grabbed their laptops and headed out the door. Buck pulled out his phone and dialed a number. The governor answered right away.

Chapter Twenty

The social media invite asked all who wanted to attend the vigil at the drag club to be on-site by noon. They planned to start promptly. The sheriff had been gracious enough to carve out a section of the parking lot so that the families would not interfere with the crime scene, and he had his deputies pull back the crime scene tape. A makeshift memorial of flowers, cards, candles and stuffed animals was growing in one of the parking spaces, and it would soon overflow that space and require additional spaces.

By noon several hundred people, locals and out-of-towners, had gathered in the parking lot. The occasion was solemn. Many people held up signs with pictures of their loved ones who had been lost. A local preacher led those gathered in prayer, and a local religious duo played and sang several songs of praise. Tears flowed like water.

County Commissioner Ellen Thompkins spoke to the crowd and offered them hope and a promise from the county government to do everything they could to find the person responsible. Sheriff Foley took his place next to her and gave the families a review of where the investigation was and what their next steps would be. He also promised that the sheriff's department would do everything possible to find those who committed this horrendous crime.

The vigil was peaceful, but as some of the families approached the podium to talk about their loved ones, several charter buses pulled to a stop on the highway, and numerous protesters exited the bus carrying signs calling the shooting fake news and calling for the sheriff to be fired for perpetuating a lie. Leading the group was radio host Donny Truex, his megaphone booming over the small amplifier the families were using.

Sheriff Foley directed his deputies, standing in the background, to get between the protesters and the families. Their presence did little to stop the protesters. Donny Truex was now the center of attention, and his charisma and his claims enthralled the news agencies that had been reporting on the shooting.

"This is a fraud being perpetrated on the people of Mesa County," said Truex. "The government has staged this with the help of the Hollywood radical left so they can push their agenda to take your guns. This entire event is a fraud. And none of these people at the vigil had family members involved. These people are all actors hired by the Hollywood elite to make sure you believe that this is real. Don't be fooled by the blood. This is all fake."

The families screamed back at Truex, but he just turned up the volume on his megaphone, and his protesters, and they drowned out the voices of the families. Several family members waded into the crowd of protesters, and the pushing and shoving began.

Truex continued. "You are all snowflakes, and you have been duped by your government. You have been indoctrinated to believe everything the government says is true, and you are fools. Go back to your fake homes with your fake signs showing pictures of people you found on the internet and bury your heads in the sand. The world is watching you, and they know the truth."

Fights broke out, and the deputies tried to stop them, but they were outnumbered on both sides. The sheriff yelled for peace and had a bottle thrown at him for his efforts. He keyed his mic and put out a county-wide assistance call. Within minutes several officers arrived from the Grand Junction and Montrose police departments, as well as additional sheriff's deputies.

Harlan Groves waded through the crowd with the picture of his grandson and got into Truex's face.

"My grandson is real," yelled Harlan Groves. "You have no right saying he doesn't exist. You don't know the pain we are going through. You should be ashamed."

Truex laughed in his face. "You're a fucking idiot. That's not a picture of your grandson; that's a picture you pulled off the internet. Your grandson was not killed in that building. Go back to Hollywood where you belong." Someone behind Truex threw a punch, and Harlan fell to the ground. The crowd closed around him and started chanting, "SNOWFLAKE, SNOWFLAKE, SNOWFLAKE!"

People on both sides were yelling, screaming and crying, and several men in the family group attempted to help Harlan to his feet, only to be pushed down, punched and kicked. The arriving officers, dressed in riot gear, formed a skirmish line and waded into the crowd, using batons and pepper spray. The crowd pushed back, and several officers went down. Truex yelled for his people to return to the buses, and the crowd broke up and raced to the buses. The police officers were stuck trying to help the families and couldn't follow.

The police cleared space so the paramedics could get to the family members who had been hurt in the commotion. Harlan Groves and several other family members were helped to the waiting ambulances and taken to St. Mary's Medical Center. Harlan was barely conscious. His wife went in the ambulance with him.

Sheriff Foley stood by the command center and looked at the carnage left in the wake of the riot. He shook his head and looked at SWAT Commander Martinez.

"What the hell happened?" he asked.

"That fucking Donny Truex came in organized and ready to fight. The families had no chance," said Commander Martinez.

"I'm going to talk to the DA about arresting him for inciting the riot. We look like idiots in front of the news media; worst of all, we couldn't protect the families," said the sheriff.

All the families wanted was to honor their deceased and injured family members, and he had let them down. He felt like shit. He noticed the members of the media racing back to their trucks and vans. He feared what his people would look like on the nightly news. He also knew what it would look like on the internet. He hated how he felt and stepped back into the command center. The past two days had been the worst in his career, and today didn't make it any better. He pulled out his phone and dialed his public information officer. He asked her to prepare a statement for the media. He knew that no matter what he said, the only one to blame was himself.

The door opened, and Ellen Thompkins walked in and stood looking at him.

"What the hell happened, Jack?" she asked. "Where did all those people come from?"

Sheriff Foley shook his head. "We expected some pushback from the right, but they came in organized and with a plan to cause as much disturbance as possible. We'll issue a statement and see what happens. I don't know what else to do."

"I'll tell you what we need to do," said Ellen Thompkins. "We need to let the press know that Congressman Royal Sanders was killed in the drag club. We need to spin this so the media vultures have something else to chew on."

"We promised the governor we would keep a lid on it for now," said the sheriff.

"Well, the governor isn't here, we are, and this is our county. I'll take care of it so your hands are clean." She stormed out of the command center, and Sheriff Foley couldn't help but think this was going to be a big mistake.

Chapter Twenty-One

Bax parked along the curb opposite the modest ranch house that belonged to Congressman Sanders and his wife, Michelle. The house, small by many standards, had belonged to the Sanders family for more than thirty years. They'd purchased it before he pursued his first elected office as the state senator from Montrose County. He lost that election but went on to bigger things, including spending twelve terms in the U.S. House of Representatives. He prided himself on being a regular person, and the people in the third congressional district thought the world of him.

Bax grabbed her backpack and slid out of the Jeep. She made note of the five cars parked in the driveway or along the opposite curb. She walked up the sidewalk and rang the bell.

Darin Phelps answered the door and frowned when Bax presented her ID. "What can I do for you? This is not a good time."

"I'd like a few minutes with Mrs. Sanders." She stared at Phelps. "It's important if we want to find out who murdered him."

"It's okay, Darin. Please let the officer in," said a voice behind him.

Darin Phelps stepped aside reluctantly and waved her in, closing the door behind her. Michelle Sanders, dressed in jeans and a T-shirt and barefoot, stepped up and introduced herself to Bax.

"You have my deepest condolences," said Bax. "I

hate to intrude at a time like this, but if you are up to it, I'd like to ask you some questions that might help our investigation."

Michelle Sanders wiped the tears from her eyes and escorted Bax into a small but comfortable living room. The TV mounted to the wall over the wood-burning fireplace was tuned to one of the conservative news channels, and Bax glanced to see if they were reporting anything about the congressman's death. She sat in a leather chair opposite the couch. Michelle Sanders sipped from a glass containing water or another clear liquid. She set the glass on the table and looked up as two younger people entered the room.

Darin Phelps hovered over Bax. "Mr. Phelps, would you be so kind as to take the rest of the family into the kitchen and give us a little privacy?"

Darin Phelps started to object, but Mrs. Sanders waved him off and told the two kids she would be fine. They all disappeared into the next room.

"They all mean well," said Michelle Sanders. "They've been hovering over me since the coroner left." Tears filled her eyes.

Bax removed her phone and opened her recording app. She set the phone on the arm of the chair.

"Mrs. Sanders, you're aware of the circumstances surrounding your husband's death. Do you have any idea why he was in that club last night?"

"I didn't know my husband was in town," said Michelle Sanders. "I thought he was still at our town house in Washington. He never said a word to me when we spoke the other night."

Bax looked surprised. "He told his chief of staff, Mr. Phelps, that he was going to a lodge near Steamboat Springs for a couple of days of fishing. Was that typical?"

Now it was Michelle Sanders's turn to look surprised, but she said, "It doesn't surprise me, Agent Baxter. The lodge belongs to a dear friend of his, and he goes up there a couple of times a year to let off a little steam and relax. He usually leaves his phone here at the house or in the car. He wasn't planning on being up there until the fall."

"I take it it's not like him to come home and not stop here at the house?" asked Bax.

Michelle Sanders shook her head. "He's never done it before. At least, not that I know of. Makes you wonder, though, doesn't it?"

"Mrs. Sanders, is everything all right in your marriage? Any issues or concerns that would have led him to come home and not tell anyone he was here?"

Michelle Sanders didn't look up at first, as if she was pondering the question. When she looked up, she said, "We've had our difficulties being separated a lot over the years. I'm not much of a politician's wife, never have been, but I believe our marriage is sound."

"Mrs. Sanders," said Bax. "Your husband was killed in a drag club; that, from my understanding, was something he was opposed to. Any idea why he would have gone to the club?"

Mrs. Sanders was staring at the television screen.

Bax looked over her shoulder and saw that the story was about the shooting at the club. She looked at Bax. "Did he suffer? The coroner would only say that he had been shot and most likely died instantly. Is that true, Agent Baxter?"

Bax turned back and faced her. "I'm sorry, ma'am, I haven't seen the coroner's report yet.

"Just a few more questions, if I could," said Bax. "Your husband had asked the governor for a security detail. Had he received any death threats that you know of?"

Michelle Sanders, once again, looked confused and surprised. "Not that I'm aware of, but his staff and the Capitol Police would have handled anything like that. Have you spoken to the security officer?"

"I'm afraid the trooper assigned to your husband was killed in the shooting. Your husband was meeting with a gentleman we have identified as George Billings. Does that name mean anything to you? Could he have been a friend or business associate of your husband?"

Michelle Sanders made a weak attempt to smile. "It seems, Agent Baxter, that my husband might have been keeping a lot of things from me."

Darin Phelps stepped out of the kitchen. "Will that be all, Agent Baxter? Mrs. Sanders needs to lie down, and we still need a few minutes to craft a statement for the press. The governor has been kind enough to allow us to make the announcement instead of it coming from official channels."

Bax stood, picked up her backpack and phone and thanked Michelle Sanders for her time, again expressing her condolences. She followed Darin Phelps to the front door and thanked him. He went to close the door behind her. Bax stopped and turned. "Mr. Phelps, you told us in the command center that the congressman was going to stop at home and pick up his truck." She pointed to the truck in the driveway. "Would that be his truck?" she asked.

Phelps stepped up to Bax and looked at the truck in the driveway. His confusion was obvious, and so was the way he stammered until he said, "Yes, but I don't understand. It shouldn't be here."

Bax pulled out her phone and dialed Duke Morgan. "Duke, have you released all the cars in the parking lot?"

"Not yet," said Duke. "We are still going through them. Why?"

"We need to figure out which cars the congressman and Billings were driving."

She disconnected the call, walked across the street and slid into her Jeep just as the mutual aid announcement came over her police radio for a riot at the drag club. She started her Jeep, flipped on her emergency lights and hit the gas.

Chapter Twenty-Two

Paul pulled his Jeep onto the gravel parking lot for Tyson Electrical Contractors and parked next to the entrance door. There were several green and yellow trucks in the yard, all with the Tyson logo on the doors. Several men and women were loading the trucks for the day's assignments. He grabbed his backpack and exited the Jeep. He pulled open the door, entered the lobby and asked to speak with the owner.

A medium-height, gray-haired man wearing chinos and a light blue button-down shirt walked through the door behind the receptionist and extended his hand.

"Pat Tyson. How can I help?"

Paul presented his credentials and asked if there was someplace private they could talk. Pat Tyson led him back through the door, and they entered a wood-paneled office with a large desk in the middle. Pat Tyson pointed to one of the leather chairs in front of the desk, and Paul sat. He pulled out his phone, opened his recording app and placed the phone on the desk. Tyson looked at him suspiciously.

"Mr. Tyson," said Paul. "I understand you have an employee by the name of Bryce Tanner. What can you tell me about him?"

"Is Bryce in some kind of trouble?"

"I assume you heard about the shooting at the new drag club. I was told your company did the electrical work. As part of that investigation, we are doing background checks on several people who have come to our attention."

"Do you think Bryce was one of the shooters?" asked Tyson.

"Mr. Tyson, this will go much quicker if you let me ask the questions. Now, what can you tell me about Bryce Tanner?"

Pat Tyson looked like he had just been spanked, and he wasn't used to not being the guy in charge. He leaned back in his chair and studied Paul for a few seconds. He leaned forward and tented his hands on his desk.

"Bryce is a good guy. Been with us for more than ten years. He is a skilled electrician and does an awesome job with the computerized lighting and sound packages we install. He did a lot of work at the new club. I'm sorry, Agent, but I need to ask. Was Bryce one of the victims?"

"Bryce was not one of the victims," said Paul, and relief showed on Tyson's face.

"That's great to know." His expression changed as another thought entered his head. Before he could ask the question that was on his mind, Paul spoke.

"Mr. Tyson, we are looking at Bryce Tanner as a suspect in the shooting. Is Bryce at work today?"

Tyson picked up the desk phone and punched a couple of numbers. He asked the person on the other end of the line if Bryce Tanner was working today and listened without responding. He thanked the person on the other end and hung up.

"Bryce never showed up or called in sick. That's not

like him. He really is a great guy. A little quiet, and he keeps to himself, but I don't see him as a killer. That's not the Bryce I know." Tyson looked sad and confused.

"Mr. Tyson. Do you have a copy of his paperwork? We are looking for an address for Tanner. We got an address from Norman Wingate, but it turned out to be an empty house."

Tyson picked up the phone again, dialed the receptionist and asked her to bring Bryce Tanner's file into his office. The receptionist entered moments later and handed the file to Tyson. He opened the manila folder, leafed through the papers and found Bryce Tanner's last pay stub. He handed it to Paul.

Paul picked up his phone and took a picture of the pay stub. The address was the same as the one they'd raided late last night. He handed the stub back to Tyson.

"Sir, have you ever been to Bryce's house?"

"No," said Tyson. "Now that you mention it, I never have. Some of the other guys might have."

"Was he close to any of the other people that work here?"

Tyson thought for a minute. He hadn't thought about it until now, but he had never seen Bryce Tanner socialize with his coworkers. He thought that was odd, and he told Paul the same thing.

"Does Bryce have a locker here on the property?" asked Paul.

Tyson nodded, and Paul asked if he could see it. He picked up his phone and backpack and followed Tyson through the office and into the shop space in the yard. They walked into a cleanup area, and Tyson looked at a note on his phone, walked over and opened locker 112. The locker was empty. They took a few minutes to talk to some of the employees who were still in the yard, and Paul walked away with the same information he had received from Tyson. Bryce Tanner was a great guy and a hard worker, but no one seemed to know much about him.

Paul thanked Pat Tyson, walked to his Jeep and slid in. He was thinking about the conversation when the mutual aid request went out on his radio. He pulled out of the parking lot, hit his flashers and siren and headed for the drag club.

Chapter Twenty-Three

I can't believe how stupid I was to believe anything that Donny Truex had to say. I thought I found someone who understood what I was going through, and I believed he wanted me to help change the world. Listening to him gave the voices clarity. I felt like I belonged, and just like everyone else in my life, he betrayed me.

He looks so smug, standing in the middle of a bunch of his followers, yelling with his bullhorn at the families of the people I killed, who were murdered because he told me to do it. I made hundreds of families suffer, all because I believed in what Truex was saying.

He's a fraud. I need to make his listeners and followers understand that. I need a plan to hurt Donny Truex the same way I made all those families hurt.

The voices in my head are screaming at me as I sit here and watch the crowd of his followers push into people who lost loved ones. Loved ones whose lives I took because I listened to him.

I should drive my car right over there and smash into his followers. If I had another pistol, I could walk over there and put a bullet in his head in front of all the people who believe in him. That would show them. The newspeople would get a big kick out of that. If it bleeds, it leads. Isn't that what they always say? I could make him suffer in ways he never could have imagined.

I can't believe what I am watching. His people are fighting with those who lost loved ones. They are knocking people on the ground and kicking them. He is screaming over his bullhorn that they are being duped by the government that wants to take their guns. He is screaming at people that their loved ones didn't exist and this is just some Hollywood production.

He is calling it fake news being spread by the lamestream media. He is calling them snowflakes. I'm not even sure what a snowflake is, but for some reason, his words are making me angry. I didn't kill and injure all those people because I was angry. I did it because the voices in my head needed to be silenced, and Donny Truex gave me a way to silence them. He led me down the path, then hung me out to dry.

He has ruined everything I did and trivialized it for his ratings. I feel horrible and want to vomit, but I'm scared to get out of the car. Someone might recognize me. I have no intention of going to prison. What I did had to be done to get rid of the vileness and evilness of that club.

It's so weird. Even after being betrayed by Donny Truex, I still believe in what he said. I still believe that I did the right thing, even if he thinks what I did never happened.

I hear sirens as several police vehicles pull into the parking lot. Cops of all kinds, in riot gear, are piling out of the vehicles and forming a line. They are marching into the crowd using batons and pepper spray to separate the groups. This has ruined everything. This is all the news media will focus on.

Look at Donny and his band of ruffians running to their buses—bunch of cowards. There are a lot of people on the ground. It looks like some are hurt. Donny Truex, the scared little rabbit. I will figure out a way to make him suffer.

There are a lot more cops arriving, and even though I don't think any of them would recognize me sitting in this parking lot, I should get out of here.

Chapter Twenty-Four

Buck stopped in front of the Shipman residence and slid out of the Jeep. He looked around and waved to Marla Scott, the neighbor across the street, who was peeking out from behind her curtains. She closed the curtains.

Buck walked up to the front door, pulled his pocketknife and slit the red warning sticker that sealed the door. He used the key they had gotten from the locksmith and unlocked the door. He stepped inside and stood for a minute. Buck typically approached a crime scene by just standing for a while and looking around, letting his mind absorb what his eyes might not see. He hadn't been able to do that at this location because it wasn't a crime scene, but he decided to start the same way he always did.

He left the front door open behind him and scanned the room from right to left. After a few minutes, he stepped into the room and looked at the pictures hanging on the wall. The frames were dusty, like everything else in the house, but it was the people he was interested in. Many of the pictures were taken in front of a white Cape Cod–style house that did not appear to be taken in Colorado.

The four people in the photos made a nice-looking family, except Buck could see a lot of sadness in the young boy's eyes. In almost every picture, he stood away from the other family members. Buck had seen children affected by trauma before and felt that this was what he was looking at.

He continued through the house, looking in each room, not sure what he was looking for. He checked the bathroom medicine cabinet and the kitchen cabinets but found nothing of interest. He opened the door to the basement, left the light off and pulled out his flashlight. The flashlight would narrow his focus, which sometimes revealed more than looking at something with all the lights on.

Buck moved down the stairs and stopped at the bottom. He scanned the room with his flashlight and then moved around the room, looking in every nook and cranny. The basement was orderly and neat, with several shelves of canned goods and books. It looked like someone at one time was a voracious reader.

He scanned the concrete walls until he came to a brick chimney. He almost walked away from the chimney until his flashlight revealed a subtle difference in the color between two mortar joints. He got closer to the chimney and widened his flashlight beam. It was almost imperceptible, but he was certain there was a difference in the mortar of several of the joints. He flipped on the basement lights and looked at the joints.

Buck pulled out his phone and dialed Franklin Williams. He asked Franklin to gather his forensic team and head his way. He would wait for them at the house. He hung up and called a number from his list.

"Judge Morgan's chambers, Janelle speaking. How may I help you?"

"Hey, Janelle, it's Buck. Is the judge in?"

"Hi, Agent Taylor; please hold on for a second, and

I will see." Buck liked talking to Janelle. For someone so young, she was very poised and professional on the phone and equally so in person. Of course, at Buck's age, everyone seemed young.

"Hey, Buck," said Judge Morgan. "Hell of a couple of days. What can I do for you?"

"Hi, Jane. I'm gonna need a warrant."

Buck explained what he'd found in the basement, and Jane listened without comment. She knew from years of experience to trust Buck's intuition.

"Is this related to the shooting at the club?" she asked.

"Yeah. This is the address one of our suspects gave, but we found out he doesn't live here. The woman who owns the house has been in a nursing home, and sometime before the shooting, she was beaten to death. The neighbors say they haven't seen her husband since her son, our suspect, came home years ago, and I think I might have found him."

"Jesus, Buck. You get yourself into the weirdest situations. I'll have Janelle type up the warrant request, and I'll text it to you. You are good to go. Let me know how things work out."

Judge Morgan disconnected the call, and Buck clipped his phone back on his belt. While he waited, he read the spine information on many of the books. Whoever read these had very eclectic tastes, ranging from romance to thrillers to science fiction, and he even found a couple of books that appeared to be erotica.

He looked at the shelves of canned foods, most of which didn't look very appetizing. He was about to head upstairs when his phone chimed. He checked the number and answered the call.

"Hey, George. What's up?"

"You have a problem," said George. "The internet just exploded with the news that Congressman Royal Sanders was killed in the drag club shooting. The right is going crazy."

"Fuck," said Buck. "We were going to let the family release that information first. The governor is not going to be happy. Any idea who released it?"

"Pretty good guess. There was a riot at the family vigil today at the club. I spoke to Bax a few minutes ago. The sheriff had to call in mutual aid. I guess things got ugly. I'm surprised you didn't get the radio call."

Buck explained that he was in the basement and not near his Jeep.

"The information came out right after the riot. Sounds like someone trying to make a point."

"Or cover their ass," said Buck.

"One other thing," said George. "Mel wasn't able to get the judge in Michigan to unseal the juvy record of Roger Shipman. The judge told her it was a fishing trip, and unless we had hard evidence of his involvement in the club shooting, he would not unseal the document."

"Shit," said Buck. "Where does that leave us?"

"Not sure," said George. "But we might have a little information from a different source. Mel spoke with the chief of police in Marquette, Michigan. He wasn't the chief back then, but he remembers the case. It seems Roger Shipman found his pastor fishing and decided to bash his head in with a rock. He said a person walking their dog on the other side of the river saw the whole thing and called the police. They found Roger Shipman at home trying to burn the bloody clothes. He was fourteen at the time and was sentenced to a juvenile home until he was eighteen. We had speculated about a possible second crime; well, there was one, and the warrant is still open.

"A year before he was to be released, Roger Shipman used a hammer and bashed in the skull of the resident director of the youth facility. The story the cops got was that Roger Shipman and some of the other boys discovered that one of the younger boys in their section was sexually abused by the director, and Roger flipped out. After beating him with a hammer he got from the maintenance closet, Roger Shipman took the director's keys and escaped. No one has seen him since that night.

"The police chief also told Mel that the family owned several nightclubs and one burlesque club in the area. There had been rumors about some strange parties that went on in the Shipman house involving some of the entertainers and some special guests. It was speculated, but unconfirmed, that the pastor was involved in those parties, which is why Roger Shipman killed him. The chief told Mel the last he heard, the family had moved someplace out west after Roger was convicted. Mel's trying to track down the psychologist assigned to Roger after his incarceration."

"That sure explains some things. That's three victims, all connected to Roger Shipman, who were beaten to death. What are the odds he has advanced to guns? The question that remains is, why, after all these years, did he decide to kill a bunch of drag queens and the customers?"

"Unfortunately, Buck," said George, "that's a question for the psychiatrists."

"Hey, do me a favor and run background on Congressman Royal Sanders and his chief of staff, Darin Phelps. Go real deep."

"Real deep?" asked George.

"Yeah, real deep," said Buck.

George knew what Buck was talking about. A few weeks back, Buck's team had investigated the death of a state brand inspector who was found surrounded by several dozen dead cows. The investigation led in several directions, but one of those directions involved a secret government lab that was built in the Colorado mountains to replace the lab at Plum Island.

The director of the lab, a full general, had asked Buck to investigate some of the people in the lab once it was determined that a deadly biotoxin was the cause of death for the cattle. Towards that end, the general had given Buck's team access to software that could open any encrypted file. After the investigation was over, the general had left the encryption software in Buck's hands to use as he saw fit. Buck was willing to let George use the software if it became necessary to determine what the congressman was involved in and why he was in a drag club instead of on a fishing trip.

George acknowledged the request, and Buck disconnected the call. He heard the screen door open and Franklin call out. Buck told him he was in the basement, and Franklin and two members of his team came down the stairs. Buck showed him the discoloration and explained that he thought Roger Shipman's father might be inside the chimney.

Buck's phone chimed, and he opened the text from Judge Morgan. He showed the search warrant to Franklin and told him he was clear to get started. Franklin led his team back upstairs so they could put on their Tyvek suits and gather the equipment they would need to take down the chimney. Buck followed them up the stairs and asked Franklin to call him as soon as they had anything. He headed for his Jeep, slid in and headed for the command center. They had a lot to talk about.

Chapter Twenty-Five

"What the hell are we waiting for?" asked Harlan Groves.

"The doctors are busy, hon," said his wife. "Quite a few people were hurt."

"I'm fine. Let's get the hell out of here," said Harlan Groves.

A voice came from behind the curtain and a deputy stepped through. "You need to stay here, sir. The detectives need to speak with you."

The young deputy smiled at Harlan and his wife, but Harlan Groves wasn't amused. He touched the bump on the back of his head and flinched. "Well, let's get a move on," he said.

His wife tried to calm him down, but he was having none of it. "I'm fine. I just want to get out of here," he said.

He stood up and leaned back against the bed. The room was spinning, and the nurse stepped in and helped him sit back down. The emergency room doctor walked in looking frazzled and stepped behind Harlan Groves. He put on a pair of latex gloves and pushed Harlan's thinning hair aside. He ordered the nurse to clean the wound and bring him a suture kit.

Duke Morgan pushed the curtain aside and stepped in. He looked at his notepad. "Mr. Harlan Groves?" he asked.

Harlan Groves nodded. Duke introduced himself

and stepped behind the doctor, who was suturing the small split in the back of his head. The doctor finished and told Mr. Groves to take it easy for a day or two in case he had a slight concussion. His wife took the prescription for the pain pills from the doctor and put it in her purse.

"Mr. Groves, who did you lose in the shooting?"

Harlen Groves wiped the tears from his eyes. "My grandson, Jeremy Maxwell. He was a bartender." He looked at Duke. "Who does such a thing? Killing people because they want to be different. And who attacks people at a vigil? My god. All we wanted to do was honor our lost family members, and those arrogant pricks show up and tell us the whole thing was fake. What the hell is that all about?"

His wife put her hand on his arm and told him the doctor didn't want him getting excited. He shrugged her hand off.

Duke Morgan looked at their daughter Irene, who had just stepped into the space. "Was Jeremy your son?"

"No," she said. "He's my nephew. My older sister's son."

"Mr. Groves. Was your grandson into drag?"

Mr. Groves looked sad. "I don't know for sure. He was a bartender and a damn good one. What difference does it make? He had his whole life ahead of him."

Duke took down their names, addresses and phone numbers. He gave them his business card and told them he would be in touch to let them know about any progress. He moved on to the next victim.

Harlan Groves, his wife and his daughter checked out with the nurse and left the hospital. His daughter drove him home, where his wife smothered him with attention until he couldn't stand it anymore. He sat on the couch and picked up his laptop. He searched for information on the riot and, after a few minutes, found what he was looking for. Donny Truex.

He watched a couple of Donny's podcasts and understood why the shooting at the club had occurred. Donny Truex may not have killed anyone, but his words were enough to incite someone to act on his behalf. He spent the next hour doing an internet search for anything related to Donny Truex. He found Donny's website, but it took a while to find out where he produced his podcasts. A plan started to form in Harlan Grove's brain.

His wife and daughter were in the kitchen consoling his oldest daughter and her husband, so he grabbed his van keys and slipped out the door. He slid into his van, started the engine and pulled away from the curb. He was angry, and his head hurt, but he knew what needed to be done. He checked his watch and headed south of town to a small gun shop he remembered from the time they lived in Colorado.

He pulled into the parking lot, turned off the engine and sat for a minute. Satisfied that he was doing the right thing, he slid out of the van and walked to the store. He pushed open the door and listened as the bell sounded, announcing his arrival.

Harlan Groves walked along the glass case until he

found what he was looking for. The guy behind the counter walked over, and Harlan pointed to the full-sized Beretta 45-caliber PX4 Storm. They chatted about the gun while the clerk took it from inside the display case, removed the magazine and opened the slide. He checked to ensure the pistol was empty and handed it to Harlan. Harlan racked the slide, moved into a Weaver stance and, using both hands, aimed into the mirror behind the counter. He pulled the trigger, worked the action several times and told the clerk he would take it along with two boxes of shells.

Harlan Groves hadn't changed his address when they moved to Arizona, so he handed the clerk his Colorado license and waited while the clerk completed the background check with the Colorado Bureau of Investigation. A half hour later, Harlan Groves left the gun shop with his new pistol, a hundred rounds of ammunition and a plan. His next stop was a gun range he had found online.

Chapter Twenty-Six

Buck pulled into the parking lot, grabbed his backpack and headed for the command center. He pulled open the door as his phone rang. He looked at the number and answered.

"Hey, Franklin. That was fast," he said.

"Yeah. We found your missing husband. Been dead a long time," said Franklin.

"Nice," said Buck. "Is he mummified or bones?"

"Mostly bones. We can say for certain that his head was bashed in. The pieces of the skull are lying at the bottom of the chimney. Must be fifty pieces."

"Okay. I'll call Sima and see if I can pull her away from one of the autopsies," said Buck.

"Don't bother. I already called her, and she said she'd be here in about an hour. In the meantime, we'll finish tearing down the chimney so we can get to all the pieces."

Buck thanked Franklin, disconnected the call and entered the command center.

Bax, Paul, Sheriff Foley and Duke Morgan looked up as he entered.

"What happened?" he asked no one in particular.

"That right-wing conspiracy theorist podcast guy Donny Truex showed up with a bunch of his wacky followers and got in the faces of the families gathered for the vigil," said Sheriff Foley. "Couple of people got hurt. He said some vile things and called the entire thing a fraud."

Sheriff Foley was frustrated, and it showed in his voice. They were all dog tired, and crap like this did not make any of their jobs easier. He averted his eyes and looked at the tabletop.

Bax stood, walked to the coffee machine on the counter and poured herself a coffee. She turned and looked at Buck.

"The governor called the sheriff. Not sure if you're aware, but the congressman's name was released along with the manner of his death. The governor is getting a lot of flak from the family and the media. He was not pleased when he called the sheriff, and he wants some answers."

Buck's phone chimed, and he looked at the number. He looked at Bax, raised his eyebrows and stepped out the door into the parking lot.

"Yes, sir," said Buck.

"Any idea how the congressman's name got released?" asked Director Jackson. "The governor just jumped all over my ass. What's going on?"

"I can't say for sure, but I'll get you an answer, sir," said Buck. "I learned about it a few minutes ago and just returned to the command center."

Buck told him about the body in the chimney at the Shipman home. The director was quiet for a couple of seconds.

"You think it's the husband?" asked the director.

"Good a guess as any at this point, sir," said Buck. "According to the neighbors, the husband hasn't been seen in more than a decade, which coincides with the last time anyone saw Roger Shipman at the house. Franklin says the skull is in a bunch of pieces. He thinks the victim was beaten to death. That seems to be a trend with any of the lives that have touched Roger Shipman."

Buck gave him a quick debrief on the information Mel had gotten from the chief of police in Michigan.

"So, you're convinced that this Bryce Tanner is Roger Shipman?" asked Director Jackson. "How the hell did he stay hidden for all these years, and what activated him to shoot up a nightclub?"

"We may never know, sir," said Buck. "Mel is trying to get his juvy record unsealed so we can look at his psych information since he killed his therapist. So far, not much luck with the judge in Michigan, so George is going to try a different approach."

"I'm not going to like that approach, am I, Buck?" asked Director Jackson.

"No, sir. You will not, which is why I'm not going to tell you about it. Have a nice afternoon, Director."

Buck disconnected the call and stepped back into the command center. He told them about the body in the chimney.

"Seems like Roger Shipman likes to beat people to death," said Bax. "How do you go from that to shooting three hundred people?"

"That's what we need to find out," said Buck.

"Anything from the congressman's wife or the company Bryce Tanner works for?"

Bax tapped a couple of keys on her laptop. "According to the wife, she didn't know he was in town. The congressman told his chief of staff that he was going fishing for a couple of days and would stop at the house to pick up his truck. The truck is still in the driveway. I got the feeling the wife was holding something back. She seemed surprised when I told her he was home, but she said she wasn't surprised. I called the lodge, and they said the congressman was expected but hadn't shown up."

"Any issues in their marriage?" asked Duke Morgan.

"The usual with long-distance marriages," said Bax. "She said everything was good, but I got the impression that she was not happy with being in the public spotlight."

"Bax," said Buck. "Have Mel run background on the wife. Paul, anything at the job?"

"Not really. He'd been working there for more than ten years. He installed specialized sound and lighting systems. Everyone on the job said Bryce Tanner was a nice guy, but no one knew him well. He didn't seem to socialize much. His locker was empty. The address they had in his personnel folder was the same one you raided, and he didn't show up for work today."

"Okay," said Buck. "What else do we know about Bryce Tanner or Roger Shipman?"

Paul shook his head. "Not much. We can't find a

cell number listed for either name. This guy is a ghost. We need a break."

"Duke," said Bax. "Were you able to locate the congressman's car?"

"Yeah," said Duke. "We have two rentals in the parking lot. One in the congressman's name and one rented by George Billings. The forensic team is on them right now."

"Great," said Buck. "Did we get the background on Corporal Cordova?"

"Yes, sir," said Duke Morgan. He clicked on a computer file. "Cordova had been a trooper for ten years, the last five in executive protection. He was well thought of, with a spotless record. He was twice decorated for bravery."

Buck sat back and looked at the picture of Cordova's ID that Duke had put up on the big screen. Something was nagging at the little bug in his brain, but he couldn't put his finger on it. He tuned Duke Morgan out, opened his laptop and pulled up a website. He clicked a few more keys and stared at the image on the screen.

He grabbed one of the cables on the table and connected it to his laptop. He tapped a button, and the image moved from his laptop to the big screen.

"We have a problem," he said.

Everyone looked at the big screen and stared. "We confirmed his identity with his state police ID," said Duke Morgan. "We never checked his driver's license. Fuck."

Buck unclipped his phone and speed-dialed a number.

"Hey, Buck," said Director Jackson.

"Sir. Can you have someone go to Corporal Cordova's address right away?"

"What's going on, Buck?" asked the director.

Buck explained what they had just discovered. The director listened without interruption. He gave the director the address off the license.

"Okay, Buck, I'll get someone over there right away. I'll let you know what we find."

Buck thanked the director and disconnected the call. He looked at everyone around the table, all eyes still on the driver's license photo on the screen. The resemblance between the two photos wasn't even close. The case had just taken another interesting turn.

Chapter Twenty-Seven

Bax, Paul and Duke Morgan closed their laptops. It had been a long day with little to show for it. They told Buck they would meet him at the restaurant, and they grabbed their backpacks and headed for the door.

Buck finished reviewing the evidence logs in the investigation file and looked over the top of his laptop. Sheriff Foley looked deep in thought. Buck closed his laptop.

"You want to talk about it?" asked Buck.

Sheriff Foley stared off into the distance. Buck leaned back in his seat. He could see that Sheriff Foley was feeling troubled, but he wasn't going to push him until he was ready.

Buck was a patient man who had made patience into an art form. There had been a story circulating the CBI offices for years about Buck getting a murderer to confess just by sitting at the table opposite him and not saying a word for four or five hours. Of course, the time got longer or shorter depending on who told the story, but it was always told as a sign of respect.

Sheriff Foley seemed to snap out of his gloom and looked at Buck. "I feel like my career has hit the shits. First, the worst mass shooting in history happens in my backyard, then we find out one of the vics is a congressman, then there's a riot during the family vigil and then the governor jumps my ass for revealing that fact to the press."

"You want to tell me about it?" asked Buck.

Sheriff Foley got quiet again. He sipped his now-cold coffee. "I told her not to do it. That we had promised the governor, but she insisted."

"Told who?" asked Buck.

"Ellen Thompkins. She wanted to give the press something to chew on other than the riot at the family vigil. She wanted to take some of the pressure off the county. She released the congressman's name to a friendly reporter so it wouldn't blow back on her. I should have stopped her."

"I doubt you could stop Ellen once she sets her mind to something. In the long run, she might have done us a favor."

"How's that?" asked the sheriff.

"Maybe someone will come out of the woodwork and tell us what the hell the congressman was doing here."

"We sure could use a break," said Sheriff Foley.

Buck's phone chimed. He unclipped it from his belt and looked at the number.

"Hey, George. What's up?"

"Hi, Buck. Can you talk?"

Buck looked at the sheriff, once again lost in thought. "Yeah, go ahead."

"I was able to access the juvy file for Roger Shipman. I'm going to send it to your email. I'd rather it didn't get into the investigation file."

Buck's phone chimed with another incoming call.

He checked the number.

"George, let me call you back. The director is calling me."

Buck disconnected the call with George and answered the director's call.

"Yes, sir."

"Cordova's dead," said the director. "We found him in his apartment. One shot to the chest and one to the head. He was executed. Buck, what the hell is going on?"

"I wish I knew, sir," said Buck. "None of this makes any sense. Something was going on between the congressman and the guy Billings. Something that got them both killed."

Buck stopped talking for a few seconds.

"Buck, you still there?"

"Sorry, sir. I need to call the governor. Do you want to call him first?"

"What are you thinking?"

"I need to know if the congressman requested the executive protection on his own or if someone from his office requested it. According to Bax's interview with the wife and the chief of staff, they were unaware of any protection requests. I'd also like to call the Capitol Police and see what they can tell us," said Buck.

"Go ahead and call the governor," said Director Jackson. "I'll call the Capitol Police and see what they have to say. Keep me posted."

Buck disconnected the call and dialed the governor's cell phone.

"Evening, Buck."

"Evening, Governor. I hate to call you during your dinner. Do you have a minute?"

"No worries, Buck. Heading into a late-night dinner meeting with some of my staff. What can I do for you?"

"First, sir. The leak of the congressman's name was Ellen Thompkins. She wanted to get some of the pressure off the county because of the riot at the family vigil."

"Thank you, Buck. I will call Sheriff Foley and apologize for the ass chewing I gave him earlier today. Is there anything else?"

"Yes, sir. Do you recall who called your office with the executive protection request for the congressman? Was it him or someone else?"

"I don't offhand. I can check with my staff and see who took the request. Is it important?"

"Yes, sir," said Buck. "Corporal Cordova was found earlier today in his apartment. He was executed."

"Fuck, Buck. How is that possible? He was killed at the drag club."

Buck explained the state police ID and the license comparison. He told the governor that it was important to get the information as soon as possible. The governor told Buck he would check with his staff and get back to him later this evening.

"Sir, one last question. You know most of the political stuff going on in this state and with both parties. Can you think of any reason the congressman would meet in secret with George Billings?"

The governor was quiet for a few seconds. "Maybe it wasn't about politics. I need to go, Buck, but I will call you back with the information."

Buck thanked the governor and disconnected the call. Sheriff Foley still sat at the end of the table, but his focus was on Buck. "What's going on?" he asked. "Is the trooper dead?"

Buck explained both calls, and the sheriff looked more bewildered than he had been earlier. "What do we think is going on here? I can't believe the shooting at the club was just to cover up the murder of a congressman."

"I don't think it was," said Buck.

"You think it was a coincidence? Most cops don't believe in coincidences."

Buck smiled. "I think sometimes, things happen that we have no control over."

Buck's phone chimed, and he checked the number but didn't recognize it.

"Buck Taylor."

"Hi, Agent Taylor. My name is Julie Kincaid, and I work for the governor. He asked me to give you a call."

"What can I do for you, Ms. Kincaid?"

"I took the call about the executive protection for Congressman Sanders. Governor Kennedy said you had some questions."

"Thanks for calling, Ms. Kincaid. Did the congressman call himself to request the protection detail?"

"No, sir. The call came from his office. I was kind of surprised. Usually, those kinds of requests come from the protectee."

"Who called from the congressman's office?"

"The call came from his chief of staff, Darin Phelps. He told me the congressman had received death threats, and since he would be traveling in the state for a few days, he was requesting a protection detail."

"Ms. Kincaid, how is the protection officer assigned? Is that random, or is the trooper requested by name?"

"We normally do not allow the protectee to request a specific trooper, but in this case, Mr. Phelps was very insistent. It was odd. He said the congressman liked working with Corporal Cordova, but I checked with the executive protection office, and Cordova had never been assigned to the congressman. Fortunately, Cordova had just finished an assignment and was available, so the governor approved the request. Does that help?"

"It does, Ms. Kincaid. Thank you very much."

Buck disconnected the call and looked at the sheriff.

"Well, that's interesting," he said.

"Didn't he tell Bax that the congressman hadn't received any death threats?" asked the sheriff.

Buck nodded. "Yeah, he also said he wasn't aware of the request for the protection detail. We need to have another talk with Darin Phelps."

Chapter Twenty-Eight

Harlan Groves sat in his van and watched the stream of people leaving the studio in downtown Grand Junction. He was looking alternately at the picture he had printed off the internet and the faces of the people leaving the building. So far, he hadn't seen Donny Truex leave the building.

He snacked on organic energy bars and washed them down with spring water. As darkness settled around him, he prepared himself for the job at hand. He removed the pistol from the carrying case, inserted the magazine and chambered a round. He lit up what was left of a joint that he found in the cupholder and took a few tokes. He could feel his nerves start to settle down. He stubbed out the joint and slid out of his van, closing the door as quietly as possible.

The studio was in the Truex Entertainment building, a block off Main Street at Fifth Street and Colorado Avenue. The reconditioned brick building still had some of its turn-of-the-century charm, and Harlan Groves was pleased to see that whoever did the remodel had taken a lot of pains to make sure it was done well.

Harlan Groves strolled past the building twice and noticed there was no security guard stationed in the lobby. He figured Donny Truex wasn't concerned with his safety since he was so all-powerful.

He walked up to the front door and pulled on it, but nothing happened. He spotted the push button security panel next to the door. He was going to need a plan B.

He walked around the building and found a metal door painted to match the color of the bricks. He pulled the pry bar out of his back pocket, put on a pair of vinyl gloves, slid the bar into the crack between the door and the frame and applied pressure. The door popped open, and he hesitated and looked around. He waited a full minute to make sure he hadn't triggered an alarm. Satisfied he was in good shape, he pulled open the door and stepped into a back hall.

He walked to the front of the building and found the information he was looking for on the board hanging on the wall. The studios were on the top floor, next to what he assumed was Donny Truex's office. He spotted the staircase next to the elevator and entered the stairwell.

He had to stop twice to catch his breath. Living in Arizona had messed with his altitude tolerance, and he stopped next to the fourth-floor stairwell door for a minute. He opened the door and stepped into the hall. He followed the hall past a set of double wood doors and a receptionist's desk and continued until he spotted the sign for Studio A.

He spotted Donny Truex sitting behind the table with his headphones on. He was talking into a large microphone that sat on the table in front of him. Harlan looked at the picture and confirmed he was looking at Donny Truex. He looked through the glass panel in the door and spotted the sound engineer sitting in a small booth next to the studio. His back was to the door.

The red light above the door was on, and a sign next to the door that said RECORDING was lit up. Harlan Groves pulled the pistol from his waist and pushed into the room. He raised the pistol as he entered and shot the sound engineer. Anyone who worked for Donny Truex was fair game. The sound engineer slammed into the large panel with dozens of sliders and switches and hit the floor. He died, never knowing why. Harlan Groves trained his pistol on Donny Truex.

Donny Truex looked shocked and stared at the sound engineer slumped on the floor. He turned and faced Harlan Groves.

"What the fuck, man? Who the hell are you, and what do you want?" asked Donny Truex—all the color draining from his face.

Harlan was composed. It had been a long time since his time in the Marines, when his job was to kill the enemy, but the muscle memory came roaring back like it was only yesterday.

"Is that thing on?" he asked, pointing to the mic.

Donny nodded but didn't say a word.

Harlan Groves stepped closer to the table. "What's the matter, Donny? Cat got your tongue? You had no problem talking yesterday when you and your squad of thugs attacked a group of families trying to honor their murdered family members."

Donny Truex opened his mouth, but no words came out. He looked over at his engineer and then back at Harlan.

Harlan Groves stepped closer to the table, and Donny slid his chair back as far as the cord on the headphones would allow. Harlan reached out and turned the mic so it was facing him. The pistol pointing at Donny Truex never wavered.

"For those of you wondering what just happened, I'm going to tell you. My name is Harlan Groves, and my grandson was one of the people killed at the drag club the other night. Most of you listening to this show believe the vile bullshit that this asshole Donny Truex has been spreading about government conspiracies and Hollywood productions. But for those of us who lost family members in the shooting, we know the truth you people are too ignorant to believe. So that we do not have a misunderstanding, I want to make sure you know what's going on. I just killed Donny's sound engineer and am now holding my pistol on Donny Truex, so you understand completely. Donny Truex is going to die. No government conspiracy. No Hollywood production. Just one pissed-off grandfather who has had enough.

"You people follow this fraud and believe everything he says. You think you are the spear tip in the revolution to take back America, but you have no idea who you are even taking it back from. You think you have all the answers, and anyone who disagrees with you is the enemy. You think the Second Amendment only applies to you, and yesterday when you attacked a group of families honoring the fallen, you called us snowflakes. You didn't believe we would fight back because you are the right and the powerful. The one thing you never counted on was a snowflake with a gun."

Harlan Groves fired one shot into Donny Truex's forehead, and Donny slammed against the wall— blood, brains and pieces of skull spattering the wall behind the table. Harlan reached over to a switch on the wall that said RECORDING and flipped it. The sign outside the door went dark. He walked past the engineer's body and noticed the call-in panel. Every light was lit as the followers of Donny Truex tried to reach their idol. Harlan laughed. He heard sirens after he exited the studio, and he walked down the hall to Donny's huge office.

He placed the pistol on the receptionist's desk and pushed open the double doors. He walked around the big kidney-shaped desk and sat in one of the most luxurious leather office chairs he had ever sat in. He spotted the bottle of twenty-year-old scotch on the credenza behind the desk, picked up a glass and poured it full. He sat back, sipped his drink and waited for the cavalry to arrive.

Chapter Twenty-Nine

I waited for the people leaving the office to disperse. I wasn't sure how I was going to do it, but whatever I decided, I didn't want a lot of witnesses. I was parked across the street from the Truex Entertainment building, and I was waiting till dark. I had my hat pulled down so no one would recognize me, but I didn't think they would. This old Jeep Wagoneer belonged to my father, but he didn't have any use for it anymore, so I figured I would use it. The registration belongs to someone else.

I looked at the big knife on the seat next to me. Everyone always talked about shootings and mass casualty events, but I wondered how many people you could kill with a knife. Silent but deadly.

Darkness had settled over downtown, and I was about to get out of my car when I spotted the old man getting out of an old van parked across the street. I sank lower in the seat and watched as he scoped out the area. He looked like he was making sure no one was watching him. I wondered what he was up to.

He had long hair in a ponytail, and his van was covered with bumper stickers, flowers and peace signs. Save the whales, feed the children, legalize pot, protect abortion rights, don't make Mother Nature mad, respect each other, love one another. It went on and on. It looked like this guy was into every cause imaginable. So, what was he doing walking up to Donny Truex's office? He didn't look like the typical Donny Truex follower.

He tried the door and then headed around the building. I was undecided if I should follow him or not. I was intrigued. I decided to wait in the Jeep. I turned on the radio and tuned in to the Donny Truex show.

Donny was talking about the conspiracy behind the drag club shooting and rambling on and on about who was involved in the conspiracy and about the Hollywood production. I sat back and listened, and then something interesting happened.

There was a noise that sounded like a shot, and Donny Truex was quiet. I turned up the volume to see if I could hear what was going on. There was dead air for several minutes, and then a voice asked Donny if the mic was on.

A voice came over the radio, and it was not Donny Truex. I leaned closer to the radio.

"For those of you wondering what just happened, I'm going to tell you. My name is Harlan Groves, and my grandson was one of the people killed at the drag club the other night. Most of you listening to this show believe the vile bullshit that this asshole Donny Truex has been spreading about government conspiracies and Hollywood productions. But for those of us who lost family members in the shooting, we know the truth you people are too ignorant to believe. So that we do not have a misunderstanding, I want to make sure you know what's going on. I just killed Donny's sound engineer and am now holding my pistol on Donny Truex, so you understand completely. Donny Truex is going to die. No government conspiracy. No Hollywood production. Just one pissed-off grandfather who has had enough.

"You people follow this fraud and believe everything he says. You think you are the spear tip in the revolution to take back America, but you have no idea who you are even taking it back from. You think you have all the answers, and anyone who disagrees with you is the enemy. You think the Second Amendment only applies to you, and yesterday when you attacked a group of families honoring the fallen, you called us snowflakes. You didn't believe we would fight back because you are the right and the powerful. The one thing you never counted on was a snowflake with a gun."

The next sound was a gunshot, and I almost jumped out of my seat. Is it possible that the old guy I watched had just killed Donny Truex? Holy shit.

I heard sirens approaching from several directions, and I started the old Wagoneer and turned down the next street. I needed to get as far away from downtown as possible. The last thing I wanted to do was get stuck behind a police blockade. I made several left and right turns to make sure no one was following me, and I headed north. I found a small park with a parking lot on the street I was on and pulled in. I turned off the Jeep and just sat there. I couldn't believe what I had just heard. Wow!

My hands were shaking, and I couldn't understand why. Someone had beaten me to it. Someone had killed Donny Truex. It was so crazy. Some old geezer killed the guy I was going to kill. How worlds collide. The worst part is now he'll never get the chance to see what I do next. I would have liked to see him try to steer the story when it's his people that die. That would be a neat trick. I was now torn about whether I should go through with the next event. The smart move would be to get in the car and head for someplace far away where no one knows me. That would be the smart move, but then I wouldn't get to hit his people, and I need that for my satisfaction.

I picked up the brochure and looked at it again. This should be a piece of cake, and they won't be expecting it. Explosives can be devastating in the right or the wrong hands. I put the brochure on the seat, calmed my nerves and pulled out of the lot. I have a lot to do and very little time to do it.

Chapter Thirty

Bax and Paul were sitting in the restaurant with Duke Morgan, enjoying their steaks and salads, when Bax's phone chimed. She pulled it out of her pocket and pressed the green button.

"Hey, Buck. We saved you a seat," she said.

"Hi, Bax. Finish your dinners, and then I need you guys back here."

"Sounds serious. Something happen?" she asked.

"Yeah. I hate it when someone lies to us," said Buck.

Buck disconnected the call, and Bax told Paul and Duke about the call. They finished their dinners, paid the bill and headed for the command center.

Buck and Sheriff Foley stepped out of the command center when Bax, Paul and Duke Morgan pulled into the lot and parked their vehicles.

Bax was the first to reach them. "What's going on, Buck?"

Buck waited for the others to reach them. "I had a conversation with one of the governor's aides. She was the one who took the call about the protection detail. The call didn't come from the congressman but from Darin Phelps."

"Wait a minute," said Bax. "He told me he had no idea why the congressman called for a protection detail, and he didn't know anything about any death threats. What the fuck?"

"Bax," said Buck. "You and Duke see if Phelps is at his hotel. During the initial interview, he told us he was staying at the Marriott Downtown. Pick him up. I'll take Paul and Sheriff Foley with me and see if he is at the congressman's house."

Bax and Duke headed for Bax's Jeep. They slid in and drove out of the parking lot. Buck and Paul, in Buck's Jeep, followed Sheriff Foley south to Montrose and parked in front of the congressman's house. There were several cars parked along the curb on the opposite side of the street.

They walked across the street, along the sidewalk, and stepped up on the front porch. Buck knocked.

"May I help you?" asked the young woman who answered the door.

Buck identified the team and asked to speak with Mrs. Sanders.

"I'm her daughter, Diane. She's not feeling well. Can I tell her what this is all about?"

"We're looking for Darin Phelps," said Buck. "He wouldn't happen to be here, would he?"

"I haven't seen Darin since this morning when I threw him out. Why are you looking for him?"

"Why did you throw him out?" asked Buck.

Diane Sanders hesitated. "He was bothering my mother." She pointed to the cars along the street. "See all these cars? This is my father's staff. Darin moved the entire Washington office out here without asking my mother. They are here to figure out how to spin my father's death. A lot of big Republican donors are upset because of the circumstances. The right-wing Christians are up in arms, and the party leadership is trying to figure out how to hang on to his seat. My mom doesn't care about any of that, but they just moved in and set up a war room in her living room."

"You sound like you don't approve?"

Diane Sanders smiled. "My dad was pretty cool when we were growing up. He was a good guy through his first couple of elections, but that's changed over the last four years. He was hanging out with radical right-wing ultraconservatives, and his attitudes changed dramatically. I blame a lot of this on Darin. This is a solidly Republican district; Dad could have won no matter what. He didn't need to become a radical."

Buck was about to ask another question when a voice behind her said, "Diane, please let them in."

Diane looked surprised but pushed open the door and waved them in. Looking frazzled, Michelle Sanders placed her finger to her lips and then indicated for them to follow her. She led them past the temporary war room, which was abuzz with young people working on laptops, talking on cell phones and having animated conversations with one another.

They passed through the kitchen, and Michelle Sanders slid open a sliding door and stepped onto the patio. The heat hit them hard after walking through the cool house. She invited them to sit and slid the door closed. Buck introduced himself and the others.

"Gentlemen, I apologize for my daughter. She can

be a little overprotective sometimes. How can I help you?"

"Mrs. Sanders," said Buck. "You have our condolences. We came here hoping to find Darin Phelps, but your daughter informed us that she threw him out earlier today. Do you know where he might be?"

"I am afraid I was asleep when Diane asked him to leave. I assume he went back to his hotel. Have you tried there?"

"We have a team on the way to the hotel," said Buck.

"That sounds ominous, Agent Taylor," said Diane Sanders. "Why are you looking for Darin?"

"Mrs. Sanders," said Buck. "You told one of my colleagues that you were not aware that your husband was home. Is that correct?"

Diane Sanders interrupted. "Mom, don't answer that." She looked at Buck. "Agent Taylor, as her attorney, I will not let her answer anything further until you tell us what is going on."

Michelle Sanders put her hand on her daughter's arm, but Diane shrugged it off. Diane stared at Buck. She was waiting for the fight, which never materialized.

"Fair enough, Ms. Sanders," said Buck. "Mr. Phelps has lied to us on several occasions, and we need to find him to clear up some of those lies. I am not here to interrogate your mother as a suspect in your father's death, but when my colleague Agent Baxter questioned your mom earlier, she felt like your mom was holding something back. Since we are trying to solve your father's murder as well as the murder of seventy-some other people, we were hoping your mother might be willing to help us."

Diane leaned into the table, but Michelle Sanders pulled her back. "It's okay, Diane. These men are just doing their jobs.

"Yes, Agent Taylor, I was holding back when I spoke with Agent Baxter. You see, my husband and I have been separated for about a year now. Because of his position and political leanings, we had to be very careful and keep our cards close to our chest. I have gotten so used to telling the same lie that I thought I could conceal it better than I did, since your agent figured something was up. The truth is, I don't know my husband anymore, and I do not keep track of his comings and goings. I was being truthful when I said I had no idea he was home."

"Mrs. Sanders," said Buck. "When was the last time you spoke to your husband?"

"About a week ago," she said.

"How did he seem?" asked Buck.

She thought back to the call. "I got the feeling he was concerned about something. He seemed distracted, like he was having trouble focusing. He wouldn't tell me what was bothering him. Said he was taking care of it."

"Did your husband ever mention a man by the name of George Billings?" asked Buck.

"What does George have to do with what happened to my husband?"

"George Billings was killed with your husband, as was an unidentified man we assume was a bodyguard," said Buck.

Michelle Sanders glanced up and looked at her daughter. Diane Sanders tried to hide her surprise.

Buck looked at Michelle's reaction and then at Diane Sanders. "You're not her daughter, are you?" he asked. "FBI, DOJ?"

Paul and Sheriff Foley looked from Buck to Diane Sanders. She smiled at Buck.

"What gave me away?" she asked.

"Micro-tics when I mentioned George Billings had died with the congressman. You weren't aware because we hadn't released his name yet. You almost covered the surprise."

Diane Sanders looked at Buck. She slid a business card across the table. "Diane McMahon, Department of Justice."

Buck picked up the card and looked at it for a minute, memorizing every word. He set the card down on the table.

"What can you tell us about the meeting between the congressman and Billings?" asked Buck.

"Nothing. The congressman was supposed to make arrangements with us when Billings was ready, but he never called us about the meeting. That's why I'm here. That was out of character. He was never supposed to put himself in harm's way."

Buck looked across the table. "Why would a meeting with George Billings put him in harm's way?"

Diane McMahon realized her mistake. She stood up. "If you'll excuse me, I need to make a phone call." She left the patio and walked around the house.

Buck looked at Michelle Sanders. "How much did you know?"

"None of it until Diane showed up here this morning. We've met before. She works with one of Royal's committees. I still don't know what's going on, but she did ask Darin Phelps to leave. He was getting on my nerves."

Buck looked at her, and then his phone chimed. He looked at the number, answered the phone and listened. He disconnected the call and looked at the sheriff.

"Donny Truex is dead, and the grandfather of one of the deceased employees at the club is being held for his murder."

Chapter Thirty-One

Bax turned her Jeep into the driveway of the Marriott Downtown and parked along the curb. She and Duke Morgan slid out, and she was about to close her door when the valet ran up and told her she couldn't park there. She smiled and flashed her badge. Told him they wouldn't be long, and they walked into the lobby.

Bax approached the desk, placed her badge on the counter and asked for Darin Phelps's room number. The desk clerk called the manager, who stepped out from behind the wall behind the desk. He spoke with Bax, looked at her badge and ID and clicked a few buttons on the computer.

"Mr. Phelps is in room four-oh-five," he said.

Bax thanked him, and they headed for the elevator. Duke Morgan pushed the up button, and as they waited, Bax looked around. The bell chimed, and she was about to turn towards the door when she spotted Darin Phelps walking across the lobby towards the front doors.

She tapped Duke on the shoulder, and they headed for the doors. Darin Phelps turned just before exiting the building, spotted them and raced out the doors.

Bax spotted the move and said, "Fuck. He's gonna run." They took off after him. They ran through the doors just as a silver Range Rover tore out of the parking lot. The valet was picking himself up off the sidewalk where he had fallen when Darin Phelps stole the SUV parked in the driveway. Duke helped him as Bax jumped into her Jeep and started the engine. She pulled forward, and Duke jumped in, pulling his rover radio from his belt. Bax hit the lights and siren and tore out of the driveway. She spotted the Range Rover turning off Main Street onto North Fifth Street. She took the corner on two wheels.

Duke looked at the slip of paper he got from the valet and raised his radio. "Grand Junction Dispatch. This is Detective Morgan, sheriff's office. We are in pursuit of a possible murder suspect." He gave a description of the vehicle.

"All available units," said the dispatcher over the radio. "Sheriff's office is in pursuit of a murder suspect. Vehicle is a silver Range Rover, Colorado plates, Charlie, Baker, Nancy, one, four, seven. Heading north on North Fifth Street, just passing Grand. Requesting roadblocks at Highway Six, Glenwood, Kennedy or Elm."

"This is Morgan, suspect vehicle just turned east onto Glenwood."

"Units eleven Charlie and fourteen Charlie. Set up stop strips at Glenwood and Seventh."

"Eleven Charlie, ten-four."

Two minutes went by. "Eleven Charlie, suspect vehicle hit the stop strips and overturned. We need paramedics and an ambulance."

"Roger, eleven Charlie. Paramedics and ambulance en route."

Bax stopped behind the two Grand Junction police

cars parked across North Seventh Street. She shut off the engine, and she and Duke Morgan slid out and raced across the street to the overturned vehicle lying on its side. It had rolled several times and was sitting in a parking lot. She looked into the driver's side window and didn't see Darin Phelps.

She looked up to see Duke Morgan talking with one of the Grand Junction police officers. The ambulance and paramedics pulled into the lot and stopped next to them, and she noticed the lump lying next to them. She ran over.

The paramedics went to work on Darin Phelps as soon as they exited their vehicle. Darin Phelps was in bad shape, but he was still alive. They controlled the bleeding from his leg and head, loaded him on the gurney and raced for the ambulance.

"Duke, go with them in case he says anything. I'll follow after I talk to the state police accident investigator."

Duke nodded and jumped into the ambulance. Bax pulled out her phone and dialed Buck, but the call went to voice mail. She left a quick message, hung up and went to talk with the police supervisor who had just pulled into the lot.

The state police accident investigator finished interviewing the two officers and Bax, took a copy of Bax's GPS data and confirmed that the chase had never exceeded sixty miles an hour. He released the scene, and Bax followed two Grand Junction detectives back to the hotel. They picked up the key to Darin Phelps's room and headed up in the elevator.

"Any idea what we're looking for?" asked Detective Alice Monroe as she opened the door. Her partner, Hank Whitmer, who stood a foot and a half above her, stepped through the door and stopped.

Bax looked past them both. The room was a disaster. It had been searched, and not in a good way. Furniture was overturned, the mattress and pillows were torn to shreds and clothes were everywhere. Bax asked the detectives to step out of the room and lock the door. She pulled out her phone and called Franklin, who said he would roll his team.

"What do you think about that?" asked Monroe. "Sure explains why he ran. What was this guy into?"

"That's a damn good question," said Bax. "Hopefully, the science will give us some answers. Any word on Phelps?"

"Last we heard, he was in surgery. I'll give our guys at the hospital a call and get an update. Did you guys bag up what we took from the car?"

"Yeah," said Monroe. "All we found was a backpack and laptop. The owner of the Range Rover identified everything else as belonging to him."

"I'd like to get that to our tech guys. If you wouldn't mind."

"No problem, Bax. I'll pull it when we leave here, and you can take it. Would have ended up with your guys anyway. Any thoughts on who might have been after him?"

"That's the first question as soon as he's out of surgery," said Bax.

"You said this guy was Congressman Sanders's chief of staff. Then it's true that he was killed in the drag club shooting. You think this is related?" asked Monroe.

Bax nodded. "Could you grab the surveillance tapes for the hotel lobby and the hallways for today? I'd like to see if we can identify who trashed Phelps's room."

"No worries," said Monroe. "Did you hear that that right-wing podcast guy who caused the riot yesterday at the vigil was killed last night? Some eighty-year-old related to one of the club victims took him out in his studio and then waited for our guys to show up. The whole thing was broadcast live."

Bax stared at her. She hadn't heard about Truex being killed. That was a lot of people dead who were connected to the club shooting. She pulled out her phone and called Mel.

"Hey, Bax. What's up?"

Bax told her she was going to drop off Darin Phelps's laptop.

"Mel, can you do me a favor? Pull all of Donny Truex's podcasts for the past two weeks or so, and let me know if you find anything interesting."

"Already on it. Buck called with the same request. He also asked us to check all the callers as well. See if we can ID anyone."

Bax thanked her and disconnected the call. That was odd. Buck must be at the Truex crime scene. That was why his phone went straight to voice mail. She wondered what he was looking for.

Chapter Thirty-Two

Diane McMahon stepped up onto the patio. She looked at Buck. "Where is your associate?"

"We have another murder that's related to the drag club shooting. I sent Paul over to meet the investigators."

Buck's phone chimed. He looked at the number and then at Diane McMahon.

"You're going to want to answer that," she said.

Buck stood, walked away from the patio and answered the call.

"Governor," he said.

"Good evening, Buck. I have Hank Clancy on the line with us. Go ahead, Hank."

Hank Clancy was the special agent in charge of the Denver Field Office of the FBI and one of Buck's closest friends. Hank had been a deputy director until earlier in the year when he fell on his sword and took the blame for a rogue FBI agent. The agent, while working out of the Denver Field Office and fighting Buck at every turn during the investigation of the Christmas Day bombings, caused the deaths of several FBI agents and serious injuries to many others.

Buck had asked the Colorado governor to intervene on Hank's behalf, and as a result, they were able to save his job, but they couldn't prevent the demotion. Hank had a long career with the FBI, and he was involved in many high-profile cases, and even though his wife wanted him to retire, Hank refused to end his career with a black eye.

"Buck," said Hank Clancy. "I hate to do this to you, but I need you to pull back on the congressman's investigation."

"What's going on, Hank?" asked Buck.

"Look, Buck. I can't go into details except to say that this involves national security."

Buck laughed. "C'mon Hank. Are you *really* going to feed me that national security shit?"

"Buck, I know this stinks," said Hank, "but it's important. You know I would fill you in if I could, but I take orders, just like you do. I need you to give anything in your investigation file concerning the congressman to Diane. She'll take it from here, and if anything leads back to the drag club shooter, she will give it to you."

The governor came back on the line. "Buck, I need you to do as they have requested."

"Yes, sir," said Buck. The line went dead, and Buck went to clip his phone on his belt when it chimed again.

"Sir," said Buck.

"Buck," said Governor Kennedy. "Under no circumstances are you to stop investigating Royal Sanders's murder. Royal was a good friend, despite being on the other side, but more important than that, whoever killed him killed one of my troopers, and that I have a real problem with. Cooperate with the DOJ as much as possible, but I want to know who killed my friend and my employee. Do you have a problem with any of that?"

"No, sir," said Buck. "I'll take care of it."

"I knew you would, Buck. Call me if you need anything." The governor disconnected the call, and Buck had to keep himself from laughing. Governor Richard J. Kennedy had won reelection by one of the largest margins in the history of Colorado elections. Part of the reason was that he was not afraid to butt heads with the folks in Washington if it came to protecting his state. And he hated it when the Washington government tried to throw its weight around in his state.

Buck walked back to the patio. "Ms. McMahon, I will have my tech people reach out to you, and you can let them know where you want the files sent." He picked up her business card and put it in his pocket. He looked at Michelle Sanders.

"Mrs. Sanders, you have our condolences. If there is anything you need, please reach out to Ms. McMahon. Thank you both for your time."

Buck and Sheriff Foley stepped off the patio and walked around the house. They reached the sheriff's SUV.

"What the hell was that all about, Buck?"

Buck laughed. "The DOJ tried to strong-arm the governor. Once again, they are going to find out it won't work. Let's go talk to the guy who shot Donny Truex."

Chapter Thirty-Three

Sheriff Foley turned left off Ute Avenue and pulled into the Grand Junction Police Department parking lot. He pulled into a visitor space, Buck grabbed his backpack off the back seat of the SUV and they walked across the lot and entered the front door.

Chief David Cutler, a twenty-year veteran of the force, met them in the lobby, and they shook hands. The chief was in his dress uniform and explained that he had been to a meeting with the mayor and the city council to fill them in on what he knew about these most recent events.

He led them through a security door behind the front desk, and they followed him down a long hall to a sign that said DETECTIVE DIVISION in black letters over a double door. He pulled open the door, and they passed through the bullpen, which was buzzing with activity.

Detectives Jessie Maldonado and Mark Ridgeway stood outside the interrogation room waiting for them. They shook hands.

"Jessie," said Buck. "Can you give us a quick review of what happened?"

"No problem, Buck. Mark and I got the call at nine thirty-five P.M. The call was a shooting at the Truex Entertainment building on Fifth and Colorado. We got there just after SWAT cleared the building. They had arrested an older man for killing the sound engineer and Donny Truex. Believe it or not, the old guy was sitting in Donny's office, behind his desk, drinking a large glass of scotch. SWAT said they found the pistol he used on the receptionist's desk. It looked like he didn't have a care in the world.

"Both victims died from a gunshot wound to the head. Based on the recording, the sound engineer died as soon as the old guy walked into the studio. Truex died a few minutes later, and it was all broadcast live. You can hear on the podcast that the old guy even asked Truex if he was on the air."

She stepped over to her desk, picked up her laptop and hit a key. The recording was of Donny Truex rambling on about the government cover-up at the drag club, and then there was a shot. A moment later, a new voice came over the air.

"Is this thing on?" A moment of silence. "For those of you wondering what just happened, I'm going to tell you. My name is Harlan Groves, and my grandson was one of the people killed at the drag club the other night. Most of you listening to this show believe the vile bullshit that this asshole Donny Truex has been spreading about government conspiracies and Hollywood productions. But for those of us who lost family members in the shooting, we know the truth you people are too ignorant to believe. So that we do not have a misunderstanding, I want to make sure you know what's going on. I just killed Donny's sound engineer and am now holding my pistol on Donny Truex, so you understand completely. Donny Truex is going to die. No government conspiracy. No Hollywood production. Just one pissed-off grandfather who has had enough.

"You people follow this fraud and believe

everything he says. You think you are the spear tip in the revolution to take back America, but you have no idea who you are even taking it back from. You think you have all the answers, and anyone who disagrees with you is the enemy. You think the Second Amendment only applies to you, and yesterday when you attacked a group of families honoring the fallen, you called us snowflakes. You didn't believe we would fight back because you are the right and the powerful. The one thing you never counted on was a snowflake with a gun."

This was followed by another shot, louder this time, and then silence. Buck asked her to play the recording a second time, which she did. He listened closely.

"There is no waver in the shooter's voice. Sounds like Donny Truex messed with the wrong people this time. What have you got for background on the shooter?"

"Very little," said Ridgeway. "Guy refuses to talk. Said everything we need to know is on the tape. He hasn't even asked for a lawyer. Was pissed because we wouldn't let him finish the scotch."

Jessie Maldonado took over. "Driver's license is from Colorado, name is Harlan Groves, with an address in Westminster, but he sold that house twenty years ago. We found his van on the street in front of the building, but the same thing. Still registered in Colorado with the same address. We're running his prints, but so far nothing."

"Do me a favor and send those prints over to George at the office. We've got access to some of the databases that you don't. George may have better luck," said Buck.

Jessie Maldonado typed a quick email, attached the fingerprint file and hit send. Buck pulled out his phone and texted George and Mel to check George's email. He clipped his phone to his belt.

"You okay if I take a crack at him?" asked Buck.

Chief Cutler nodded, and Buck removed his pistol and holster and handed it to Sheriff Foley. He pushed open the door to the interrogation room, walked in and sat down opposite Harlan Groves.

"Harlan. May I call you Harlan?" he asked.

Harlan Groves nodded. "Harlan, looks like you've had a busy night. Is there someone I can call for you? A friend or a relative?" Harlan Groves shook his head.

"Okay, Harlan. My name is Buck Taylor, and I work for the Colorado Bureau of Investigation. I've been investigating the shooting at the drag club and listened to the tape of Donny's podcast. It sounds like someone you cared a great deal about was among the victims. Is that correct?"

Harlan Groves's eyes filled up with tears, and Buck reached behind him to a small table, picked up a box of tissues and slid the box towards Harlan. Harlan pulled out a tissue and wiped his eyes.

Buck sat back and let Harlan Groves have a minute to reflect on his loved one. After a few minutes, Buck leaned into the table.

"Harlan, no one is trying to jam you up here. We're all concerned about you. It's been a long day, and there must be people who are worried about you. You cared enough about your grandson that you felt it was important to get him justice. I'm sure someone out there cares about you just as much."

Buck sat back, and Harlan Groves pulled another tissue from the box. He wiped his eyes and looked up at Buck. "You have my phone. If you can bring it to me, I can give you a number."

Buck knew that Jessie and the team were watching through the window. He sat still for a few minutes until there was a knock on the door, and Jessie stepped in and put the phone on the table. Jessie stepped out of the room, and Buck slid the phone over to Harlan Groves. Harlan activated the screen, pulled up his contact list, clicked on a number and slid it over to Buck.

Buck looked at the name Harlan had chosen and held the phone up, indicating to Jessie to come back and get it. Jessie walked into the room, took the phone from Buck and walked out.

"Harlan, can you tell me about your problem with Donny Truex?" asked Buck.

Harlan sat quietly, staring at the handcuffs wrapped around his wrist and the bar bolted to the table.

"Two bullets, two kills," said Buck. "That's good shooting. Were you in the military?"

Buck sat back in his chair.

"Marines," said Harlan Groves. "Did two tours in Vietnam. Left a gunnery sergeant."

"Looks like you kept up your skills. Do you hunt?"

"Used to. Getting too old to be out traipsing around in the woods. Besides, the place we live in now is all about peace and love." Harlan laughed. "Guess that doesn't fit with tonight, does it?"

"Harlan, what happened that set you off?"

"That Donny Truex said my grandson didn't exist, never had, and that the government was duping us so they could take our guns. Have you ever heard such stupid shit in your life? I fought for this country, and he had the nerve to call me a snowflake. I guess I just had enough."

"From the black eye and the bruises on your arms, it looks like you got caught up in the altercation at the family vigil. Is that what started all this?" asked Buck.

"Maybe. The beating I took at the hands of his followers didn't help matters. I needed someone to blame for my grandson's death. Truex made it too easy."

"You said where you live now. Do you still live in Colorado?"

"Nah. Wife and I moved to a kind of commune in Arizona. Came up when we found out about the vigil."

"Did you bring the pistol with you?" asked Buck.

"Nope. Bought it all nice and legal in Montrose this morning. My only purpose was to kill Donny Truex and any of his followers I ran into."

"You sound like you think Donny Truex was leading a cult."

"What would you call it? He sits behind his

microphone, spouting some of the stupidest conspiracy theories one could imagine, and these idiots follow him blindly. All we wanted to do was pay tribute to our dead family members, and here he comes with his band of thugs, and he unleashed them on us. Words kill, Mr. Taylor. In your line of work, you see that all the time, but evil people like Truex never see the harm they cause. Well, he won't be causing anyone any harm ever again."

There was a knock on the door, and Buck excused himself, stood and exited. Jessie Maldonado handed him a file folder, which he opened.

"Nice job in there. We've spoken to his wife and daughter, and they're on their way. We've also called a public defender, who should be here in a few minutes. Everything he told you was true. He was in the Marines for five years, between sixty-seven and seventy-two. He received two Purple Hearts and a Silver Star. Spent forty years in the trucking industry in Denver and moved to Arizona twenty years ago. We found the receipt in his wallet for the pistol. All nice and legal, as he said, except that he doesn't live here anymore."

Buck handed her back the file. "We're gonna run over to the crime scene. If you need anything else, give me a holler."

Buck and Sheriff Foley left the building, and the little bug in Buck's brain started dancing around. Buck wasn't sure why, but he always listened to the bug.

Chapter Thirty-Four

Sheriff Foley pulled up to the Truex Entertainment building and parked behind Buck's Jeep along the curb. Buck walked up to the Jeep, unlocked it with his phone and grabbed his backpack off the back seat. They signed in with the officer at the door and proceeded into the building.

They had just passed through the entrance door when his phone rang. He pulled it from his belt, checked the number and answered.

"Hey, George," said Buck.

"Hey. Got your message and found Harlan Groves's prints in the military database. Passed the info on to Detective Maldonado. Also, got into Roger Shipman's juvy record. You can decide what you want to put into the investigation file. Nothing beyond what we already knew. He killed his preacher at fourteen, was sentenced to five years in a juvy facility, spent four and then supposedly killed the facility director, who was also his therapist. That's the outstanding warrant that Mel told you about.

"Read through the therapist's reports. There's a lot of disturbing stuff in there. The kid was a real wacko—pardon my characterization. He was troubled. There was a lot of information about his family life explaining what happened at the drag club. Lots of sexual and physical abuse by his parents and others. The guy was a walking time bomb. Disappeared from the facility at eighteen and was never seen or heard from again."

"Great work, George. Are you in the office?"

"No. Paul asked me to meet him at the Truex crime scene."

"We're just walking in. We'll see you upstairs." Buck disconnected the call, and they stepped into the elevator, which let them off on the fourth floor. Paul was talking with two detectives in the elevator lobby, and Buck and Sheriff Foley walked up.

"What's going on?" asked Buck.

The two detectives thanked Paul and walked down the hall. Paul asked Buck and Sheriff Foley to follow him. He led them into Truex's office. Buck noticed the glass of scotch still sitting on the desk.

"It was strange," said Paul. "According to the SWAT commander, when they entered the floor, they spotted the pistol sitting on the receptionist's desk, and Harlan Groves was just sitting behind the desk drinking scotch. He surrendered without a fight?"

Paul turned and walked out of the office, and Buck and Sheriff Foley followed. They made their way to the studio.

"Forensics cleared the space, so you don't need to suit up. The coroner is waiting for transport. The pathologist just left."

Buck stepped into the outer studio area and kneeled next to the body of the sound engineer. There were two holes in the engineer's head—one in front and one in back. The one in the back appeared to be the entry wound. "The guy never saw it coming," thought Buck.

He stood and stepped into the studio, where the

body of Donny Truex was now lying on the floor under a white sheet. He walked over, lifted the sheet and saw that Donny Truex had a single gunshot wound to his forehead. He replaced the sheet.

Buck exited the studio. "Paul. George said you asked him to come over here. What's going on?"

Paul waved for them to follow him, and he walked a short way down the hall, pushed open the door and stepped into what looked like a computer server farm. George was sitting at a table working on his laptop. He had a cable running from his laptop into a hub on the server. He turned and waved to Buck.

"Paul had an idea," said George. "Donny Truex had taken a lot of interest lately in bashing anything related to drag. Paul wondered if that was the catalyst that set off the drag club killer. He asked me to go through Truex's podcast library for the past two months and see if anyone took a particular interest in his podcasts. Maybe got involved in commenting on things Truex said. You and Bax both asked for the same information, and when we found out Donny Truex had been killed, it made more sense to do the research right at his mainframe."

Buck looked at the laptop. The letters, numbers and symbols on the screen made Buck's head hurt.

"Anyone stand out so far?" asked Buck.

"Nothing yet, but there's a lot of information here. If there's anything here, I'll find it for you."

Buck stepped into the hall, followed by Paul and Sheriff Foley.

"What led to that thought, Paul?" he asked.

"Just a whim. We were discussing over the last couple of days what might have set the shooter off, and when I listened to the entire podcast from before Truex got shot, it got me thinking. His disgust for drag was evident, and I wondered what that might sound like to someone who might be vulnerable to manipulation."

"Well, let's hope someone shows a lot of interest in the drag club," said Buck.

He told Paul what had happened with the DOJ lawyer and the governor's response.

"You know, I thought there was something odd about the daughter. She seemed overly aggressive. What do you think is going on?" asked Paul.

"I wish I knew, but the congressman was involved in something he didn't want a lot of people knowing about, especially his handlers at the DOJ."

Buck checked his watch and suggested that they call it a night and get some sleep. Sheriff Foley agreed and headed for the elevator. Paul said he would stick around and work with George for a while and get a ride home from one of the detectives.

Buck was beat and realized he hadn't had anything to eat since breakfast. He said good night to Paul, took the elevator to the ground floor and decided to walk over to his favorite Italian restaurant, which was just a couple of blocks from the crime scene. It felt like the nighttime temperatures were starting to break—the heat was not nearly as unbearable.

Buck unlocked his Jeep and placed his backpack on

the back seat. He locked the Jeep and headed for the restaurant. His phone chimed as he walked. He pulled it from his belt and checked the number.

"Hey, Bax. How is Darin Phelps?"

"Hi, Buck. He's out of surgery, it's still touch and go, but the doctor is hopeful," said Bax. "Where are you?"

Buck told her where he was heading, and she asked if he wanted company. He told her he was okay with that and said he would hold a place for her. He disconnected the call and pushed open the door to the restaurant. Even though it was late, the owner was happy to see Buck and had no problem keeping the kitchen open late. He led Buck to the table in the back corner and brought him a large glass of Coke.

Buck took a big gulp of Coke, not realizing how thirsty he was, sat back in his seat and took a deep breath. It had been a long couple of days, and it was not over yet.

Chapter Thirty-Five

After getting a hug from the restaurant owner, Bax slid onto the chair opposite Buck. The owner brought a glass of cabernet, and Buck and Bax ordered their usual: Buck ordered chicken parmesan, and Bax ordered the spinach ravioli in vodka sauce. They dug into the bread sitting in the middle of the table.

"You look like you haven't slept in a while," she said.

Buck broke off a big chunk of bread and dipped it in the olive oil and seasoning from the bowl on the table. "Yeah, I could use a couple of hours, but things are breaking."

Buck filled her in on the conversation with Michelle Sanders and Diane McMahon.

"And the governor wants us to back off the investigation into the congressman's death?" asked Bax.

"Just the opposite," said Buck. "He called me back after we hung up and told me in no uncertain terms that we were to cooperate with the DOJ but to keep investigating."

The owner brought their meals and refilled their drinks. He stepped away and left them to their conversation. Buck knew he wouldn't come to the table again until they were ready to leave.

"Buck, what do you think is going on with the DOJ? The whole thing seems odd."

"I was thinking about that before you got here. I think the DOJ lost control of the situation. For some reason, the congressman chose not to involve them in his meeting with Billings, yet he must have confided in his chief of staff, who convinced him he needed protection."

"Since Darin Phelps asked for Corporal Cordova by name, do you think he set up the murder of the congressman?" she asked.

"It's the only thing that makes sense. He was the one who knew the congressman was coming to Colorado, he made the security detail arrangements and he ran when you and Duke approached him. The thing that bothers me is how quickly he was able to set up the hit. This had to take planning. He had to get someone set up to take out Cordova. He needed a quality ID for the trooper and had to make travel arrangements that no one would find out about. We don't know when this all began, but it couldn't have been that long ago."

They ate their meals in silence, and when they were finished, they slid their plates to the center of the table.

"So," said Buck. "What made Darin Phelps steal a car and run, and who trashed his apartment?"

"I'm hoping Mel can find something on his laptop," said Bax. "He bolted as soon as he saw us. Forensics didn't find anything in his hotel room, and I checked every hidey-hole after they finished. The detectives sent me the surveillance videos from the lobby and the hotel hallway. You can see one person enter the lobby wearing a dark hoodie and sunglasses, and you can see that same person enter Phelps's room, but it looked like that person knew where the cameras were because we didn't get a clear view of the face. I can't tell if that person is male or female. I'm waiting for an update from the hospital so I can get in to talk to Phelps."

"Let's pull his life apart," said Buck. "Have Mel go deep. Social life, finances. Everything. And see if Grand Junction can put a guard on his room at the hospital. If someone ransacked his room, then his life could be in danger. Right now, he's the only one who can tell us what's going on."

"Okay. Any luck on the mystery man in the dressing room?" asked Bax.

"Nothing yet. Duke ran his picture by some of the entertainers, and no one recognized him. His prints are not in the system, which is not unusual since many law-abiding citizens do not have their prints on file. Right now, he's just one more mystery in a mess of mysteries."

Buck waved over the owner and paid the tab, and Bax left a nice tip that she knew he would share with his staff. They stood, exited the restaurant and Buck walked Bax to her car, parked down the street. They said good night, and Buck headed for the Truex Entertainment building to retrieve his Jeep. The air was cooling off enough to be comfortable. Paul's Jeep was still parked in front of his, and he was tempted to head into the building and see if he and George had found anything in the podcast library.

Crime scene tape still surrounded the building, and a Grand Junction officer stood by the door, holding a clipboard. Buck decided to let Paul and George work undisturbed, so he slid into his Jeep and headed for his hotel a couple of blocks away. Halfway to the hotel, he turned south and headed for Highway 50, where he turned south and headed for Montrose.

Buck's mind was focused on too many things, and he needed to sort them out. He knew the only way to clear his head was to spend a little time standing in a river and fly-fishing.

Fly-fishing was Buck's coping mechanism. When his wife, Lucy, passed away, Buck lost himself in fishing. Now he used it to clear his head. Once you stepped into the river and made that first cast, all your focus had to be on the interaction between the fly and the fish. You had to block out everything else to be successful.

Buck reached the town of Delta and pulled off Highway 50 at the sign for Confluence Park. He pulled into the park and stopped his Jeep at the boat ramp. Since it was late, the ramp was empty, and Buck had the place all to himself.

Buck put on his waders, grabbed his fly vest and fly rod and stepped into the Gunnison River. He studied the water for a few minutes and then cast the fly to land behind a rock that was sticking out of the water. The line jerked, and the fish was on. For the next two hours, Buck caught fish after fish, and his mind started to clear.

Around one A.M., he loaded his gear into his Jeep and headed back to Grand Junction. With a clear head, he might be able to get some sleep.

The ringing in Buck's ears didn't want to stop. He tossed and turned, trying to get it to stop, until he realized it was his phone sitting on the nightstand next to the bed. He looked at the alarm clock. Six A.M. He grabbed the phone.

"Taylor," he said, trying to focus on not falling off the bed.

"Hey, Buck. It's Paul. You sound like I woke you."

"That's okay," said Buck. "What's up?"

"We may have found something in the podcast library."

Buck took a sip from the warm bottle of Coke next to his bed. "I'll be there in fifteen minutes."

He set his phone on the nightstand, finished the bottle of Coke and grabbed a quick shower. He found a clean T-shirt in the go bag next to the bed, clipped his badge and gun onto his belt and headed out the door.

Fifteen minutes later, he signed in with the officer guarding the door, walking past the gaggle of journalists that had formed outside the crime scene tape, and entered the building. Paul and George were where he had left them several hours ago; they looked tired but excited. Buck stepped into the library and stood behind them.

Paul and George finished reviewing whatever they were looking at on George's laptop, and Paul stood and handed Buck a sheet of paper with four names on it.

"We went through six months of podcasts to make sure the information held up," said Paul.

Buck looked at the four names on the paper.

Paul continued. "Most of the comments are what you would expect. Every day people ranting and raving about everything that upsets them: conspiracies, UFOs, bigfoot, Democrats, liberals, diversity and inclusion. You name it; they're pissed off about it. Donny Truex took those fears and anxieties and played on them, reinforcing their feelings of being left behind. Kind of sad, actually.

"Three months ago, after the opening of the drag club was officially announced, Donny Truex made it his sole mission in life to get it closed down. He organized virtual rallies on his podcast, went after politicians that took a stand in favor of the club and made a pest of himself. Although upset by the idea of the club, most of his listeners didn't really get deep into the weeds about it. Those four names are men who did."

George clicked a few keys, and a printer in the corner of the room lit up. Paul lifted the papers from the discharge tray and handed them to Buck.

Buck took a few minutes to read the comments, finally looking at George and Paul.

"Pretty vile stuff," said Buck. He read aloud from the list. "We should burn the building to the ground, drag queens should be castrated and set on fire, an abomination that needs to be crushed and their broken bones scattered to the wind."

Paul pointed to a comment on the last page. "This was dated a week before the shooting. "I am ready to slay the queer drag(ons). You will guide my hand as I follow your wishes. You have told me what to do, my plan is ready, and I am prepared to show everyone that there are still good people in the world. Anyone who attends opening night should fear for their lives because I am the angel of death come to smite them."

"Was there any response from Donny Truex?" asked Buck.

Paul shook his head. "No, but if you look at the whole string, you can see that Donny Truex encouraged this person from the beginning. The comments and Donny's responses get more aggressive as the weeks go on."

"So, what are you thinking?" asked Buck.

"This guy had fallen under Donny's spell. I think he carried out the shooting at the club because he believed that was what Donny wanted."

Buck thought for a few seconds. "I agree, but that adds to my concern. Donny did a one-eighty on the shooting, calling it a government cover-up and a Hollywood production. I wonder how that made our suspect feel?"

"Yeah, but if he was pissed, wouldn't he go after Donny himself? Harlan Groves killed Donny," said Paul.

"Maybe he planned to," said Buck. "Have you been able to trace the IP addresses?"

George looked up from his laptop. "Yes. Three are in the city, and one is in the county. I just got the last one, and I should be able to finish the background check now that I have his name. I have the background on the other three."

"Can you pull up their license pictures?" asked Buck.

George opened the DMV website and entered each name into the search engine. He pulled up their license photos, and Buck looked over his shoulder. All four men were white; two had bald heads, and one had long hair and a long beard. The last one caught Buck's attention.

"Can you pull up the DMV photo of Bryce Tanner?"

George pulled the photo from the investigation file and put it next to the other picture. "And we have a match," said Paul.

"That sure looks like Bryce Tanner," said Buck. "What's this guy's name?"

"Mitchell Evans lives in the city," said George. He pulled up Google Maps, entered the address, sat back and whistled. "Guy lives two blocks from the Shipman house. Give me a couple of hours to run his background."

"Okay," said Buck. "Load everything you have in the investigation file. I'll call the sheriff and Chief Cutler. Let's meet at the command center, and we'll set up a plan. I want to talk to this Evans guy, but I also think we should talk to the other three in case there's a connection.

"George, see if you can find any cameras or CCTV that cover the area around the Truex building. Check the pictures against the CCTV footage and let's see if any of them have been in the area around the time of the shooting." Buck stood up.

Buck stepped out of the room and pulled out his phone. He speed-dialed a number. The director answered on the first ring.

"Morning, sir. We may have some information on the club shooter."

Buck quickly debriefed him on what Paul and George found in the podcast library.

"So now this guy has a third name," said the director. "What? Does he work for the CIA or something? Fuck, Buck. What's your plan?"

Buck went through how he wanted to handle it, and the director told him to call if he needed anything. Buck disconnected the call.

Chapter Thirty-Six

Buck pulled into the parking lot, parked next to the command center and slid out of his Jeep. He reached in and grabbed his backpack just as his phone chimed.

"Hey, Mel. What's up?"

"Hi, Buck. I finished running deep background on Darin Phelps and Diane McMahon. You got a minute?"

Buck pushed his backpack onto the passenger seat and slid back into the Jeep. "Go ahead, Mel."

"Darin Phelps got his degree in political science from the University of Pennsylvania. He worked on several political campaigns before landing on the first campaign for Royal Sanders. People I spoke with said he is the reason Royal kept getting reelected. He's smart, arrogant and considered a serious political operative. He lives way beyond his means. I found an offshore account in the Caymans but can't get into it. But he drives a Mercedes and lives in a very exclusive high-rise in Alexandria, Virginia. Rents in the building start at forty-five hundred a month and go up from there. His salary would make that kind of rent difficult at best."

"Call your contact at the financial crimes division at the FBI. Let's see if they can get anything from the Caymans," said Buck.

"There are also several encrypted emails on his laptop that I haven't been able to break yet. Still working on those."

"Okay," said Buck. "What about McMahon?"

"Diane McMahon is an enigma. She graduated from Yale Law School, but I can't find where she ever took the bar exam in any state. She works for the DOJ, but her paycheck comes from a congressional fund. It appears that she has been working as an investigator for several congressional committees, but I can't get anyone to say what she's working on. She's trained in several martial arts. Beyond that, there is nothing. No boyfriend or girlfriend and no work history before she started with DOJ. I'm still digging."

"Okay, Mel. Let me know if you find anything else. Thanks."

Buck disconnected the call, grabbed his backpack and headed for the command center. He walked in, set up his laptop on the table and waited for the others to arrive.

Bax walked in and closed the door. "Did you get any sleep, or did you go fishing?" she asked.

Buck smiled, and his phone chimed. He looked at the number and answered.

"Hey, George."

"Buck, pull up the investigation file."

Buck opened the file, and Bax stepped up next to him.

"What am I looking for?" he asked.

"Open the video file marked Truex CCTV."

Buck clicked on the video file and pushed the start button.

"Donny Truex must have been paranoid," said George. "He had multiple cameras placed around the building, but he also had two cameras placed across the street watching the front of the building. Stop the video at nine forty-four."

Buck stopped the video and moved frame by frame until he got to the time. He looked closely.

"Son of a bitch," said Buck. "That's Bryce Tanner."

"Maybe," said George. He pulled up a driver's license photo of Mitchell Evans, one of the four people identified by their IP addresses.

"That's the guy we identified as Mitchell Evans," said George. "Whether he is Bryce Tanner, Roger Shipman or Mitchell Evans, he was sitting across the street watching the building at the same time Harlan Groves was entering the building to kill Donny Truex. We did get a clear picture of his license plate from one of Donny's street cameras. The plate came back registered to Mitchell Evans. I think you were right, Buck. I think he was there to kill Truex, but Harlan beat him to it."

"Shit, George," said Buck. "Is that a good ID?"

"Yes, we ran his license, and it's all legal, just like the licenses we have for Tanner and Shipman. We now have three legitimate IDs for the same man. Who the hell is this guy?"

"We need to find out," said Buck.

He disconnected the call as the door opened, and Paul walked in, followed by a small army.

Buck recognized everyone, so there was no reason

for introductions. Buck asked everyone to gather around.

"We have four people we need to interview. We do not have arrest or search warrants, so we need to be careful. Let's keep the interviews friendly until something happens to change that. Right now, we stick to the same story. Their names came up during the investigation, and we need their cooperation to clear their names from our list."

Paul gave every team a written copy of the email comments, a picture of the person of interest and that person's address. Paul and Duke Morgan would handle the one person of interest who lived in the county. Two teams of Grand Junction detectives would handle the two guys who lived in the city, while Buck and Bax would interview Mitchell Evans.

Buck continued. "You can tell from the comments that these people are a little off. We don't know if any of them are dangerous, but be on high alert. We need to determine if any of them were working with Bryce Tanner or had any knowledge of the club shooting. Remember, keep it low-key, but be careful. Everyone goes home tonight."

Buck pulled up the picture of Mitchell Evans's driver's license and put it on the big screen. There was a noticeable gasp from those gathered. He looked around the room.

"Our fourth person of interest is Mitchell Evans. As you can see, he looks just like Shipman and Tanner. We have confirmed that his ID is legitimate. We believe this is another identity for Tanner and

Shipman, but whoever he is, he was outside the Truex building when Donny Truex was killed."

"What the hell are we dealing with?" asked Bax.

"Not sure," said Buck, "but we need to be very careful when we interview him."

They gathered their information sheets, left the command center and headed for the vehicles.

Buck and Bax slid into Buck's Jeep and pulled out of the parking lot. They were both quiet as they followed the same route he'd taken to get to the Shipman house, but instead of turning onto Seventeenth Street, he turned onto Fifteenth and pulled up in front of the house.

They slid out of the Jeep and walked up the walk. They both unsnapped the thumb break on their holsters. Buck knocked on the glass window in the center of the door, and they waited.

The door opened, and Mitchell Evans looked at his visitors.

"Can I help you?" he said.

Buck and Bax held up their IDs. "Mr. Mitchell Evans?" asked Buck. Evans nodded.

"Sir, your name came up during an investigation, and we'd like to ask you a couple of questions to help eliminate you from our inquiry. May we come in, sir?"

"What's this about?" asked Evans. He stepped aside and waved them in. He led them to a neat living room and pointed to two side chairs. He sat on the couch opposite them. Buck stayed standing and watched him closely as Bax asked the questions. He stepped over to the wall and looked at the diploma hanging there.

"Mr. Evans. We are investigating the death of Donny Truex, and your name came up in the course of our investigation. Where were you last night between nine and eleven?"

Evans looked at them slightly sideways. "Do I need an attorney?"

"I don't know," said Buck. "Do you need an attorney?"

Evans stared at Buck and then smiled. "No. I'm good. Last night I was here. I got home from work at six, watched the Rockies game until eleven or so and went to bed."

"Can anyone verify that?" asked Bax.

"No. Afraid not, I had a project to finish for one of my clients and was here alone. The Rockies lost eight to five if that helps, and the game went twelve innings."

Buck smiled.

"Do you own any guns?" asked Bax.

"Just an old hunting rifle that I used to use when I went hunting with an old boss, but after he passed away, I had no interest in hunting anymore, so it sits in the closet collecting dust."

"What do you do for a living, Mr. Evans?"

"I'm an electrical engineer. I work under contract to several builders and developers and design building circuitry and electrical systems."

Buck pulled the papers from his back pocket that contained the comments and handed them to Evans. He did not show him the picture from in front of the Truex building.

"Sir, we traced these messages back to your IP address. Did you send those?" asked Buck.

Evans read the emails and sat back in the chair. "Not my finest hours. I got angry when I heard about the drag club. Donny Truex has a way of firing people up, and I'm afraid I got caught up in all the hype. That's one of the reasons I stopped listening to his podcast. I realized what a terrible person he was."

"Did you ever correspond with any of his other listeners?" asked Bax.

"No. I would have no idea how to even contact anyone."

"Where were you the night of the club shooting?" asked Buck.

Evans's eyes darted around. "What does that have to do with someone shooting Donny Truex?"

"We think Truex might have been the catalyst that caused the shooter to kill all those people, so we're asking anyone who had contact with Donny Truex where they were."

Buck noticed some stress in his answer.

"I was here, same as always. I rarely go out."

Bax asked a few more questions, and the answer stayed consistent. They thanked him and followed him to the door.

Buck thanked him again, and they followed the sidewalk to the Jeep. They slid in, and Buck pulled away from the curb, made the next right and pulled to the curb. He looked at Bax.

"What did you think?"

"I think he was nervous, but he covered it well. The question about the club shooting caught him off guard. Did you see the diploma on the wall when we first walked in? This guy has his backstory down rock solid."

Buck opened the camera app on his phone and held up the picture he had secretly taken of the diploma. He dialed Mel, told her he was sending the pictures and asked if she could check and see if the diploma was legit.

Bax looked at him when he disconnected the call. "What do you want to do?" she asked.

"He lied to us about his whereabouts last night. I'm going to call the judge and request a warrant, then we are going to get the SWAT guys, and we're going to arrest him."

Chapter Thirty-Seven

Shit. That was the last thing I expected today. Cops at my door. I gave them solid answers to their questions, but I think they were still suspicious when they pulled away. I need to think about what brought them to my door.

I had everything covered at the shooting. I know I didn't leave any evidence that would point them in my direction, so what was it? They acted like they didn't know who I was. Maybe I'm just being paranoid.

Those comments were interesting. They shouldn't have been able to trace those back to my IP address. I'm not sure how they did that. I was very careful. I should have known better than to get into online conversations with Truex.

Reality jumped up and hit me between the eyes. I'll bet that fucking Truex had cameras on the building. He was paranoid; of course he'd have cameras. I'll bet they spotted me when I was watching that old man scope out the building. Shit. They know I lied to them.

I don't have much time. I'll bet they are working on getting a warrant right now. Damn. I may have to put my plans for the next attack on hold. I need to get out of here for a while. I have two other identities I can use. I can head to Wyoming or Idaho and disappear for a while.

I need to look around the house and see what I need to take with me. I know my other identities are sound. There's enough money in various accounts that I should be able to stay off the grid for a while. It's time to pack up and hit the road.

I stand still for a minute and listen to the voices in my head. They need to be satisfied, but I can't do it now. I'll need a plan when I get to wherever I end up to make the voices go away. But I need to hurry. They could be back any minute, and I can't be here.

I take a look out the window. I expect to see a SWAT team mobilizing in the street in front of the house, but there's no one there. Maybe they don't know who I am. Maybe I'm in the clear and can go on with my life.

No. I need to get out of here. They are coming to arrest me. The voices in my head are warning me. I have always listened to the voices. They can't be wrong now.

It's time to go!

Chapter Thirty-Eight

Paul and Duke Morgan pulled to a stop in front of the driveway to the Johnny X residence. The chain-link fence with the razor wire along the top made the property look like a prison. The signs in several languages that warned of physical violence for trespassing made it clear that Johnny X was not interested in having company.

The house was a nondescript concrete block house with a metal roof. It was run-down, needed a coat of paint, and was surrounded by a yard that needed a lot of work. The property at the end of the dirt road looked abandoned, except for the four cameras that moved and tracked Paul and Duke Morgan.

Paul held up his badge so the cameras could see it. He kept his hands up, hoping that Johnny X would know he was not a threat. They stood at the gate and waited.

They walked back to the SUV and slid in, and Duke picked up the microphone and flipped the switch to speaker.

"This is the Mesa County Sheriff's Office. We would like to come up to the house and ask you a few questions regarding an investigation in which your name came up. This is just a formality and should only take a minute or two to clear up." His voice echoed off the cliffs behind the house.

Duke looked at Paul. "What do you want to do?"

That question was answered as the first bullet

slammed into the front windshield of the SUV. Glass shards followed the bullet as it slammed into the back of the driver's seat.

Paul dropped below the dash and looked at Duke Morgan. Blood dripped down the side of his head.

The second and third bullets hit the windshield on the passenger side, and pieces of glass fell around Paul. He shook them off and grabbed the mic from Duke Morgan, who was holding his hand up to the side of his head. Paul flipped the radio to the emergency channel.

"Shots fired! Officer injured. Need backup!" He gave the dispatcher the address.

Paul didn't wait to hear the reply from the dispatcher. He told Duke Morgan to slide across the seats and get on the passenger side, and he worked his way around the SUV, slid into the driver's seat, shifted into reverse and slammed his foot down on the gas.

The car blew backward as more bullets hit what was left of the windshield. He spun the wheel and sped down the dirt road. When he stopped, he hoped he was far enough away to avoid getting shot.

He shut off the engine, ran around the SUV, pulled open the passenger door and lifted Duke Morgan's head. Like with any head wound, the blood poured out of the gash that ran just above his left ear.

Paul grabbed the first aid kit off the back seat, pulled out several gauze pads, stacked them together and pushed them against the gash.

"Looks like you got hit by a piece of glass," said Paul. He lifted Duke's hand and pushed it against the pads. "Keep pressure on that."

Duke Morgan nodded and leaned back in the seat, holding the gauze pads to his head, blood still dripping down his neck.

Paul heard the sirens approaching and stepped to the back of the SUV. The SWAT truck pulled up behind him, and Commander Martinez jumped out of the passenger seat, looked around and walked up to Paul.

"What the hell happened?"

"Guy opened up on us as soon as we identified ourselves. Duke's got a nasty gash on the side of his head from glass that blew out of the windshield."

Commander Martinez walked to the back of the SWAT vehicle and called for one of his SWAT deputies, who was trained as a paramedic. The deputy raced to the SUV and kneeled next to Duke. He opened his emergency kit and started working on Duke's head.

Commander Martinez walked back to Paul. "Any idea how many shooters we are dealing with?"

Paul shook his head. "All our background says this guy is a loner. He's bought a lot of prepper products in the past year: food, lots of bottled water, emergency supplies."

"What do you want to do?"

"I think we need to end this now before it gets out of hand. All we need is for him to call some of his prepper buddies, and we could end up with a war on our hands. I think our best bet is to hit the house hard."

Martinez pulled out his laptop and pulled up the

address. They looked at the property on Google Earth.

Martinez pointed to the front yard. "There is nothing in the yard to give us any protection. Guy has a perfect kill zone. The back of the house is too close to the cliffs to give us any advantage to come in from the back."

"The front is the only way," said Paul.

"I was afraid you were going to say that. Luckily, we have bulletproof glass and a big-ass bumper," said Commander Martinez. He walked back, discussed the plan with his other deputies and returned to Paul.

"You stay here with Duke and Deputy Hauser. We'll call you when we have the situation neutralized."

He didn't wait for an answer but walked to the truck and slid into the passenger seat. The big diesel engine roared as the driver stepped on the gas, and they tore up the dirt road. There was no hesitation as they turned towards the gate and hit it at full speed.

Paul heard three rifle shots in rapid succession, followed by a loud crash as the SWAT vehicle hit the front door and smashed into the house. Even though he couldn't make out the words, Paul heard lots of yelling and heard several rifles firing in rapid succession. Within seconds there was silence.

"Dispatch, SWAT one. The threat has been neutralized. We need an ambulance; notify the sheriff and call the coroner."

"Ten-four, SWAT one. Sheriff and ambulance en route."

Sheriff Foley pulled in and parked behind Duke Morgan's shot-up SUV. He slid out of his SUV and walked over to check on Duke.

"He gonna be all right?" Sheriff Foley asked Deputy Hauser.

"Yes, sir. A piece of glass from the windshield raked him across the side of his head. Lots of blood, but I have that under control. There might still be a piece of glass in the wound. Ambulance is on the way."

The sheriff patted Duke on his shoulder and thanked Deputy Hauser. He looked at Paul.

"I thought we were going in low-key and friendly. What happened?"

"Guy opened up on us as soon as we announced ourselves," said Paul. "Duke was bleeding before the second round hit the glass. Got him moved over and called for help as I backed us out of there. Totally unprovoked."

"Okay, let's go see what they found."

Paul and Sheriff Foley walked to his SUV, and the sheriff headed for the house as the ambulance stopped behind Duke's SUV. He drove past the gate, which was now bent and twisted and hanging off the fence by one hinge. He parked behind the SWAT vehicle that had been backed out of the house. The damage to the front of the house was extensive, and Paul was surprised the house was still standing.

Commander Martinez approached them and handed Paul an evidence bag containing a wallet. The Colorado driver's license sat next to the wallet.

"John Singletary," said Martinez. "Twenty-four years old. We should wait for forensics, but you should see this."

He led them around the SWAT vehicle and into what used to be the living room. The first thing Paul noticed was that the windows were covered with newspaper, blocking the view.

The second thing he noticed was a series of printed pages secured to an interior wall with tape. Paul stepped over to the wall, followed by Sheriff Foley.

"What is this?" asked Paul.

"Grand Junction High School," said Sheriff Foley. "Looks like he printed the whole school off the internet. Notice the x's in several locations."

"I think those are targets," said Martinez. "And the red lines are escape routes."

One of the SWAT deputies walked over carrying a laptop. "Sir, found this in an office in the back. I took a quick look. He must have two hundred hours of Donny Truex's podcasts on here. He also has saved several news articles from some pretty off-the-wall websites, discussing drag kids being allowed in the school, transgender restrooms and kids dressing up as animals. Every article mentions the high school."

Paul walked over to the body of John Singletary lying on the kitchen floor. "He's so young. It's amazing how quickly kids can be radicalized. It looks like we stopped a potential mass casualty event at the high school."

Sheriff Foley shook his head. "I'll never understand

this, but I'm grateful we found out before he had a chance to activate his plan. Looks like a good day's work. Deputy, put the laptop back where you found it, and let's clear out of the building."

He pushed the button on the mic on his shoulder. "Dispatch, sheriff one, we're going to need forensics at this location and let the coroner's office know we have one fatality." He thought about what he just said and that this had been an officer down call. "Dispatch, also pass the word that Detective Morgan is on the way to the hospital and his injury is not life-threatening."

Paul and Sheriff Foley walked to his SUV and slid in. He turned around in the front yard and headed for the street. "We're lucky we found this guy. Could have been another bad week," said the sheriff. "Thanks for taking care of Duke."

Paul nodded as they headed back to the command center.

Chapter Thirty-Nine

Buck and Bax sat in Buck's Jeep around the corner from Mitchell Evans's house and watched the front door. They were waiting for the warrant and the Grand Junction SWAT team. Buck was uncomfortable. He hated stakeouts. He focused on the job at hand.

"You think he'll try to rabbit?" asked Bax.

Buck looked at her. "I wish I knew. If he does, we could lose him forever. If he is Roger Shipman and Bryce Tanner, he has been able to hide in plain sight for a dozen years. No telling how many more identities he has."

Buck pulled out his phone and texted Franklin to roll the forensic team.

Buck's phone chimed, and he looked at the number and answered. "Hey, Mel. Whatcha got?"

"Those diplomas you sent me the pictures of are fake. I spoke with the admissions office at Duke University. Mitchell Evans was never a student at the university. But get this. Just for laughs, I checked on Roger Shipman and Bryce Tanner. Bryce Tanner was enrolled in their electrical engineering program. He only spent two semesters there before he dropped out. They sent me his transcripts. For the two semesters he was there, he took several advanced engineering classes, and he carried a four-point average. There are some comments from conferences he had with his professors. They called him brilliant, forward-thinking, an exceptional problem solver."

"Sounds like he stayed long enough to get the jargon down. Anything else?" asked Buck.

"Yeah. This is interesting. A psychologist teaching one of the classes he was required to take said he was aloof and had some deep-seated anger. The teacher believed he was faking his way through school to avoid some kind of trauma. She said he was brilliant but easily manipulated, and she believed, after working with him for a semester, that he had faked his way into the school. She had recommended a disciplinary hearing to determine if he should remain in school. He quit school before they could hold the hearing. There's one final note from her. She felt he was a danger to himself and others."

"Thanks, Mel," said Buck.

"Buck, before you hang up. I just Googled the psychologist. She was found beaten to death a few weeks after she made this recommendation. Her death is listed as active, unsolved."

"Mel, get hold of the detective who ran the investigation and see if he will send us his file?"

Buck disconnected the call, and Bax faced him. "How many bodies has this guy left in his wake?"

"I have no idea," said Buck. "But it seems like anyone who threatens his secret ends up dead."

Buck speed-dialed the director. "Sir, we got more information on our main suspect in the shooting."

He told the director what Mel had discovered and what their interview revealed. The director listened without comment until Buck was finished.

"How did this guy live three separate lives simultaneously?" asked the director. "Sounds like we are dealing with one sick son of a bitch, who might also be the smartest person in the room. You and Bax need to be careful."

"Once we have that answer, sir," said Buck, "we'll let you know."

"One other thing, Buck," said Director Jackson. "I heard back from the Capitol Police. Congressman Sanders had not told them about any recent death threats and had not asked for additional security while in Washington. They said he gets the usual ugly fan mail, but nothing outrageous or worrisome."

The director disconnected the call, and Buck set his phone on the dash as it chimed again. He picked it up.

"Paul. What's up?"

"We ran into an issue when we tried to speak with Johnny X. Turns out John Singletary, his real name, didn't want to talk to us. He opened fire on us when we got to his gate. Duke caught a piece of windshield glass, and it took a slice out of his head. He'll be all right. SWAT took the guy out, but when we looked around his house, we found a map of the high school and a target list. He also had a bunch of Donny Truex podcasts on his laptop. Forensics is on the way."

"Fuck," said Buck. "What the hell is going on around here? Is Duke going to be okay?"

"Yeah," said Paul. "He may have a headache for a day or two, but he should be fine. Could have been a lot worse.”

“Paul,” said Buck. “Go grab a couple of hours of sleep and then meet us back at the command center.”

Buck disconnected the call. He looked in the rearview mirror and saw two black SUVs pull to the curb behind him. He and Bax exited the Jeep and met the SWAT leader, Sergeant Jeffries, as he slid out of his SUV. They shook hands.

“So, Buck, what do we have?”

Bax pulled her laptop out of her backpack and opened the investigation file. She pulled up the picture of Mitchell Evans.

“We’re waiting on the arrest warrant. We believe this guy is the drag club shooter,” said Buck.

“What do we know about weapons?” asked Sergeant Jeffries.

“There were none evident in the house. He told us he had an old hunting rifle, but we have no idea.”

Bax gave him a quick debrief concerning Mitchell Evans, and then she pulled up the Google Maps view of the house. They studied the layout and discussed a couple of scenarios.

Buck’s phone chimed with an incoming text. He read the text.

“We have the warrant. We are good to go as soon as you feel ready.”

Sergeant Jeffries walked back to his team and told them the situation. He sent half his team around to the next street so they could enter the backyard from the neighbor's house. The rest of his team would make entry through the front door.

Buck walked to his Jeep, opened the rear hatch and pulled out two ballistic vests. He handed one to Bax. He strapped a backup pistol to his thigh and took the safety off his primary pistol. Bax did the same.

"You can come in after we secure the suspect and I give you the all clear," said Jeffries. He raised his hand and made a circular motion with his finger, and his guys moved back into the SUV.

He stood next to Buck and waited. "SWAT one, SWAT three. We're in position, backyard is clear."

"Ten-four, SWAT three. We are moving." He climbed into his SUV and pulled around Buck and Bax, who headed for Buck's Jeep. Buck stopped at the corner and watched as Jeffries stopped his SUV in front of the suspect's driveway. The doors opened, and his team raced across the lawn to the front door. They positioned themselves on both sides of the doors, and then the front SWAT officer slammed the ram into the door, and it flew off its hinges. They raced into the house. Buck could hear shouts coming from the house, and then Jeffries stepped out onto the front walk and waved for Buck.

Buck parked his Jeep in front of the house, and he and Bax climbed out and walked towards the door.

"Suspect is secure. We found him in the basement with a go bag. He surrendered without incident. I took a quick look in the go bag, and I spotted two passports and driver's licenses. I left the bag where we found it," said Jeffries. "Give my guys a minute to clear the rest of the house, and then you can go in."

Two Grand Junction patrol units pulled up to the house, and four uniformed officers slid out of their patrol units and waited at the curb. Buck and Bax stepped aside as one of the SWAT officers escorted Mitchell Evans from the house with his hands cuffed behind his back. He stopped abruptly when he got to Buck and smiled. The SWAT officer pushed him and turned him over to the patrol officers.

They placed him in the back of one of the patrol units, and then both units left the scene and headed for police headquarters.

Buck pulled out his phone and texted Franklin, telling him that the house was ready for him. Franklin responded that they would be there in ten minutes. He clipped his phone back onto his belt and waited.

Jeffries and his team came out of the house. "House is clear. It's all yours."

Buck thanked him, and he and Bax waited at the door for Franklin.

"What do you think was up with the smile?" asked Bax.

"He thinks he's the smartest person in the room, and he's been getting away with whatever this is for so long now that he thinks we can't touch him."

Buck's phone chimed; he checked the number and answered. "Hey, Chief."

"Hi, Buck. Darin Phelps is awake. Thought you'd like to know," said Chief Cutler.

"Thanks. I'll head to the hospital now."

Buck disconnected the call. "I'm going to see what Darin Phelps has to say. Work with Franklin, and let's see what we can find in the house. If you have to, take it down to the studs and tear up the floors."

Bax nodded, and Buck headed for his Jeep.

Chapter Forty

Buck gave a voice command to call Paul, who answered right away. "Hey, Buck."

"Have you left the crime scene yet?"

"Not yet," said Paul. "Why?"

"Now that I have a minute to focus," said Buck. "Tell me about the possible school shooter. You mentioned he had plans of the school and a target list."

"It might be worse than that," said Paul. "The county forensic team just sent Jack some pictures. He has twelve barbecue-sized propane tanks in his basement and a bunch of material to make pipe bombs. They took another look at the school's floor plan hanging on the wall and the red x's that we thought were possible targets. Well, there are twelve x's. They think those were locations where he intended to place his IEDs. Would have caused huge damage."

"Looks like you guys might have saved a bunch of kids. Any idea what his timeline was?" asked Buck.

"Nothing at first glance. It's gonna take some time to get through all the stuff on his computer. Forensics will drop it off at our office, and George and Mel can go through it. It was one crazy afternoon."

"Okay, the main reason for my call. Darin Phelps is awake. I'm gonna see if I can get him to talk. If you feel up to it, meet me at the hospital; otherwise, go home, kiss your family and get some sleep," said Buck.

"I'll pick up my Jeep from the command center and

head right over."

Buck hung up and pulled into the hospital visitor's parking lot, grabbed his backpack and slid out of the Jeep. He walked into the lobby, presented his ID to the volunteer at the desk and was directed to a secure area on the third floor. He headed that way.

Chief Cutler was standing in the waiting area talking with Detective Jessie Maldonado. They turned as he entered the room.

"Heard the county got in a shootout with the guy they went to interview. Duke gonna be okay?" asked Detective Maldonado.

"Yeah," said Buck. "He should be downstairs in the ER getting some stitches. From what I understand, a piece of the windshield sliced his scalp when the bullet hit the window."

Buck told them about the floor plans, the propane and the bomb materials.

"Does Paul think he was a potential school shooter?" asked Chief Cutler.

"Looks that way. Paul said the floor plan was marked with target locations; the number coincides with the number of propane tanks."

"Fuck," said Chief Cutler. "Looks like Paul and Duke might have saved us from becoming part of a growing list that no one wants to be on. I'll be sure to thank them."

Buck nodded. He had been to several school shootings in his career, and he hated that anyone should have to go through that, especially the kids.

"What do you want to do with Mitchell Evans?" asked the chief.

"Let's let him stew in holding for a while. Ask your guys to keep the video and audio running. Has he asked for a lawyer yet?" asked Buck.

"Not yet," said Chief Cutler.

"I don't think he will," said Buck. "If I read him right, I don't think he believes we have enough to hold him. We'll see if he's as smart as he thinks he is. How did the other two interviews go?"

"Waste of time," said Chief Cutler. "The one guy is seventy years old and in a wheelchair. He has nothing to do all day but get fired up. He listens to several podcasts and sends comments to them all. The other guy is a fourteen-year-old kid. He was using his father's laptop without permission. The DMV photo was the father since that was whom the IP address led us to. The kid's parents were upset when the detectives showed up. They had no idea he listened to Donny Truex, and they were not happy about it."

Buck laughed.

A doctor in blue scrubs walked into the waiting room. "Gentlemen, Mr. Phelps is awake. You have ten minutes, and if you upset him in any way, I will pull the plug on the interview."

They thanked the doctor and followed him down the hall and into ICU room four. Darin Phelps was lying in the bed with a drip line in his left arm. His head was bandaged like a turban, a brace kept his head from moving and he had a cast on his right arm and left leg.

He had a variety of scrapes and some nasty-looking bruises.

Buck walked up to the side of the bed and pulled the table closer. He pulled out his phone, engaged the recording app and set it on the table. He looked at Darin Phelps and told him that he was going to read him his Miranda rights. Buck pulled a laminated card from his pocket and read Darin Phelps his rights. He asked Darin Phelps if he understood his rights, and Darin, with a weak voice, said he did.

"Darin, I want to start with the most obvious question. Why did you run?" asked Buck.

"I can't tell you," said Darin Phelps. His voice quivered.

"Why can't you tell us?"

Darin Phelps was quiet for a couple of seconds. "My life could be in danger."

"Darin, who ransacked your room? Who are you afraid of?" asked Buck.

Darin Phelps closed his eyes.

"Darin," said Buck. "What do you know about the death of Congressman Royal Sanders?"

Darin Phelps opened his eyes, and tears rolled down his face.

"Darin, we know you were the one who ordered the protection detail from the governor's office, and we know that Corporal Cordova, the real Corporal Cordova, was executed. What was the congressman involved with?"

The machines monitoring his blood pressure and heart rate started to increase, and the doctor stepped into the room and looked at Buck. Buck nodded to him.

"One last question, Darin. How much money were you paid to have the congressman killed?"

The monitors spiked, and the doctor intervened and asked everyone to leave. Darin Phelps looked scared to death. Buck picked up his phone but left the recording app on. He turned to leave Darin's bedside.

"Only Billings was supposed to die. They promised me," said Darin Phelps.

Buck stopped and turned.

"Who promised you, Darin?"

The doctor asked Buck to stop, but Buck held up his hand. He stepped back to the side of the bed and leaned in closer to Darin Phelps.

"Darin, we can't protect you if we don't know who to protect you from," said Buck. "Tell me who you are afraid of."

"McMahon," said Darin Phelps, then he passed out. The doctor asked everyone to please leave as he attended to Phelps.

Buck turned off his recording app and stepped through the door. He looked at Jessie Maldonado and Chief Cutler.

"Who is McMahon?" asked Jessie.

Buck stepped away and stared into space. The more they learned about what happened at the drag club, the more questions came up. Now this.

Buck faced the chief and Jessie Maldonado. "Diane McMahon works for the DOJ. She's assigned to one of the committees that Royal Sanders was chairman of," said Buck. "She got the governor to turn over the investigation into Sanders's death to her. The FBI stepped in and wouldn't take no for an answer. Governor Kennedy told us to cooperate but to not stop investigating."

"What's her angle?" asked Chief Cutler.

"I don't know, but I think it's time we had an in-depth conversation with the lady."

Buck pulled Diane McMahon's business card out of his pocket, pulled out his phone and dialed her number. When she answered, he asked her if she would be willing to meet him at the command center later in the day. He told her he wanted to share additional information their investigation had revealed. She told him she would be there.

Buck put his phone away. "She'll meet me later today. Now, let's talk to Mitchell Evans and see what lies he wants to tell us."

Chapter Forty-One

Buck, Chief Cutler, and Jessie Maldonado went into police headquarters through the back door to avoid the press gaggle that had formed outside the front doors. As soon as word got out about the death of Congressman Royal Sanders, the press went nuts. They poured into the police department parking lot. The sheriff's office didn't have as big a lot, and it was hard to get the department SUVs in and out of the lot with all the press trucks blocking the space.

Buck grabbed an empty seat in the detective division and pulled his laptop out of his backpack. He opened the investigation file and reviewed everything that they had on Mitchell Evans, as well as the files on Bryce Tanner and Roger Shipman. He could tell when Evans passed him on the way to the patrol car that he was going to be a tough nut to crack.

His phone chimed with an incoming text. He opened the text from Mel and saw that she had entered the file from the detective in North Carolina who led the investigation into the murder of the psychologist.

He opened the file. There was a note from the detective on the cover. He wrote that he was sorry there wasn't more information. They had found some unknown fingerprints on the murder weapon but could not find any prints to compare them to. Buck realized the prints were sealed with Roger Shipman's juvy record, which is why they didn't show up in AFIS.

The woman, Elizabeth Burrows, had not been sexually assaulted, and there were no signs that she tried to defend herself. The detective felt it was a blitz attack. According to the medical examiner's report, there were no defensive wounds, and any of the five or six blows to her head could have killed her. She was twenty-eight years old at the time of her death, and she was pregnant. The detective pointed out that the investigation was still open and active, and any help from the folks in Colorado would be greatly appreciated.

Buck sat back from the file. He picked up his phone to make a call, and it chimed with an incoming message. Mel had sent the print card to the Grand Junction forensic lab and asked them to compare the prints from the murder to the ones they had just taken at booking. The prints were a match. Mitchell Evans, or one of his alter egos, had killed the psychologist in North Carolina. Buck was pleased. No matter what happened with the drag club shootings, the murder of the psychologist meant that he could keep Mitchell Evans in prison while they worked on the club shooting.

Buck showed the information to the chief and Detective Maldonado. He then pulled up the North Carolina detective's email address and sent him an email requesting a copy of the arrest warrant. The detective must have been sitting by his laptop because the return email with the warrant was instantaneous, along with about a dozen smiling emoji faces. Buck laughed.

The door to the detective division opened, and Duke Morgan walked in. He had a bandage on the side of his head, and there was blood matted in his hair and on his shirt. He walked over and shook hands.

"Should you be here?" asked Buck, looking at the side of his head.

Duke Morgan smiled. "Yeah, I'm good. Took a couple of stitches, and the doc told me I'd have a headache for a couple of days, but otherwise, I'm good to go. I heard you arrested Bryce Tanner."

Now it was Buck's turn to smile, as did Detective Maldonado. "Well, we arrested somebody. We're still working on who he is."

Duke Morgan cocked his head and looked at Buck. Before he could say anything, Buck continued. "We arrested a guy named Mitchell Evans for lying to us about his whereabouts on the night Donny Truex died. He looks like Roger Shipman and Bryce Tanner. We found a go bag in his house with two additional sets of IDs."

He told him about the psychologist in North Carolina and that fingerprints had just connected that death to Mitchell Evans. Duke looked surprised.

"How do you go from beating people to death to a mass shooting? Seems like a leap," he asked.

"That's what we're going to try to figure out," said Buck.

"Where's Paul?" asked Duke Morgan. "I need to thank him for saving my life back there. If he hadn't gotten that car out of there . . ."

"I sent him home to get some sleep," said Buck.

He closed his laptop. "Let's get this show on the

road."

He picked up his laptop, and Jessie Maldonado picked up an envelope with some of the things they'd found at Evans's house following the raid. Buck turned his phone to vibrate and clipped it back onto his belt. Buck never got upset if someone interrupted his interviews as long as the information was pertinent to the case. He always laughed watching police dramas on TV when someone would knock on the interview room glass, and the detective always looked pissed. Buck had found over the years that sometimes that intrusion was good for the interview.

They stopped outside the interrogation room and placed their weapons in the lockers, and Buck pushed open the door. Mitchell Evans lifted his head off the table. He looked like he had just woken up and used the little slack in the handcuffs to wipe his eyes. Buck kept his laugh to himself. He had dealt with some evil characters in his long career, and they all wanted to come off at first like being in an interrogation room was no big deal. Mitchell Evans was no different.

Buck set his laptop on the table, opened it and opened his recording app. He made sure the camera was pointed at Mitchell Evans. He pulled his Miranda warning card out of his pants pocket and read Mitchell Evans his rights.

He asked Evans if he understood his rights, and Evans said he did. Buck then asked if he wanted an attorney, and Mitchell Evans laughed and told Buck he was fine without one. Jessie Maldonado pulled a sheet of paper from a manila folder sitting next to her and slid it across the table with a pen. Mitchell Evans read the waiver of counsel form, signed it and slid the paper and the pen back to Jessie.

Buck looked at Mitchell Evans. "Mitchell, may I call you Mitchell?"

Mitchell Evans nodded.

"Great," said Buck. "Mitchell, do you know why you were arrested today?"

"No," said Mitchell Evans.

"Well, sir. You were arrested for lying to a police officer. Does that ring any bells?"

"No," said Mitchell Evans.

"Let me refresh your memory. Earlier today, Agent Ashley Baxter and I interviewed you at your home regarding information we received about the death of Donny Truex. You told us you were home all night working on a project for a client. Do you remember that conversation?"

"No."

Buck clicked a couple of keys on his laptop, and Mitchell Evans's voice came through loud and clear. Buck shut off the speaker and asked him if that was his voice. He said it sounded like him.

"So, just to be sure. Where were you the night Donny Truex was killed? That would be the night before last."

"I was home all night working on a project for a client," said Mitchell Evans. He smiled.

Buck spun his laptop around and showed Mitchell

Evans the picture of him in his car across the street from Donny Truex's office. Mitchell stared at the picture.

"Mitchell, is that you in the picture?" asked Buck.

"Looks like me," said Evans. "So what. I didn't kill him. I heard on the news you arrested an old man for the murder. So what if I was there or not."

"So, why did you lie to us?"

"Guess I forgot. Are we through now?" asked Evans.

Buck laughed, picked up the evidence envelope and removed two bags containing passports, driver's licenses and credit cards. He set the bags on the table.

"Mitchell, why do you have two complete identity kits? We found these in your go bag," said Buck.

"So I have a couple of other identities. Who cares?" asked Mitchell Evans.

"Well, for one," said Buck, "we do, but we'll come back to that in a little while."

Buck could see Mitchell Evans was getting irritated. He wasn't sure why, but he intended to use that to his advantage. His phone vibrated on his hip. He checked the message and clipped it back on his hip.

"Mitchell, we're going to stop this interview for a few minutes. Can we get you something to drink?"

He shook his head, Buck closed his laptop and they left the room.

Chapter Forty-Two

These fucking cops. I'm not sure how long I've been sitting in this shitty little room. I wonder what they're waiting for. I bet they want to see how long I can sit here before I piss myself. Well, two can play that game. I won't give them the satisfaction.

I laid my head down on the table, pretending I was asleep. I saw it on a TV show. It makes the cops think you're not guilty because you're relaxed and quiet. I wonder if it will work. The problem is that when I lie still for any length of time, the voices start up again. Right now, they are screaming at me, and I have no way to make them stop.

I'm not sure how long I lay like that, but the door opened, and in walked two cops. The one I recognized. He was the one who came to my house this morning with that cute blonde. He's old but in good shape. The other one is a woman. Boy, she's a big girl. Probably lots of fluff under that frumpy suit. I should remember what she looks like. If I ever decide to become a drag queen, I could make my character look like her.

They sit down across from me, and they look so serious. I wipe the sleep out of my eyes and yawn. I fake looking disinterested. He reads me my rights, and I tell him I don't need an attorney. The voices are deep in my head, and I'm having trouble concentrating.

The old guy starts asking me questions, and I give him short one-word answers. I'm in control of this conversation, but for some reason, I'm getting irritated. It must be the voices. They want me to do something, They are trying to warn me, but I'm not listening. I'm too smart to listen to the voices. I satisfied them before; I can do it again. I just need to get out of here.

I had all my answers ready for when he asked me about the club shooting, but he's not doing that. He's asking me about why I lied to him this morning. What the fuck is he asking me about? When did I lie to him? He's screwing up all my answers. The voices are making me crazy. I need to get out of here.

Shit, now he's asking me about my other IDs. What the hell? No one cares about fake IDs. They are supposed to ask me about killing all those people at the drag club. He's making me confused with his questions. I want to scream that he's making a mistake.

I hear buzzing, and the old guy looks at his phone. They get up and walk out—something's up. I don't know how to respond. I'm smarter than them, but he's making me crazy. I need to get out of here. The voices need to be satisfied. And now I'm alone again. I don't want to be alone with the voices. I don't want to be alone.

Chapter Forty-Three

Bax and Franklin were standing by the interrogation room window when Buck and Jessie Maldonado exited the room.

"He looks irritated," said Bax. "He's trying to hide it. What got him so riled up?"

"Not sure," said Buck. "I noticed it too. What have you guys got?"

Franklin held up an evidence bag and handed it to Buck. The hammer in the bag was covered with dust. He looked at Franklin.

"We did a quick test on the head," said Franklin. "That is definitely human blood. It's old and degraded, so we may not be able to get any DNA off of it. Found it in the bottom of the chimney."

Franklin's face turned into a huge smile, and Buck waited for the next surprise. Franklin took out his phone and opened his gallery. He pulled up a picture and handed the phone to Buck.

Buck looked at the picture. "What am I looking at?"

"Our suspect was new at this when he killed his father and walled him up in the chimney. He left us a present in the mortar between two layers of bricks—a perfect thumbprint preserved for all eternity or until we found it. My guys found it when they took the chimney apart brick by brick. The print belongs to Mitchell Evans."

Buck looked at Bax and Franklin. "That's

awesome. We can charge him with the murder of the psychologist and now with the murder of his father. Nice work."

"That's not all," said Bax. "We found a laptop hidden in a compartment under the floor in Mitchell Evans's house. I ran it over to the office, and Mel and George got to work on it. He has a complete set of blueprints for the drag club. Now, Bryce Tanner was the electrician on the job, so that could be explained away. However, he also had floor plans for a Presbyterian church on Patterson Road."

"Did he do work there?" asked Jessie Maldonado.

Bax shook her head. "No." She handed Buck another evidence bag containing a brochure. He flipped the bag open and looked at the brochure.

"What's the Christian Freedom Council of America?" asked Buck.

"Well," said Bax. "That depends on who you talk to. According to several watchdog groups, the CFCA is an extremist group bordering on domestic terrorism. According to the group's website, they promote religious freedom. Take your pick. According to the brochure, they are having their annual meeting in the church next week."

"What's the connection to Mitchell Evans?" asked Buck.

"We're not sure," said Bax. "But here's the interesting part. Donny Truex was going to be one of their guest speakers."

"Was Evans part of this group?" asked Chief Cutler.

"Nothing we found indicated he was," said Bax. "Evans uploaded the information on the group and printed the brochure after the riot at the club."

"Interesting," said Buck. He asked Jessie to follow him back into the interrogation room. Mitchell Evans looked up as they entered. He had a smile on his face, but Buck could see that the irritation was still present. They sat at the table, and Buck opened his laptop and hit the recording app. He had an idea and wanted to see if he was right.

"Mitchell," said Buck. "Tell me about growing up. Have you always lived in Colorado?"

Mitchell Evans gave Buck a side-eye look. "Yeah. Born and raised right here in Grand Junction."

Buck asked a few more inane questions about growing up in Colorado. He was gauging the level of irritation that Evans was showing. Evans answered them, but Buck could see that he appeared confused. He had trouble remembering details, like where he went to high school and who his friends were.

What the hell is this guy doing? He can't be that stupid. Why does he care where I grew up? In the grand scheme of things, it's not important.

"So, tell me, Roger, did you like growing up in Marquette, Michigan?" asked Buck.

Evans looked at him. "I'm sorry, what?"

"Growing up in Michigan. I understand your parents owned several bars. They must have been busy a lot."

Now Evans looked confused. "Who the hell is

Roger? I told you I grew up here in Colorado, and my name is Mitchell Evans. What's going on here?"

"Tell me about your parents."

"Nothing to tell," said Evans. "They were ordinary people; Dad worked, Mom stayed home."

He's trying to confuse me. I told him I grew up here. Why is he asking about Roger? They should have brought in a better interrogator, or maybe they should let the fat broad ask the questions.

"Bryce," said Buck. "Where did you go to school to become an electrician?"

Evans was getting more and more aggravated, and Buck could see that tiny chinks were developing in his story.

"I'm an electrical engineer, not an electrician, and who the hell is Bryce? You can't be that stupid, or are you just not listening?"

"I'm sorry, Roger. I thought maybe you might have learned the electrical trade at the juvenile home in Michigan."

"I've never been to Michigan. I got my degree from Duke University in North Carolina. I'm not Roger. My name is Bryce; sorry, now you're confusing me. My name is Mitchell."

"That's right, Bryce. I remember reading about the unsolved murder of a psychologist who worked at Duke. Do you remember her name? I understand it was a pretty brutal murder. Someone beat her to death with a hammer."

What the hell is this now? Does this guy have no idea who he is talking to? Maybe he's having a stroke or something. He's getting himself all confused. The voices are making my head hurt, and this idiot isn't helping.

"I have no idea what you're talking about. And why do you keep calling me Bryce or Roger or whatever?" said Evans.

The voices are screaming at me to escape. To get out of this room. This guy is driving me crazy. What is wrong with him? I'm not sure how much more of this I can take.

"When did you graduate from Duke, Roger?"

"Don't remember," said Evans. "Sometime around twenty-ten. Why."

"And that qualified you to be an electrician?"

"No," said Evans. "It was a degree in electrical engineering. You saw the diplomas in my house."

"Which house is that, Bryce?" asked Buck.

"I only have one house," said Evans.

"Is that your parents' house on Seventeenth?" asked Buck.

"No, my parents don't own a house here. I live on Seventeenth."

"Then who lives in the house on Fifteenth? We show it was owned by the Shipmans. Your parents," said Buck.

"My parents lived in Michigan. I mean Colorado,"

said Evans. He shook his head and scratched his brow.

"Did your parents also live in North Carolina, Bryce, or did they move straight from Michigan to Colorado?"

I don't understand what's going on. I can't tell if it's the voices that are confusing me or if it's this idiot cop. None of this had anything to do with the shooting at the drag club. Why won't he ask me about that?

"I never lived in Michigan, and my name is not Bryce; it's Roger. I mean Mitchell."

Buck closed his laptop and signaled for Jessie to leave the room. He looked at Mitchell, whose head was lying on the table, and walked out behind her. He knew it was time to finish this.

Chapter Forty-Four

"Fuck, Buck. How the hell are you keeping up with this? You had me confused there a couple of times. Watching him is like watching an egg crack," said Jessie Maldonado.

"Do you think he's ready?" asked Bax.

Buck smiled at her. "Yeah. He's right about where I want him."

"What are you hoping to accomplish, Buck?" asked Duke Morgan.

"He wants us to know how smart he is. I think he already had a head full of answers if we asked him about the club shooting. Right now, he's confused because I haven't asked him about the club shooting. I think that's what's getting to him. I'm just adding a little confusion into the mix."

Buck leaned against one of the desks, his brow furrowed. He thought about the evidence from the house and the computer. Adding the church into the mix might be enough to get him to open up. "The riot at the club was the first time Truex called the shooting a fake." He was quiet for a minute. He walked over to the window and watched Mitchell Evans make-believe he was asleep. He walked over to the desk, picked up the hammer and brochure and asked Jessie to follow him. He pushed open the door to the interrogation room, walked to the table and dropped the hammer onto the table. It landed with a bang, and Evans jumped back in the chair, a shocked look on his face. He stared at Buck. Buck knew it was time to come on strong.

"You screwed up, Roger. We found the hammer you used to kill your father at the bottom of the chimney. What a rookie move. You would think after killing your preacher, the director of the youth facility and the psychologist in North Carolina that you would be smarter than to leave evidence around for us to find."

Mitchell Evans looked surprised; Buck took advantage of that. "You were also sloppy when you bricked in the chimney." Buck pulled out his phone and opened the picture he'd sent to himself from Franklin's phone. He slid the phone across the table, and Mitchell Evans stared at it.

"You left us a beautiful thumbprint in the mortar. We have matched it to you. And your prints match Bryce Tanner and Roger Shipman."

Buck hesitated a minute to let that sink in. He slid the evidence bag across the table. Evans looked at the brochure.

"What's your connection to the Christian Freedom Council of America?"

Mitchell Evans stared at the brochure. He looked at Buck. "I don't have one."

"We found this in your house, Bryce, just like we found your laptop. By the way, my tech people tell me that your encryption software sucks. We found the blueprints for the church. Were you that pissed off at Donny Truex that you decided to attack the church during their meeting? If you attacked a right-wing

Christian group, the right wing would be hard-pressed to call it a fake. You would get the recognition you wanted. Everyone would know your name. You would have to kill all those Christians because someone else beat you to killing Donny Truex."

I can't figure out what he's doing. He's asking me about old crimes and this church group that I haven't done anything about. The voices are screaming at me. My head hurts from all the yelling. Why won't he ask me about the drag club shooting? He's making me confused. What is he after? Has he not figured it out yet?

"I didn't attack any church," said Evans, his anger building.

"But you were planning to," said Buck. "Did you hate them the way you hated Donny Truex? Did you hate them like you hated your father for watching all those men having sex with your mother? Did you hate them the way you hated the preacher for having sex with you while your mother held you down and prayed to save you from the devil?"

Why is he asking me about crimes I haven't committed yet? The voices want me to escape, I need to get out of here, but I need to tell him why I killed all those drag queens. He's asking me the wrong questions. Who cares about old crimes and fake IDs? I have to get rid of the voices; they're making my head hurt. Suddenly the words are screaming out of my mouth, but I'm not saying them. It's the voices.

Mitchell Evans's face turned red, and he stared at Buck. He leaned across the table and strained at the handcuffs attached to the bolt. Spit flew from his mouth.

"YOU'RE ASKING THE WRONG QUESTIONS! NO ONE CARES ABOUT THOSE OLD CRIMES! EVERYONE I KILLED DESERVED TO DIE! MY PARENTS WERE SICK AND TWISTED! THE THINGS THEY MADE ME WATCH WERE HORRIBLE! MY MOTHER WAS A WHORE, AND SHE WATCHED THAT PREACHER RAPE ME REPEATEDLY! ALL IN THE NAME OF GOD! THEY BOTH HAD TO DIE! AND DONNY TRUEX! I THOUGHT HE WAS MY FRIEND! HE SPOKE DIRECTLY TO ME AND MADE THE VOICES EASIER TO LIVE WITH! HE GAVE ME A SENSE OF PURPOSE AND THEN BETRAYED ME! HE TURNED ON ME! CALLED ME A FAKE! I WAS GOING TO KILL HIM JUST FOR FUN UNTIL THAT OLD GUY BEAT ME TO IT! YOU DON'T EVEN KNOW ABOUT ALL THE OTHER PEOPLE I KILLED! WHY AREN'T YOU ASKING ME ABOUT ALL THE PEOPLE I KILLED AT THE DRAG CLUB? THE PEOPLE I KILLED BECAUSE DONNY TRUEX TOLD ME IT WAS OKAY AND IT WAS THE ONLY WAY TO STOP THE VOICES! I DID IT TO SAVE THE CHILDREN! TO PROTECT THEM FROM PERVERTS AND PEDOPHILES! I'M A HERO! A SAVIOR!

Mitchell Evans started to babble incoherently, slumped into his chair and laid his head on the table. Softly he said, "You asked the wrong questions," and tears rolled down his face. His mouth moved like he was talking to himself, but the words were jumbled. Buck tried to get his attention, but there was no response.

Jessie Maldonado looked at Buck, and her shocked expression said it all. Buck gave Mitchell Evans a couple of minutes to calm down. He made some notes on his laptop. Buck asked Jessie to stay in the room, and he stood and walked out.

The stunned faces in the room stared at Buck.

"Shit," said Chief Cutler.

"Buck, what do you want to do?" asked Bax.

Buck walked over to the refrigerator in the corner, opened the door and pulled out a Coke. He popped the top and swallowed the entire can in one long gulp.

He walked back to the group. "Bax, would you call Hank Clancy? Let him know we uncovered a serial killer that the FBI doesn't have on their radar. No telling how many more crimes he committed and how many other personas he has. Also, call Mel and have her call the police in Michigan and North Carolina and fill them in on what we have so far. We may get the first crack at him because of the size of the crime here and because we can classify the club shooting as a hate crime.

"Chief, do you have a psychiatrist on call for the department? We're going to need someone to evaluate Roger Shipman."

Chief Cutler nodded and pulled out his phone. He stepped away from the group. Franklin was standing next to Duke Morgan. He walked over and patted Buck on the shoulder. He stepped back.

Buck looked at Duke. "Once the psychiatrist has a

chance to talk to him, call the public defender's office and let's get him a lawyer."

"Do you think any of these crimes will ever get to trial?" asked Duke Morgan.

"I wish I knew," said Buck. "We'll arrest him for the drag club murders, killing his father, the psychologist and the director of the youth facility. We'll need to wait on the science to connect him to his mother's death. It could take years, if ever, to figure out what's going on inside his head."

Chief Cutler walked back into the room. "Psychiatrist is just down the street at the hospital. She'll be here in a couple of minutes. What do we do with him now?"

"Let's see what she says, and then we can decide," said Buck.

Chapter Forty-Five

Everyone relaxed for a few minutes while they waited for the doctor to arrive. Ten minutes later, Dr. Jackie Thurston walked into the interrogation area. Dr. Thurston wore her gray hair short and was small and thin. She introduced herself to the group, then sat at one of the desks and watched the interview tape. She ran portions of it back several times and then asked to see the juvy file and the notes from the juvenile detention center. Bax opened the investigation file on her laptop and slid it over to the doctor. She read the reports and then asked to see Mitchell Evans.

Jessie Maldonado stayed with her in the interrogation room and sat next to her while she spoke with Evans. He barely raised his head during the conversation and seemed to drift off to sleep at times. Other times he just stared into space. After two hours, Dr. Thurston and Jessie exited the room and approached the group.

"Mr. Evans, and I'll call him that for now, has had his entire world turned upside down. In all my years of practice, I have never seen a case like this. He has multiple personas that he has created, but it's not multiple personality disorder. Each persona functions as a separate individual, not as part of the collective. He appears to create a new persona as the need arises and then discard the old one. They never go away; they're buried in case he needs one later.

"Now, if that isn't strange enough, here's the unusual part. He was operating as two high-functioning individuals at the same time. One a skilled electrician working with sensitive and complex systems, and one a successful electrical engineer working on complex plans for multiple clients. I don't know how he was able to function at all."

She looked at Buck. "Agent Taylor. I don't necessarily agree with your methods, but I believe you approached him the best way possible. Based on the notes from the juvenile hall, his IQ is off the charts, and I'm guessing, but an educated guess, that he can close out any interactions the other personas have had. He knows that Roger killed the preacher and the director of the youth facility, but to him, it's more like an event he saw on television or in the news. His focus now was on the club shooting, and after watching the interrogation tape, it appears the agitation was because you were not asking him about it. He most likely had already created the answers to questions you hadn't asked. He would probably never admit to killing all those people, but he wants to be associated with the event.

"When you started switching up your questions and addressing him as the other individuals, he became confused because, as I said, those were people he had seen elsewhere, not him. The more confused he became, the more agitated he became, and at the point when he exploded, all those people came together. Essentially, Agent Taylor, you broke him. He was faced with multiple personas, all wanting a piece of him, and he didn't know how to control them."

"Any chance he's faking all this?" asked Buck.

Dr. Thurston thought about her answer. "There's

always that possibility. The brain is fragile, and we all develop different coping mechanisms. He might have exploded and then closed up again as part of some scheme to show how smart he is. Only time and a lot of intervention will tell, but I don't think that's the case here. He had too much going on in his head, and sooner or later, it was going to fall apart."

"If he's not faking it," said Duke Morgan. "Will he recover enough to stand trial?"

"That's harder to say," said the doctor. "Therapy could help, but we have no way of knowing. Anticipating your next question. Does he know right from wrong? I can't say. Each persona would handle the situation differently. He could snap out of this in an hour, or he might never snap out of it. You might never get that question answered."

"What about the voices he mentioned? What is that all about?" asked Buck.

"According to the session notes from his time at the juvenile center, he hears voices or noises. The therapist's notes are pretty graphic. Whenever these voices become intolerable, he lashes out at someone. The voices push him over the edge, which is why the murders are so violent. He needs to satisfy the voices. So besides everything we've talked about, he also has to deal with the voices. His parents really did a number on him."

"You sound like you sympathize with him," said Buck.

She smiled weakly. "No, Agent Taylor. Not sympathy. Mitchell Evans, or whatever name you want to use, is a psychopath. I feel bad because he had no control over what was done to him." She looked Buck in the eye. "I'm not naïve, Agent Taylor. Despite my training, I believe some people are just born bad. I don't know if Mitchell Evans was born bad, but I do know that what his parents did to him contributed to the man he became."

She looked at Chief Cutler. "I'll make arrangements, when I get back to the hospital, to have him committed and placed in the secure psychiatric ward. Please have your officers bring him over. I'd also like copies of all the files you have on him."

She shook hands with everyone and left the office. Buck looked at his watch. He hadn't realized how late it had gotten. He called Diane McMahon, apologized for missing their meeting and asked if they could reschedule for the following afternoon. She told him that would be fine, but it needed to be early afternoon because she was heading back to Washington on the late afternoon flight.

Buck disconnected the call and looked around the room. "It's been an interesting day. Chief, if you can get Evans to the hospital, that would be great. Let's call it a day and reconvene tomorrow at the command center."

They all gathered their belongings. Duke said he was going to connect with Sheriff Foley and fill him in on what had transpired. He shook hands and left the office. Franklin said he had a few things to finish and would see them in the morning. Buck thanked him for all his help.

Buck asked Bax and Detective Maldonado if they would like to join him for dinner. Jessie Maldonado declined since she was supposed to be on vacation and needed to make things right with her seven-year-old son.

Bax and Buck grabbed their backpacks and headed for the restaurant. They may have solved the club shooting, but they still had a couple of other crimes to deal with.

Chapter Forty-Six

Buck's favorite Italian restaurant was crowded compared to the night before, when the owner had remained open later than usual to accommodate them. The owner greeted them at the door and seated them at the same table in the back of the restaurant. Tonight, they had a server dressed sharply in black pants, a starched white shirt and a black apron.

The server brought Buck a large glass of Coke and Bax a glass of Merlot. They ordered the special—lasagna with meat sauce—sat back and watched the crowd enjoying their meals.

"So," said Bax. "Do you think that was a performance, or do you think that was real?"

"I agree with Dr. Thurston," said Buck. "I think Mitchell Evans had a conflict going on in his brain, and all his personas ganged up on him at once. He lost control. I don't think it was a fake."

"So, what's next?" asked Bax.

Buck was about to answer when the front door opened and two men in suits walked in, looked around and headed for their table.

Hank Clancy introduced Special Agent James Carpenter and they shook hands, and the men took the two empty seats. Hank and James Carpenter wore the standard-issue FBI uniform, as Buck liked to kid him. Gray slacks, black shoes, white shirt, navy-blue jacket and red-white-and-blue-striped tie.

The waiter brought Buck and Bax their meals and asked the two new visitors if they would like a drink. Hank Clancy asked for black coffee, as did Agent Carpenter. They looked at the lasagna and asked the waiter to bring two more. The waiter left, and Hank put on his serious face.

"We just came from the hospital. Mitchell Evans, or whatever his name is, is a mess. He might as well be drooling in his soup. We met with Dr. Thurston, and she had him sedated. What the hell is the story?"

"I sent you a copy of our investigation file," said Bax.

Buck took a bite of his lasagna and continued. "Mitchell Evans is also Bryce Tanner and Roger Shipman. As Roger Shipman, he murdered his preacher, the director of the juvenile hall he was confined to and his father. As Bryce Tanner, he killed seventy-some people at the drag club and injured almost two hundred and fifty others. He is also suspected of killing his mother in a nursing home. As Mitchell Evans, he killed a psychologist at Duke University. We arrested him for lying to the police during a murder investigation, and we found plans for another active shooting situation it appears he was planning."

Hank sat back as the waiter delivered the two coffees to the table along with new plates of lasagna.

"A possible serial killer turned mass murderer," said Agent Carpenter. "Now, that's something you don't see every day."

"How sure are you about all of this?" asked Hank.

"We have forensics to back up our stuff. We haven't gone through the out-of-state cases, but then that's your job." Buck smiled and took a long drink from his glass of Coke.

"That's why Agent Carpenter is here," said Hank. "He heads up a task force that was put together this afternoon to dig into this guy. Agents are already en route to Michigan and North Carolina."

"We ran into Chief Cutler at the hospital," said Agent Carpenter. "He and the doctor told us this is not a typical case of multiple personalities but of someone who created different personas dependent on need. You were in the interrogation room when he broke, for lack of a better word. Do you believe that's true?"

Buck slid his empty plate to the middle of the table. He sat back and tented his fingers. "I'm no psychiatrist, but what I saw looked like someone who had a collision of personalities or personas. He wanted us to question him about the club shooting, but I kept asking him about the other crimes. I guess he had enough and wigged out."

"Buck," said Hank. "Did you get the feeling that the personas knew each other?"

"I think he operated like a spy," said Buck. "I think each persona served a purpose, but he never discarded any of them. They were all still up there in his head. He may have been able to separate them in the past, but for some reason, that changed."

Agent Carpenter's phone chimed, and he pulled it from his inside jacket pocket and opened the text. He was quiet as he read the text and then put his phone away.

"We've had a development since this afternoon," he said. "One of those other IDs you guys found is wanted in connection to a murder in Amarillo, Texas. A man was found in the desert, beaten to death. Here's the interesting part: this man was originally from Marquette, Michigan. Two of our resident agents in the area are heading there to get the particulars."

Bax looked at Buck. "This case gets stranger the more we find out about this guy." She looked at Hank.

"What is the plan going forward?"

"We're flying in a special team from the Behavioral Analysis Unit. People more qualified than us to deal with this. They'll conduct interviews and evaluate the probability of taking this guy to trial. One step at a time, Bax. One step at a time."

"Are you going to take this guy out from under us?" asked Buck.

Hank laughed. "Would I ever do something like that to my dear friends?"

They all laughed as the waiter brought them another round of drinks and removed the plates from the table. Agent Carpenter's phone rang. He removed it from his pocket and excused himself. He stepped away from the table and left the restaurant.

Hank leaned into the table. "Tell me what's going on with the Royal Sanders murder."

Buck gave Hank a quick rundown of what they knew. He told him about Darin Phelps running and about him saying the name McMahon before he passed out. He also told him about the dead state trooper and the unknown guy who was with George Billings.

"What the hell was George Billings up to?" asked Hank. "My information is he retired as the CEO of Globestar Industries five years ago. What could he have that would interest Royal Sanders?"

"I don't know," said Buck. "I'm more interested in why Darin Phelps mentioned Diane McMahon just before he passed out in the hospital. You told us to give her access to everything we had, and you got the governor to back you up. Who told you to put her in the middle of our investigation?"

Hank tilted his head to the left and looked sideways at Buck. "What are you implying?"

"I'm not implying anything, Hank. I'm asking who sent her to look into Royal Sanders's murder?"

Hank was silent for a minute. "It came down the chain of command, Buck. You know how it is."

"No, Hank. She doesn't work for you; she works for the DOJ. Why were you involved in calling us off?"

Hank was silent for a moment again. "I received a call from Assistant Attorney General Tim Gifford. After he called, I called my boss in Washington, and he said it was all cleared. I guess I was a familiar face to you and the governor and they must have thought it would sit better coming from me."

"What do you know about her background?" asked Bax.

"I know she works for several congressional committees. Why?" asked Hank. He stared at Buck and then at Bax. "You can't believe . . ."

The front door opened, and Agent Carpenter walked to the table. He sat down. "That call was the agents in Amarillo. The victim was Martin Wolford. He was murdered a month after the psychologist at Duke. He was a doctor in Marquette, Michigan, until he moved to Amarillo. He was also an investor in Randall and Olivia Shipman's entertainment business. According to the Amarillo file, he left Marquette right after Roger Shipman escaped from the juvenile facility."

He looked around the table. "Did I interrupt something?" he asked.

"No," said Hank. "We should get going. We have a lot of people coming to town, and we need to get organized."

Agent Carpenter stood and said he would wait outside. Hank stood and watched him walk out the door. He looked back at Buck and Bax.

"I'll look into what we discussed and let you know if I find anything." He reached into his pocket and left several twenty-dollar bills on the table. He walked out.

Buck looked at Bax. "The one thing I always hate is when Hank Clancy looks concerned." They left money on the table, thanked the owner on the way out and exited the restaurant. They still had a lot to do.

Chapter Forty-Seven

Buck walked to his hotel and stood outside the front entrance. He pulled out his phone and dialed the office. Mel answered.

"Hi, Buck," said Mel. "Did you get my message?"

"Hey, Mel. What message?"

"I sent you a message an hour ago. We hit a wall with Diane McMahon. George is working on some backdoor stuff, but as soon as we got into her accounts, email, finances, etc., we triggered an alarm, and a security wall went up. Luckily, we had all our security measures in place, so whoever dropped the hammer shouldn't be able to trace us, but we're keeping an eye out just in case."

"What does that mean, Mel?" asked Buck.

"It means she's got some high-level security protecting her. Buck, this was NSA-level security. You can't buy this protection on the internet."

"Were you able to get anything before the wall went up?" asked Buck.

"Not much. Her social media accounts are pretty bland. She has a few friends, but it looks like mostly family. She owns a town house in Alexandria, Virginia, that's paid for. No mortgage. She does not have a car loan on her new Land Rover. According to her tax returns, she made a little over one hundred eighty thousand last year. She's living beyond her means, but we have no idea how. As soon as we went for her finances, we hit the wall."

"What about any connection to Billings or the congressman besides the committee work?"

George came on the line. "Hey, Buck. I pulled her CV. There are some gaps in her employment history that I'm still tracking. Her schooling looks solid. She graduated from Yale Law School with honors. She went to work for the DOJ right after college. Mostly staff positions until she landed on a congressional committee. Everything after that is locked out."

"Fuck. What about our special software?" asked Buck.

"It's running now; we'll see if it's as good as advertised," said George.

"You called us, Buck," said Mel. "What did you need?"

"Any luck with any of the phones we collected from Shipman, Tanner and Evans?"

"Yeah," said Mel. "All his phones are empty."

Buck interrupted. "What do you mean empty?"

"There is nothing in the call logs, there's no text messages and no contacts. If I had to guess, I'd say the phones were for show. We couldn't even get any cell tower or GPS tracking from the providers. I don't think he ever carried these phones with him. He must have another phone someplace."

"We didn't find any other phones," said Buck. "Who the hell did this guy think he was, James Bond?"

"Good guess, Buck. With all his different identities,

he could have worked for the CIA," said Mel.

"Okay. What about his laptop?" asked Buck.

"It looks like he used it mostly for work as the electrical engineer. He has some proposals, contract documents and several sets of plans. Other than the notes about the church conference, there's nothing incriminating or interesting."

"Looks like we've hit a brick wall at every turn with this guy. How do you plan a mass shooting and not keep any records?" asked Buck.

"Probably kept it all in his head," said George. "Naval intelligence turned a guy once who kept everything in his head. He had the whole terrorist network in his head: attack plans, finances, weapons, membership. He was like a walking filing system. Until he came to us, there was no way to access any of that information. It was crazy but effective."

"Okay," said Buck. "Stay on Diane McMahon."

He disconnected the call and was clipping his phone back to his belt when it rang. He didn't recognize the number.

"Buck Taylor."

"Agent Taylor, this is Michelle Sanders. I hope it's not too late to call."

"No, ma'am. What can I do for you?"

"Would you have time to stop by my house this evening?"

"I can be there in about an hour; would that work?" asked Buck.

"That would be fine. Thank you."

The call disconnected, and Buck wondered what that was all about. He walked into the parking lot and slid into his Jeep.

An hour later, Buck pulled to the curb in front of the congressman's house and slid out of his Jeep. He looked up and down the block and didn't notice anything out of the ordinary. He walked up the front walk and was about to knock when the front door opened. Michelle Sanders invited him in and led him through the house to the back patio. The house was much quieter than the last time he had been there.

"Agent Taylor, please have a seat. Can I get you a drink—coffee, water, anything?" she asked.

Buck sat across from her at the table. "No thanks, ma'am. I'm fine."

"I was wondering if you could tell me how things are going with the investigation into my husband's death?"

Buck didn't answer right away. Something was nagging at him, and the little bug in his brain was moving around. "You know as much as we do, ma'am. The news tonight reported the arrest of Mitchell Evans, who went by several other names, and he is being questioned and will most likely be charged with the drag club shooting. We have forensic evidence that puts him at the scene."

Michelle Sanders smiled. "That's not what I'm interested in, Agent Taylor. I want to know where you are with who *actually* murdered my husband."

"Mrs. Sanders, this is an ongoing investigation, and I'm afraid I can't give you too many details."

"I understand that, Agent Taylor. My husband was a good man, and there are a lot of rumors floating around that he may have been involved in something nefarious, and that was what got him killed. I don't believe that for a minute, and I don't think you do either. The governor told me that you are a man who can be trusted to get to the truth. Is that true, Agent Taylor?"

Buck looked into her eyes. "Mrs. Sanders. What's this all about? Why am I here?"

Michelle Sanders stood and walked to the edge of the patio and looked out over the backyard. She stood there for a few minutes and said nothing.

She turned and looked at Buck. "Agent Taylor, I don't know who to trust anymore. Everyone who surrounded my husband seemed to have an agenda that did not line up with my husband's agenda. What I'm asking is, can I trust you? I've been told by several people that I can, but I want to hear it from you."

"Yes, Mrs. Sanders. You can trust me."

She smiled. "Please follow me."

She stepped off the patio and walked down a small paved walkway to a potting shed near the back fence. She opened the door and stepped inside. Buck followed her. She left the overhead light off, using moonlight to navigate the space. She stopped at a potting table full of dirt, took a small hand shovel lying there and pushed some of the dirt aside. Satisfied, she put the shovel down, reached into the depression she had made and pulled out a plastic bag. She shook off the dirt and handed the bag to Buck.

Even without any lights on, Buck could tell that there was a laptop inside the plastic bag. He followed Mrs. Sanders out of the shed and back to the patio. Michelle Sanders sat at the table and took a large gulp of the brownish liquid from her glass.

Buck set the bag on the table but didn't remove the laptop from the plastic bag. He looked at her questioningly.

"The laptop in that bag belongs to George Billings. George left it here with me a week ago. He wasn't sure he wanted to give it to my husband, but he was also afraid someone would find out about it. According to what George told me, if anything were to happen to him, everything anyone would need to know about his death is in there."

"Why would George Billings leave that with you?" asked Buck.

"George was my uncle on my mother's side. Very few people knew that. He told me that if anything were to happen to him to get this to someone I trusted. I didn't know who to trust, so I called Governor Kennedy. The governor and my husband were political enemies, but Royal always said Richard could be trusted. Richard said I should reach out to you."

"Why didn't you say something sooner?" asked Buck.

"When Diane McMahon showed up at my door and

pushed her way into my life, I was convinced she was not all she said she was. In public, she had this almost adversarial relationship with Darin Phelps, but a couple of times, I sensed that they were scheming something. To tell you the truth, I was scared to say anything."

"What do you know about Darin Phelps?"

"My husband thought Darin was a brilliant political strategist, and he helped Royal win a couple of hard-fought elections. Elections he might have lost. He also worked hard to make sure my husband was placed in the top position on several important committees, but I always felt there was something more to it than loyalty. He made my skin crawl, so I stepped out of the political spotlight."

"Could Phelps have been involved in the plot to kill your husband?" asked Buck.

Michelle Sanders closed her eyes, and Buck waited. "When I heard my husband was killed, murdered, my first thought was that Darin Phelps got what he wanted. I know that must sound terribly bitter, but I sensed that he had something going on outside of government. I overheard him speaking with Diane the other night when they thought I had taken a sleeping pill and had fallen asleep. They were talking about next steps. I didn't hear the entire conversation, but several times over the last couple of days, they have each asked me if I knew why Royal was meeting with George Billings. I sensed that George talking with Royal was getting in the way of something they had going. Something that Royal was not a part of."

"Mrs. Sanders, why would your husband meet George Billings at a drag club that went completely against what your husband believed in? It doesn't make any sense," said Buck.

"Nothing mysterious about that, Agent Taylor. Sometimes, even in the world of politics, what you see is what you are actually seeing. My uncle did not like Royal's positions on most subjects. He figured no one would know they were there because of Royal's opinions. George enjoyed nothing more than making Royal uncomfortable. By meeting at the club, George exerted power over Royal. Although I have no proof, I think my uncle left his laptop with me before going to the club because he was going to discuss something with Royal that was not connected to what's in the laptop. I wish I knew what that was.

"When my uncle dropped off the laptop, he was scared, Agent Taylor. I've never seen my uncle scared of anything. He started working in a small machine shop at seventeen and turned that company into one of the largest defense contractors in the world. Nothing scared my uncle except what was on that laptop."

"Did your husband stop here before going to the club?"

"No, Agent Taylor. I was being truthful when I told you I didn't know he was here. I was surprised when I heard the news that he had been killed at that club."

"Ma'am, is there anything else you want to tell me?"

"Just one thing, Agent Taylor. Do not trust Diane McMahon. I've spent the last three days under her watchful eye, and I wouldn't trust her with anything."

Buck picked up the laptop, thanked Michelle Sanders for her help and left her house. He slid into his Jeep, dialed George and told him not to leave the office. It was going to be a long night.

Chapter Forty-Eight

George opened the laptop and turned it on. The laptop was not password protected. Dozens of file folders appeared on the screen. Mel removed a new air-gapped laptop, having never been connected to the internet, and handed it to George. He downloaded all the files from the Billings laptop to the air-gapped laptop and set the Billings laptop aside.

Buck stood next to George and was mesmerized as he watched George's fingers fly over the keys. Lines of text flew across the screen as George entered command after command. He stopped typing and sat back in his chair.

"It's clean," said George. "What should we look at first?"

Buck pointed to the first folder on the top line. "Might as well start at the beginning."

He looked up as the door to the cyber lab opened, and Bax and Paul walked in. Buck had called them on his way to the office. They stood next to him in silence as George opened the first file folder.

George clicked on a couple of the documents and looked up at Buck. "These are testing reports for the F-41 Warbird. This is the latest, most advanced fighter jet we have in development. Most people don't even know this plane exists."

"Why would George Billings have them on an unsecured laptop?" asked Bax.

"His company is the one building it," said George.

"And he wanted people to be able to access the information without any problem," said Mel. "There's something in these files he wants regular people to see."

George had been clicking on various documents in the files when Paul asked him to stop. He leaned over George's shoulder and read the report. He stood up.

"This is a letter from a structural engineer who worked on the project. He states that at high speeds, the structural integrity of the fighter jet will deteriorate, resulting in a massive airframe failure."

Mel was typing on her laptop. She stopped and looked up. "The structural engineer who wrote that letter was killed in an automobile accident three months ago." She turned her laptop so they could all see the screen.

George looked at Buck. Mel stood, walked to the closet and returned with three more new laptops. She unpacked them and gave them to George, who split the files into four piles and uploaded each pile to a different laptop. When he was finished, he handed Bax, Paul and Mel a laptop, and they headed for separate workstations. They knew what they needed to do, which left Buck standing there with nothing to do.

Feeling left out, since technology wasn't his thing, he pulled out his phone and called someone he knew could help.

Max answered immediately.

"Buck Taylor, how's my favorite cop? Something

must be up if you're calling me this late."

"Hi, Max. I'm looking for an expert on fighter jets, specifically someone outside the government who might be able to help with some information on a secret program. I was hoping you might know someone."

"Does this have something to do with the Royal Sanders murder?" she asked.

"It might have everything to do with it," he said.

"Give me a few minutes to make some calls. Let me see what I can find out."

Max disconnected the call, and Buck clipped his phone back on his belt. If anyone could find a source for information, it was Max.

Buck returned to the group and told them about his call to Max. He watched as their fingers flew through document after document faster than Buck had ever realized it could be done. His team always impressed him with their knowledge, but watching this was fascinating. They were transferring documents back and forth on a closed net that George had put together, so all the laptops were linked.

Buck exited the lab and walked down the hall to the office he seldom used. He pulled a bottle of Coke from the small refrigerator in the corner and sat at his desk. He unclipped his phone and hit the number one button.

"Buck. What's got you up so late?" asked Director Jackson.

He filled in the director on the laptop and what his team was working on. When he finished, the director asked him if he needed additional help.

"No, sir. Not right now. I'd like to keep this confined to a small group for now, but thanks for the offer."

"Buck, is this what got the congressman killed?"

"I believe it did, sir. We're not sure why, but hopefully, the laptop will give us what we need."

His phone chimed with an incoming call, and Buck told the director he would call him back when he knew something. He disconnected the call and answered the incoming call.

"Buck Taylor."

"Agent Taylor, my name is Philip Cross. Max Clinton said you were looking for an expert on jet fighters. How can I help?"

Buck didn't bother to ask what qualified Philip Cross as an expert. He knew if Max called him, his credentials would be top-notch.

Buck explained a little about what they had discovered and were working on. He tried to keep the information close to his chest, but Philip Cross was way ahead of him.

"Agent Taylor, did this information come from the late George Billings?"

Buck was taken aback. "It might have."

"It's okay, Agent Taylor. I understand your hesitancy to answer. George and I have been talking about the Warbird program for the last several months."

He stopped talking for a minute. "You have the

laptop, don't you?"

Buck took a gamble. "Yes, sir. How did you know?"

"There have been rumors for months that George Billings had information that would scuttle this program. No one, including myself, has seen the data, and most people didn't believe it even existed. Let me give you a little background, Agent Taylor.

"The F-41 Warbird is the next generation in stealth technology. The Pentagon is investing almost three hundred billion dollars in this program. George's company is the leading development group for the project and will see the lion's share of that money. All of this occurred after George Billings stepped down as chairman and CEO of the company. George liked to keep his nose in the business and told me that he had found out some unsettling things about the program. He said he was compiling the information, and when he was ready, he would share it with the powers that be. He never told me what he discovered, but it now appears that whatever he found might have cost him his life."

He asked Buck how they were evaluating the information and Buck explained what they were working on.

"I would like your people to connect me to a secure network I have set up. Can you do that, Agent Taylor?"

Buck asked him to hold on. He left his office and headed for the lab. When he entered the lab, he noticed that the whiteboards around the room were covered with notes. He walked up to George, handed him the phone and told him who he was talking with. George took the phone, listened for a few minutes and then began typing.

After several minutes of typing, George stopped and put Buck's phone on speaker.

"Okay, Dr. Cross, you're on speaker."

They could hear keys clicking in the background, and then Philip Cross's voice came on the line.

"Agent Taylor, your team has done an extraordinary job of organizing the data, so let me simplify the information you have been evaluating. The F-41 Warbird cannot fly. All the testing data that George collected reveals significant issues in the airworthiness of this vehicle. Information that has not been shared with the Pentagon or Congress. George was spilling the beans on his own company. There is evidence of numerous crimes in these documents."

Buck looked at the whiteboards. "Looks like my team came to the same conclusions about crimes being committed. They just didn't know how to read the testing data to put two and two together."

"Agent Taylor, this fighter jet is entering the manned testing phase, and pilots are going to die. This information needs to be shared with the Pentagon, and those who have been hiding that information need to be arrested."

"We'll take care of the arrest part of that," said Buck. "But we may need your help to get the documents to the right people. You have the contacts that we believe can put a stop to this program. I need to ask you a favor, sir. Please do not reveal anything about what you have seen here. We still need to arrest the person responsible for murdering Congressman Sanders and George Billings."

"That will not be a problem, Agent Taylor. Let me know when you are ready to release the documents, and I will be ready to get them where they need to go. And thanks for not letting George Billings's and Congressman Sanders's deaths be in vain."

Buck disconnected the call and looked around the room. "Aside from the tech stuff, what have we learned?"

Chapter Forty-Nine

Bax stood from her workstation and walked to one of the whiteboards.

"George Billings was working with someone who had access to encrypted emails. There are dozens of emails in these files from Diane McMahon to Raymond Hastings, the current CEO of Globestar Industries. There are also several emails from McMahon to Darin Phelps."

Mel brought up the email strings on the two large monitors hanging in the front of the room. Buck read through them. He turned to look at the team.

"Hastings was using McMahon to spread money around Congress and the Senate to keep the F-41 program going and keep the money pipeline flowing. McMahon was getting help from Darin Phelps in exchange for a lucrative payout once the plan was approved to move into manned trials. These people were going to make tens or possibly hundreds of millions of dollars."

Bax pointed to one email string between McMahon and Phelps.

Phelps: Sanders getting info from someone questioning the program.

McMahon: Need to find out source and eliminate. Too much at stake. Can you?

Phelps: I know a guy. Let me make a call.

The next string was dated a week later.

Phelps: Info coming from Billings. Sanders waiting on info and then will defund the program.

McMahon: Need to stop the info flow. Can your contact do the job? We need a time and place to do it.

Phelps: Sanders going to Colorado next week. Meeting with Billings at fishing lodge. Will set it up.

McMahon: How?

Phelps: Not for you to worry about. I will handle it.

Mel brought up the next string. This was a transcript of a phone call that occurred after Billings and Sanders were killed. Someone was still feeding info into the secure server.

McMahon: What the hell happened? You told me this was going to happen at a fishing lodge with no one around. How the hell did we get involved with a mass shooting?

Phelps: Weird coincidence. Sanders and Billings were in the drag club. I had no idea. I guess either our guy took advantage of the situation, or they were all killed by the shooter. Who cares?

McMahon: We care. Our guy was supposed to recover the information, so there were no loose ends. We never talked about killing a cop. Did the cops find a laptop or a thumb drive?

Phelps: The cop had to go. We needed someone who could get close to the congressman, and I have no idea what the cops have. I'm heading to the airport now to head to Colorado. I need to see if anything was left with Sanders's wife or the cops.

McMahon: Are we clean on this? Is there any way this can be traced back to us?

Phelps: No. We're clean. Just make sure my money is in the account. I want to get out of here as soon as I clean up a couple of things in Colorado.

The next call was from McMahon to Raymond Hastings.

Hastings: What a clusterfuck. I thought you said this guy was dependable. We have no way of knowing if Billings talked or who he gave the information to. You need to get to Colorado and find out what you can.

McMahon: Phelps is going there.

Hastings: You listen to me. I pay you a shitload of money to make things happen. I don't deal with this Phelps character; I deal with you. I want you on the next plane to Colorado. Make sure the wife doesn't have the information, and get into the middle of the investigation and see what the cops have.

McMahon: What do I do if the wife or the cops have it?

Hastings: You're a smart girl, figure it out, but I don't want any loose ends leading back to me. If the wife has to disappear, so be it. I pay you to make things happen.

Buck looked at Bax. "We don't have enough here to arrest McMahon or Phelps for murder. We need something more."

"We're still working on Phelps's laptop," said Bax. "The encryption software is running now. I was going to check it in the morning." She looked at her watch.

"Oh, wait. It is morning."

The team laughed, and Buck pulled out his phone and ordered breakfast to be delivered to the office. He then called Hank Clancy and asked him to come by the office.

George was typing on his laptop the entire time Buck was talking. He stopped typing and clicked on a file on the screen. He sat back and smiled.

"Darin Phelps had an insurance policy," he said.

Buck turned around as George brought up the file on the big screen. They all looked at what was included in the file.

"Darin Phelps was a careful guy," said Paul. "He wrote detailed notes about the entire plan."

"Yeah," said Buck. "Right down to the bodies being found in the river with an overturned fishing raft. Alcohol, inexperience and water sports: a deadly combination. No one would have suspected, and the assassin would have been long gone."

"The bodies would have been found eventually," said Mel. "And the suspected drowning would have been listed as the cause of death. Two inexperienced fishermen out of their element. Happens all the time."

"He bought two first-class tickets to Brazil," said Paul. "He even used their real names. He and McMahon were planning to run away together. I wonder if she had the same plan?"

Their breakfast arrived, and they continued reviewing the documents while they ate. A little while later, Hank Clancy was escorted to the lab by one of the building's security guards. He looked at the workstations and all the writing on the whiteboards.

"Don't you people ever sleep?" he asked. "What the hell is all this?"

Buck and the team spent the next two hours walking him through the information they'd found on George Billings's and Darin Phelps's laptops. When they were finished, Hank sat back in the chair.

"So," said Hank. "It all comes down to money."

Buck smiled. "It always comes down to money."

"We have Phelps's own words describing the murder of Trooper Cordova and the plan to kill Sanders and Billings," said Bax. "What we don't have is anything tying McMahon or Hastings directly to the murders."

"I agree," said Hank. "We could get her on conspiracy charges, but she'll serve minimal time. We need more."

"Bax," said Buck. "Would you call Duke and see if he can assign someone undercover to protect Michelle Sanders? McMahon will have to pressure her about the laptop or thumb drive."

"What about McMahon?" asked Paul.

Hank stood from his chair. "I have requested a FISA warrant for McMahon's phone and email. I'm going to call the attorney general's office and modify it to include Hastings. Maybe we can get them to incriminate each other."

"I think I have an idea how to do that," said Buck.

Buck told them his plan and gave them their assignments, then sent everyone home to get some sleep.

After they all left, Hank asked, "Do you think it will work? She's pretty smart."

"She's also pretty greedy," said Buck. "We shall see."

Chapter Fifty

Diane McMahon pulled her rental car into the parking lot at the drag club, turned off the engine and sat for a minute. She looked once again at her phone. She couldn't believe how stupid he was. Did Darin Phelps believe she would run away with him? He must have, because she was looking at a plane reservation for tomorrow, leaving Washington Dulles airport and bound for Rio de Janeiro.

She couldn't believe it. She had never given him the slightest idea that she was interested in him. He was like a worm and made her skin crawl. Besides, she hadn't heard from him in a couple of days, and she hoped the Feds didn't have him. She touched her throat. She felt like a noose was closing around her neck. She couldn't wait to get this briefing over with, and then she was heading straight to Denver to get on a flight. She had her escape plan already in place, and it didn't involve Darin Phelps.

She slipped out of her car, grabbed her oversized handbag and walked to the command center. It was still brutally hot, and she couldn't wait to get out of Colorado. She opened the door, and the cold wave hit her like a blast chiller. She stepped inside and closed the door.

Buck, Sheriff Foley and Detective Morgan greeted her, and they all shook hands. Buck pointed towards a chair, and she set her bag on the floor and sat. The sheriff slid a bottle of water towards her, and she thanked him, opened it and drank heavily. Buck waited until she put the bottle down.

"We wanted to update you on where we stand with the death of Royal Sanders and George Billings," he said. "As you are aware, this investigation has had many challenges, not the least of which was trying to figure out why Sanders and Billings were in the drag club. I don't typically believe in coincidences, but this time it was purely happenstance that put them in the same place as the shooter. George Billings set up the meeting to give some information to Sanders, never knowing that they were walking into a shooting gallery.

"George Billings had a laptop he was supposed to give Sanders during the meeting. We are not sure if he became concerned about the congressman or if something else spooked him, but he didn't bring the laptop to the meeting, having hidden it someplace he felt was safe. We are now in possession of that laptop. We believe this laptop contains information regarding a conspiracy to cover up a crime, but it is heavily encrypted, and we are having trouble getting the information. We have contacted the FBI cybercrimes unit, and the laptop is on its way to Washington by secure courier. Hopefully, by this time tomorrow, we will know what's on the laptop."

Buck spoke for a few more minutes about the evidence they did have, then he ad-libbed and fibbed a little. "We were able to determine the name of the man who killed Trooper Cordova, the congressman, and Billings. His name was Ernesto Trujillo, and he was wanted in connection with several political assassinations in Europe and South America. We have proof that he was paid by the congressman's chief of staff, Darin Phelps. Phelps kept detailed notes on his laptop."

"What does Mr. Phelps have to say?" she asked. "I assume you have arrested him."

"Actually, we haven't," said Buck. She looked surprised.

"Mr. Phelps was involved in a traffic accident while trying to evade two of my agents. He is at Saint Mary's Hospital in the ICU in critical condition. He has been in an induced coma, which the doctors are working right now to bring him out of. I'm hoping we can question him tomorrow about who might have been involved with him."

Buck had been watching Diane McMahon the entire time he was talking. She tried hard to hide her facial expressions, but Buck was watching her body, and she couldn't hide the micro-tics that told Buck she was now scared. She had reacted when he told her about the laptop, but her reaction was stronger when he mentioned talking with Darin Phelps in the morning.

"Do you think he'll be able to talk by tomorrow, Agent Taylor?" she asked.

"Tomorrow or the next day. We recovered his laptop and phone. Both are encrypted, but not like George Billings's laptop. My tech people already accessed the laptop, and they figure they should be able to access his phone by morning. Once we get into his phone, we should be able to tell who his coconspirators are. So, it's possible we might not even need to question him right away."

More micro-tics.

"Where did you find George Billings's laptop, if I might ask? It wasn't listed on the list of evidence collected at the scene," said Diane McMahon.

Duke Morgan answered just like he'd rehearsed. "We found it last night. George Billings had hidden it in a potting shed at the Sanders home. Mrs. Sanders called us when she found it buried under some potting soil. She said she had no idea what might be in the laptop. She didn't know her husband or Billings were even meeting."

"Well, Agent Taylor. Your office and the sheriff's team should be commended for your fine work on this case. If you would forward a copy of your final report to me at my office, I would be most appreciative. I will also let the governor know how much your cooperation in these matters was appreciated."

She started to get up. "By the way. Were you able to determine the identity of the man who was killed along with the congressman and George Billings?"

"Not yet," said Buck. "We are still trying to figure that out. He is not in any of the databases we or the FBI use. We are about to go international. We'll figure it out."

"Okay," she said. "If I can be of further assistance, please reach out. You have my card."

She picked up her bag and exited the trailer. Buck hoped it was enough. From her micro-tics, he knew he had gotten her attention; now the question was, would she act on it?

"Do you think she bought it?" asked Sheriff Foley. "She hides her emotions well."

"We shall see," said Buck. His phone chimed, and he answered the call.

"Bax," he said.

"She's not heading for the airport, that's for sure," said Bax. "She just pulled into the parking lot of her hotel, and she's on the phone. She sure is waving her hands a lot. Something has her excited."

"Good, stay on her." Buck disconnected the call.

"Looks like she took the bait," said Buck. "Let's get out of here; we have a lot to do."

Chapter Fifty-One

Diane McMahon was shaking by the time she got to her car. She opened the door, slid in and sat, trying to calm herself down. She looked around to make sure no one was watching, and she put the car in drive and pulled out of the parking lot. She headed back to her hotel, glad now that she hadn't checked out, pulled into the parking lot and left the motor running. The air-conditioning felt good.

She slammed both palms against the steering wheel and screamed, and then she looked around to make sure no one had seen her. She pulled out her encrypted phone and dialed a saved number.

"What do they have?" asked Raymond Hastings.

Diane was hesitant, finally answering, "They have Billings's laptop. They don't know what's on it because it's encrypted, and knowing Billings, the encryption is high-end."

"Where is it now?" he asked.

"It's on the way to FBI cybercrimes. We don't have a lot of time," she said.

"Fuck, Diane. This is bad. How could you let this happen? Can you get hold of it?"

"No. Once it gets to cybercrimes, there's nothing I can do about it. It wasn't my fault. We always knew he had the information; we just had no idea where it was. You told me you could take care of making sure the information didn't get out. I'm not to blame for this."

"You're blaming me for your fuckup? Blame that idiot you've been working with. Where is he?"

"Darin was in an accident. He is in the ICU. They also have his phone and laptop. It's encrypted, but according to Agent Taylor, his tech team should be able to get into it by tomorrow."

There was silence on the end of the line, and she thought they'd lost the connection.

"You cannot be fucking serious. He can lead them right back to you and me," said Hastings. "You fucking moron. You need to handle this, Diane. You need to make sure that idiot is not around to answer questions. Do you understand what I'm telling you?"

"I'll see if I can find someone who can . . ."

"You're not listening to me, Diane. I said I want you to handle it. I don't want you to involve any more of your imbecile friends. You need to get this done, and then you need to find someplace to hole up."

"I don't know if I can," she said.

"Of course you can. You've done it before," said Hastings. "Do whatever you have to do, and don't call me again."

The line went dead, and she pictured Raymond Hastings running his phone pieces through the shredder in his office. She wondered how she could have been so stupid to hook up with him in the first place. Of course, she knew exactly why. Money. More than she could ever imagine.

She also knew that Hastings was probably already sending evidence against her to select people at the FBI and the DOJ who would put all the blame on her. Well, two could play that game. She had enough on him to bury him, along with all his friends who were also involved. She would make sure he suffered. She had friends at the FBI and the DOJ too.

But first, she needed to deal with Darin Phelps. He could sink them both. She needed a plan. She dialed the hospital, asked if her brother, Darin, was still in ICU and was informed that he had been moved to a regular room. She disconnected the call. She knew having him in a regular room would make her job easier. Now she just needed to gather supplies. She had sources, and she made some calls.

She had time to kill, so she grabbed her bag, slid out of the car and headed into the hotel. She never saw Bax's Jeep sitting across the street in the fast-food restaurant parking lot.

Bax called Buck and let him know where Diane was, and he told her to keep her eyes on her and hung up.

Buck called Hank Clancy, who was already reviewing the transcript of the call from Diane McMahon to Raymond Hastings. So much for encrypted phones.

"Sounds like she took the bait," said Hank. "You all set with the next step?"

"We've got it covered. What about your end?" asked Buck.

"Agents are on their way to Raymond Hastings's office and home as we speak. We'll take him as soon as you give me the word. Good luck."

Buck disconnected the call and alerted his team. There were a lot of moving pieces, and he needed to make sure each piece was in the correct place.

Chapter Fifty-Two

Diane McMahon made one stop after she left the hotel. She pulled behind a small gas station, and within seconds, she came back out and pulled onto the street. She headed for the hospital. Bax called Chief Cutler and gave him the location. Bax was hot on her tail, three cars back. She kept the team apprised.

Diane pulled into the hospital parking garage, parked, slid out of her rental car and entered the hospital through the parking garage entrance. She looked around the lobby and located the elevators. Diane McMahon stopped at the reception desk and got her *brother's* room number. She walked to the elevator and punched the up button. She stepped off the elevator on the third floor, pushed open the stairwell door and walked up to the fourth floor.

She pulled open the door on the fourth floor and walked past the nurse's station. At this time of night, the hallways were empty. She walked with purpose like she belonged there. The whole time she was trying to keep her hands from shaking. She felt the syringe in her pants pocket. She stopped outside the door to room 414 and took a breath.

Diane looked up and down the hallway and slipped into the dark room. She walked to the side of the bed and looked at the monitors. Darin was sleeping on his back, and she could see the damage the accident had caused. Both of his eyes were black, and his head was wrapped in a large bandage. He wore a neck brace and a metal halo to keep his head straight. He was probably going to die anyway from his injuries. She wished she could wait, but they were out of time.

She was saddened by what she was about to do. Darin had been a good partner in this situation, and even though she had no romantic inclinations towards him, he had become a good friend.

She reached into her pocket and removed the syringe. She pulled off the cap with her teeth, spit it on the floor and then pushed the plunger to ensure it worked. She pulled the cap off the IV line that ran into his arm and inserted the tip of the syringe into the port.

"If you push that plunger, I am going to shoot you," said a voice in the dark.

Diane McMahon froze, one hand on the port and one on the plunger. She looked behind her, and a small light came on. Buck Taylor sat in a chair in the dark corner of the room. He was holding a pistol, and it was pointed at her. Her hands started to shake, and she looked at the syringe. She put pressure on the plunger and then looked at Buck.

Buck wasn't smiling, and his hand holding the pistol never wavered.

"You need to think very carefully about the next decision you make, because I guarantee you, if you make the wrong decision, it will be the last one you ever make," said Buck.

She knew she had a decision to make, but she couldn't make her hands do what she wanted them to do. She dropped the port, and the syringe fell out and hit the floor. She raised her hands.

The door opened, the overhead lights came on and several people entered the room. She found herself lying on the floor and felt the handcuffs snap shut on her wrists. She could see the syringe lying on the floor next to her. Hands helped her up, and Duke Morgan informed her that she was under arrest for attempted murder and for conspiracy to commit the murder of Trooper Cordova, Congressman Royal Sanders, George Billings, and an as-yet unidentified man. He read her rights from his Miranda card and pushed her towards the door.

Buck holstered his pistol, and Paul, wearing nitrile gloves, picked up the syringe and put it in an evidence bag, which he sealed and signed.

Buck pulled out his phone and dialed Hank Clancy.

"We've got her" was all he said, and he disconnected the call. He clipped his phone to his belt and walked out of Darin Phelps's room.

Bax came off the elevator and looked at Buck.

"We're good," he said.

"Awesome. Narcotics busted the guy she bought the syringe off of. It's filled with insulin," she said.

Buck nodded. He needed sleep, but they still had mysteries to solve. He left the crowd on the fourth floor and headed for the office.

He pushed open the door to the cyber lab, walked in and plopped into a chair. George and Mel were still at their workstations, and Buck imagined they were running on pure adrenaline. He rubbed his forehead and leaned forward in the chair.

"What have you got?" he asked.

George turned his chair and faced Buck. "We finished with Phelps's laptop and phone. What we found so far corroborates what we got from your expert. This was all about protecting Globestar Industries. A lot of people were poised to make a lot of money once the F-41 program was approved. The plan was to keep delaying the flight tests while collecting huge payouts. Eventually, the project would have been declared a failure, and more money would have been thrown at it to fix the problems. This could go on for years.

"The congressman was unaware of what George Billings had but knew it was important. They agreed to meet at the fishing lodge, but it looks like George made the last-minute decision to change the location. That caught Darin Phelps completely off guard. He couldn't reach the shooter he hired and wasn't sure what to think until the mass shooting occurred. At that point, both he and Diane McMahon went into overdrive.

"He also has a list of other congressional committee members who received bribes to ensure the F-41 program wasn't scrapped. We'll pass that on to Hank and his team. George Billings was trying to do the right thing, even if it meant destroying the company he built from the ground up."

Buck thanked him and Mel for all their work and left the lab. He drove back to his hotel, grabbed a quick shower, finished what was left of the warm bottle of Coke on the nightstand and laid his head on the pillow. He was asleep in seconds. He slept fitfully, but when he woke up, he still felt like he was missing a lot of sleep.

Epilogue

Buck spent most of the morning on the phone with the director and the governor. They discussed the multiple personas that Roger Shipman had created to keep one step ahead of the law.

"A serial killer," said the governor, "who became a mass murderer. I don't think I've ever heard of such a thing. You have a knack for finding the strangest cases, Buck."

They were both pleased with the outcome and were saddened that so many people had died. The governor mentioned that he would be coming to town to attend several of the funerals. They told Buck to thank his team, and the governor said he would call the sheriff and the chief of police and thank them as well. He was also planning to call Michelle Sanders. He just wasn't sure what to say to her. For a man never at a loss for words, nothing he thought of seemed right.

Buck pulled to the curb in front of the Sanders house. He slipped out of the Jeep and walked up the sidewalk to the front door. The door opened before he knocked.

"Is it over?" Michelle Sanders asked.

Buck nodded. "Yes, ma'am. The laptop you gave me was the clincher."

He told her what he could about the investigation and the arrests. Tears filled her eyes. She had lost two people who had been very dear to her, and the reality of those losses was settling in.

"My uncle was a proud man," said Michelle Sanders, "and he was proud of the equipment his company had provided to the military over the years. He would have been devastated had something his company built hurt the people using it. He died trying to protect the pilots. I couldn't be prouder of him."

"Any thoughts on why he changed the meeting location and hid the laptop?"

"I think in the end, he wasn't sure who he could trust, my husband included. Knowing my uncle, he wanted to make sure he was in control, not someone else."

She invited him in, but he declined. He had a lot of work yet to do and needed to get to it. He thanked her again and headed for his Jeep. He drove to the drag club and pulled into the parking lot. He parked next to Duke Morgan's unmarked SUV. The command center trailer was no longer in the lot, and the deputy on duty at the front door had been reassigned.

Buck walked to the building and opened the front door. He stepped inside. The air-conditioning was helping keep the smell down, but death was still in the air. He thought about all the people who died here and how senseless it all was. He entered the show space and found Duke Morgan near the bar. He was staring off into space, and Buck stood there, not wanting to disturb him.

Duke noticed Buck standing in the doorway and walked over.

"So much death," he said. "And all because one man's opinions found a receptive home in another man's troubled mind." He shook his head. "The pathologists finished with the last autopsy this morning. All the bodies have been released."

"That's good," said Buck.

"We formally arrested Darin Phelps this morning. It will be a while before he can stand trial, but he's not going anywhere. My mom will make sure of that. Harlan Groves is being arraigned today for the murder of Donny Truex. I hear the Grand Junction cops are preparing for huge protests at the courthouse. It's amazing how much damage Donny Truex caused."

"What's going on with Diane McMahon?" asked Buck.

"The FBI took possession of her this morning and whisked her out of here. I got the impression she made a deal to save her ass. We'll probably never know what happens to her. Oh, one piece of news. The FBI was able to identify the unknown man we found in the dressing room. It turns out he was the boyfriend of one of the entertainers. He was there to surprise him. He was going to ask him to marry him. They found his ID in his car, parked down the street at the health club. He had been working out and forgot to grab his ID or the ring. According to his mother, he had never been fingerprinted or had his DNA tested. His boyfriend was one of the entertainers who was killed. They're going to be buried together."

"Gonna be a lot of funerals in town this coming week," said Buck. "Lots of sadness."

"Do we know anything more about the guy who was killed with the congressman and Billings?" asked

Duke.

"We're still searching, but I think we may never know who he was," said Buck. "The guy is a ghost. If I had to guess, I'd say he was the guy who helped George Billings gather all the information on the fighter jet problems and then came along to make sure the information was going to the right people, but who can say."

"Listen, Buck. I want to thank you and the rest of your team for all the help. I don't know how we would have gotten through this without you guys."

Buck smiled. "No thanks necessary, Duke. This is what we do."

They shook hands, and Buck left Duke Morgan to his thoughts. He stepped out into the heat and headed for his Jeep. He knew he should head to the office. There was still a lot of paperwork to get through. A lot of *t*'s to cross and *i*'s to dot. Buck smiled. He'd work on the paperwork later. Right now, there was a stream up on the Grand Mesa that he liked to fish, and it was calling his name.

Acknowledgments

A special thank-you to my daughter Christina J. Morgan, my unofficial collaborator. She devoted a significant amount of time making sure the book was presented as perfectly as possible.

Thanks to my editor, Laura Dragonette, whose efforts helped turn my manuscript into a polished novel. Her help is greatly appreciated. Any mistakes the reader may find are solely the responsibility of the author.

Special thanks to my daughter Stephanie Morgan, my beta reader. Stephanie has read every novel in its rough stages and rarely gets to see the completed product. Her insight and critique have been critical to making sure the stories make sense.

Also, I would like to thank my family for their encouragement. I have been telling them stories since they were little, and I always told them that someone should be writing this stuff down. I decided to write it down myself.

I want to thank my closest friend, Trish Moakler-Herud. She has been encouraging me for years to write my stories down. I hope this will make her proud.

A special thanks to my late wife, Jane. She pushed me for years to become a writer, and my biggest regret is that she didn't live long enough to see it happen. I love her with all my heart and miss her every day. I think she would be pleased.

Finally, thanks to the readers. Without you, none of

this would be important.

About the Author

2019 Pacific Book Awards Best Mystery Finalist . . . *Crime Delayed*

2020 Pacific Book Awards Best Mystery Winner . . . *Crime Denied*

2020 Chanticleer International Book Awards: 1st Place Blue Ribbon, CLUE Book Awards for Suspense, Thriller Fiction . . . *Crime Denied*

2021 Chanticleer International Book Awards Finalist, CLUE Book Awards for Suspense, Thriller Fiction . . . *Crime Conspiracy*

2021 Chanticleer International Book Awards Finalist, Book Series, CLUE Book Awards for Suspense, Thriller Fiction . . . Crime Series, The Buck Taylor Novels

2022 Chanticleer International Book Awards Finalist, CLUE Book Awards for Police Procedural Fiction . . . *Crime Spree*

2022 Chanticleer International Book Awards Finalist, CLUE Book Awards for Detective/Crime Fiction . . . *Crime Exploded*

Chuck Morgan attended Seton Hall University and Regis College and spent thirty-five years as a construction project manager. He is an avid outdoorsman, an Eagle Scout and a licensed private pilot. He enjoys camping, hiking, mountain biking and fly-fishing.

He is the author of the Crime series, featuring Colorado Bureau of Investigation agent Buck Taylor. The series includes *Crime Interrupted, Crime Delayed, Crime Unsolved, Crime Exposed, Crime Denied, Crime Conspiracy, Crime Unknown, Crime Exploded, Crime Spree* and *Crime Family.*

He is also the author of *Her Name Was Jane*, a memoir about his late wife's nine-year battle with breast cancer. He has three children, four grandchildren and a Siberian Husky. He resides in Lone Tree, Colorado.

Other Books by the Author

"Crime Interrupted: A Buck Taylor Novel by Chuck Morgan is a gripping, edge-of-the-seat novel. *Right from page one, the action kicks off and never stops, gaining pace as each chapter passes." Reviewed by Anne-Marie Reynolds for Readers' Favorite.*

Finalist . . . 2019 Pacific Book Awards Best Mystery

"This crime novel reads like a great thriller. *The writing is atmospheric, laced with vivid descriptions that capture the setting in great detail while allowing readers to follow the* intensity of the action and the emotional and psychological depth of the story." Reviewed by Divine Zape for Readers' Favorite.

"Professionally written in the style of a best-selling crime novelist, such as Tom Clancy, Crime Unsolved: A Buck Taylor Novel by Chuck Morgan is a spellbinding suspense novel with an environmental flair. Intriguing subplots of fraud, survivalist paranoia and murder weave their way through the fabric of the plot, creating a dynamic story. This is an action-filled, stimulating tale which contains fascinating details that are relevant in our present climate." Reviewed by Susan Sewell for Readers' Favorite.

"Chuck Morgan has a unique gift for plot, one that makes Crime Exposed: A Buck Taylor Novel a hard-to-put-down book. From the start, readers know what happens to Barb, but they become curious as they follow the investigation, wondering if the characters will find out what happened to her. The descriptions are filled with clarity, and they offer readers great images. The prose is elegant, and it captures both the emotional and psychological elements of the novel clearly while offering vivid descriptions of scenes and characters. This is a fast-paced thriller with memorable characters and a criminal investigation that is so real readers will believe it could happen." Reviewed by Romuald Dzemo for Readers' Favorite.

Winner . . . 2020 Pacific Book Awards Best Mystery

2020 Chanticleer International Book Awards: 1st Place Blue Ribbon, CLUE Book Awards for Suspense, Thriller Fiction

"It's really progressive to see a female serial killer portrayed with such intelligent writing and depth of character, and the cat and mouse chase dynamic is thrown off nicely by the switching of genders. What results is a really enjoyable thriller and crime mystery novel, and overall Crime Denied is certain to please fans of both hard-boiled detective tales and action/adventure crime novels." Reviewed by K.C. Finn for Readers' Favorite.

2021 Chanticleer International Book Awards, Finalist, CLUE Book Awards for Suspense, Thriller Fiction . . . *Crime Conspiracy*

"This makes for a truly dynamic story where anything is possible, and a hero you can root for even when it looks like all is lost." Reviewed by K.C. Finn for Readers' Favorite.

"This is a book you can't put down, which will entertain you on many levels, and at times make your skin crawl; the kind of book that remains in your thoughts long after you finish reading." Reviewed by Steven Robson for Readers' Favorite.

"I read Crime Unknown in one sitting. The plot is intense and the main character, Agent Buck Taylor, is a hero like no other. This book has everything a thriller needs to be and more. I thought I knew the story at the beginning. Buck will solve a tricky murder case, I thought. But Chuck Morgan adds a twist to this story that expands it and makes it one of the most enjoyable books I've read in this genre. I loved that the lead was such an awesome well-rounded fellow but that he also had a support team who were just as important to the story."* Reviewed by Maureen Dangarembizi for Readers' Favorite.

"Crime Unknown is a thoroughly enjoyable read and I would not hesitate to recommend this book to fans of the crime genre and those looking for a gateway in." Reviewed by K.C. Finn for Readers' Favorite.

2022 Chanticleer International Book Awards Finalist, CLUE Book Awards for Detective/Crime Fiction . . . *Crime Exploded*

"Action-packed and fast-paced, I was sucked into the story the moment I opened the novel. The author built the story to perfection. Chuck Morgan gave just the right amount of suspense, mystery, and action to keep readers' attention on Buck and his team. There was never a dull moment in the story.

The narrative ran smoothly until the end; it followed the development of the story and the pace set by the characters. I enjoyed the twists and turns. What I loved more than anything else in the plot was how calculating Buck was. He was smart; he didn't let the FBI discourage him and kept his head in the game. The action gave me an adrenaline rush. Absolutely brilliant!"
Reviewed by Rabia Tanveer for Readers' Favorite.

2022 Chanticleer International Book Awards Finalist, CLUE Book Awards for Police Procedural Fiction . . . *Crime Spree*

 "**It is one of the best crime novels I have read in a long while**, with real characters developed in a way to let you get to know them intimately, understand them, and appreciate their strengths and weaknesses. The plot is tight, exciting, and tense, with plenty of action, and it will grip you from the start."
Reviewed by Anne-Marie Reynolds for Readers' Favorite.

"*Crime Family is the tenth book in the Buck Taylor series. Chuck Morgan had me hooked from the first page until the end.* There was never a dull moment with all the action; one chapter flowed into the next. The story was fast-paced and kept me on the edge of my seat. I kept turning the pages to find out what would happen next. I was intrigued, and with all the twists and turns, I could not predict what was looming. The characters were well-developed. Each had a background description, and it was fun getting to know some of them. The story was excellently written with a fitting ending." Reviewed by Alma Boucher for Readers' Favorite.

www.ingramcontent.com/pod-product-compliance
Lightning Source LLC
Chambersburg PA
CBHW070623300726
48975CB00006B/1909